For
Susan & Mike

JACOB JUMP

To the best days
and the fun of it!

Ems

STORY RIVER BOOKS

Pat Conroy, Editor at Large

JACOB JUMP

A Novel

ERIC MORRIS

Foreword by Pat Conroy

The University of South Carolina Press

© 2015 Eric Morris

Published by the University of South Carolina Press
Columbia, South Carolina 29208

www.sc.edu/uscpress

Manufactured in the United States of America

24 23 22 21 20 19 18 17 16 15
10 9 8 7 6 5 4 3 2 1

Library of Congress Cataloging-in-Publication Data
can be found at http://catalog.loc.gov/.

ISBN 978-1-61117-543-1 (paperback)
ISBN 978-1-61117-544-8 (ebook)

This book was printed on recycled paper with
30 percent postconsumer waste content.

To Christine and James,
for then and now.
And to our mothers and our fathers.

. . . there's only one thing that occurs to me,
the day is late and the sun is low,
and I don't know where I'll be in a year.
Of all the places I might have gone,
and soon I'll leave, please explain this to me.
And now I stand here and remember the day,
when we were young and didn't ask to be.
We searched tomorrow
with our hearts already broken . . .

FOREWORD

Few things ignite the imagination of a writer more than a river. The great American poet James Dickey told a generation of his students that he considered rivers to be the most stunning imagery of nature. In the best of Dickey's fiction and poetry, you will find yourself navigating the steep rapids of the Chattooga or wading knee deep in the tide-swollen waters near Darien before the Atlantic begins to achieve its ascendency. Coleridge moves you forward: ". . . Alph, the sacred river, ran / Through caverns measureless to man." Horatio defended the bridge to Rome over the Tiber, Balzac's boardinghouse residents quenched their thirst at the Seine, Dante eased his dark visions in the clear waters of the Arno, Jesus of Nazareth fished for souls along the Jordan, and Conrad ran his river through his own heart in search of a darkness that belonged to Africa. Rivers can serve as symbols of escape and launches toward freedom. They bring news of the world to their doorways and piers. Often, they form borders between countries and warring states, and they can feed a town as well as a hundred fields of beans or corn. You can dip a child in a river and free it of original sin. You can hide the corpse of a murderer, drown a knave, a cutpurse, or a blasphemer, and avoid the cost and trouble of a burial. A river is always alive, tide- and gravity-ruled, single-minded yet unmindful of the million eyes it gives pleasure to in its singular rush toward the mother of all waters that calls it homeward.

In his bold first novel, *Jacob Jump*, Eric Morris takes full possession of the Savannah River, which flows past his native city of Augusta as it surges through the sparsely populated borderlines of South Carolina and Georgia on its headlong rendezvous with the Atlantic, first passing through the old port city of Savannah. Few novelists writing today can equal Morris's majestic command of the language, and he writes about the beauty of his river in the immaculate descriptions of the natural-born poet. His images fly off the page like sparks leaping off struck flint. Before I read his novel, I'd never encountered a single sentence that Eric Morris had ever written, and I found myself unprepared for the sheer dazzlement of his ease with metaphor and descriptive legerdemain. His nature writing holds up well with the works of Thoreau, Edward Abbey, or Barbara Kingsolver. The darkness of his themes and characters will remind critics of the South invoked in the works of Cormac McCarthy, Ron Rash, and Flannery O'Connor herself. Yet his voice is as distinctive as it is original. The midlands city of Augusta has been underserved and undiscovered in southern letters, with some distinguished exceptions, until now. Though it is a starting-out place in *Jacob Jump*, Morris brings it to life as he prepares us to make a two hundred–mile river journey with two men who have both reached desperate points in their lives. Like many of the great voyages in literature, this one begins as an impetuous odyssey of rediscovery, to capture something lost in two lives that have suffered too many wrong turns. The trip down the Savannah River holds the promise of mystery, a connection to the memory of innocence, a time-out from the burdens of bad choices, and a prayer for one's own soul. In *Jacob Jump*, the river run is a wild and splendid thing. It is only when Morris's protagonists—Thomas Verdery and William Rhind—have to venture ashore for rest and food that the world intrudes on their voyage of escape and renewal. There they encounter the human animal, which turns the earth and its wildness against them.

Verdery and Rhind have fostered a long, Augusta-rooted friendship that has sustained them since childhood, and there is little about the Savannah River that they were not born knowing in their bones. Early in the novel, Verdery states the theme, which could serve as both coda and epitaph to the most distinguished southern fiction: "I cannot live here, but this is my home." Yet *home* is a loaded word, a storage facility for all the heavy ordnance and weaponry of the past. As the book opens, Thom Verdery is in flight from his job as theater teacher in a high-class New England prep school. He drives straight through from Connecticut to Augusta, leaving behind a woman he loved and who loved him, and leaving an unctuous headmaster on his knees after a punch to the mouth that effectively ended Verdery's teaching career. He is a man on the run who can escape from everything that has a grip on his soul except himself. But that self is excoriating, clear-eyed, and essentially moral in worldview. As we accompany him down that great brown river, he seems to record its sights and sounds like a director building a stage set in his own mind's eye.

The wife and daughter of William Rhind have abandoned him in the opening pages, and though he has worked as a cameraman for the local TV station, he is surveying the wreckage of his own life as he and Verdery make plans for their six-day trip down to the harbor of Savannah just before the Atlantic overpowers the freshwater surge of the river itself. Morris excels in the writing of dialogue between the two friends who speak to each other in the easy, almost inarticulate phrases that expose isolation from their own lives and the natural trust they have in their own shared past. They hold no delusions about the necessity of this trial by water, except that neither has ever done it, and both bear the acute insight that they need some break from the absurd dreamscape of their overwhelmed lives. Though Verdery is more contemplative and Rhind more broken, the two seem to complete something damaged by the life both men have endured without quite knowing what that life is supposed to be or why it has delivered them to the currents and tidal pull of that river. They are caught up in a whirlpool where eddies and coils make no sense to them. Thus, the river. Thus, the journey.

The boat that takes them down the Savannah River is called the Ouachita. It is a seventeen-foot aluminum craft, paint-scarred but seaworthy. A craft to be trusted. The river itself, with the aid of hurricane-borne storms, provides adventure enough, but only when Verdery and Rhind pull over for the night and encounter strangers who live out their rough-hewn lives beside the river does the human dilemma intrude to let them know why they came on the trip in the first place. They come to a nasty-tempered lockkeeper so cantankerous that before the old man relents and finally lets them pass, you long for Rhind to shoot him. Morris has a unique but generous gift in illuminating small-craft souls like this one.

When they drift in sight of the cooling towers of a nuclear plant, and its father, a bomb plant situated opposite the watercourse, where tritium is the chief byproduct of the site, we become aware of the crimes against rivers which humanity has made one of its specialties. When night falls, they pull ashore to set up camp when they spot a boy fishing for his family's dinner near a half-sunken yacht with clean aristocratic lines named the *Caron Lee;* Morris moves us into the heart of southern dread—and storytelling, where our literature began. The tale of the Covington family, its tragedy, and the detritus it leaves in its wake takes us deep into the history of the South, rife with broken lives and torn fragments. A fifteen-year-old girl, also named Caron Lee, slips out of her house and wakes up the theater teacher Thom Verdery and asks him to let her go down the river with him. Her brightness and tender beauty light up the awkwardness of the encounter, yet let us feel some of the integrity Verdery must have brought to his classroom and some of his kindness. Caron Lee's heartfelt cry is for her discharge papers from a life without fulfillment; she longs for the possibility of something she cannot name, but of inordinate value, perhaps even ecstasy. In the young girl, Verdery sees a mirror image of himself and the longingness that sometimes grabs hold of the imaginative child, gripped by the terror of being lowborn and afraid.

The father of William Rhind joins his son and Thom Verdery on the river, and the older man brings long experience on the river and a portion of wisdom as they camp together on sandbars and storm-soaked riverbanks. Dan Rhind is worried about the two boys he helped raise, and though his own life is a mare's nest of regret, he brings a solidness and wealth of knowledge to the campfire. Both young men respect the old man, and his company is welcome, yet it is Dan Rhind's fate that is the central pivot point on which the novel turns. The river has a single task, and it is subject to the law of flow. But all men and women in *Jacob Jump* become subject to these laws once they embark to test themselves on its heartless currents.

Eric Morris is a novelist with singular gifts of compression and exactitude. Whenever the Ouachita makes landfall, Morris presents us with characters both original and strange. When Thom and William meet the insane, murderous Alice Mays, he crafts a hilarious short story that is a tour de force in itself. Morris writes with a poet's unerring eye. With great ease he makes the reader fall in love with at least four women in this book, and he accomplishes this task in brilliant sketches less than ten pages long. His men seem like they are walking through minefields of their own careless making. Throughout the book, they struggle with the inarticulateness that quavers on the edge of some emotional breakthrough, but seldom reaches it. He fills you up with reluctant admiration for men who cannot find the generosity to love themselves. Morris is a writer to be closely watched, and his first novel is as finely crafted as a Swiss timepiece. It has a perfection of design that is satisfying and a scope that is as ambitious as it is finely wrought.

In the end only one man takes the Ouachita beyond the spires and riverwalk of Savannah, past the markers to the channels and where the great freighters line up to await their harbor pilots. Facing the open sea, he leaves us with them, wondering. His solitude is as great as Ishmael's after the *Pequod* sinks into the open waters. We long for the sight of the rescue ship that saved Ishmael floating on a coffin. But the wondrous Eric Morris leaves fate up to the will of the ocean and our own imaginations—and that's what the good writers always do.

Pat Conroy

ACKNOWLEDGMENTS

With sincere thanks . . .

to the good people at USC Press, and their quality work. Linda Fogle, Bill Adams, Suzanne Axland, Brandi Avant;

to Jonathan Haupt for giving it a chance and sending it forward;

to Pat Conroy for his kind words of encouragement;

to Peter Powlus for his help reading and for the company on all those starry nights on all those rivers;

to Dan Robinson for the trip and the story of it;

to Troy, for all of it . . . and he knows why;

and to Christine, for believing and believing, and believing . . .

CHAPTER ONE

This benchmark is old brass, set into the bricks, simple, precise decoration, two hundred statute miles upriver from Savannah, the Tybee lighthouse, actually. They stand upon the very same earth, the path de Soto had footsore scuffed across four hundred fifty years before, with the four hundred horses and the six hundred men—a haggard, febrile aimless search for Cufitachiqui, ancestress of the Creek, and her legendized gold.

William Rhind squatted like a baseball catcher, and Thomas Carpenter Verdery did the same, and even squatting Rhind was taller, and they searched out past the full-grown hackberry, across the river's emerald surface, seeing the same this watercourse, seeing differently the distance.

"You want to go now," said Rhind, knowing all there was to it, thinking in the same breath, *she will not be there when I go home tonight. They, will not be there, and the house will be empty, and it is nearly late August, and you should have known it would come to this. Because she asked, how much do you love it, and what did you answer.*

Verdery still held the remnant inertia of the road in his blood and bones, and he balanced himself with a fist against the unsteadiness of travel and change. When he drove home this time, he drove straight through. He left the circle of old elms at The Lake School with the long white boat strapped to the top of his truck, and he made the thousand miles, stopping only to gas up and once more, along a ridge of the Shenandoah Valley to watch the sun go low, it declining vermilion, then bruising to lavender, then slipping away into the earth's upspilling lilac dust.

"You going back?" said Rhind.

"No. I'm not going back," said Verdery, answering the same way it had been asked, without intent, a weary said-aloud fact, because fact remains even when memory has gone.

They walked the levee and the air was thick with the humid burden of the long summer, deep South, and Verdery tasted the air in his mouth and lungs, and though he did not always love the place where he was born, he knew it was home and that Nepaug, Connecticut, and any other place was not; was never.

"Dad says it's six days to Savannah," said Rhind, panning a last time the emerald river, a soft wind teasing its back into riffles, swapping, shading its hues in the low sun, he framing the shot with his trained eye as he would at his work and imagining an edit, a dissolve, and another, then a story of a place and a time that had not before been told, if there were such a thing.

"He's been all the way?"

"Halfway. To the 301 bridge. He figures six. He's heard tell of that. But, if you start here, you still have the new lock and dam to pass."

"But this is two hundred."

"It has to be two hundred."

"Yes, it has to be two hundred."

"By law they have to let you through the lock."

"I know it. We're not above dragging around."

"By law, no matter what size boat it is."

"I know it."

From atop the levee the city seemed barren to Verdery, and would until the dullness wore on—his expectations numbed by proximity, assuming and once again immune to the sorrow of homeplace abandoned and reclaimed. From the floodwall you view the old cotton row, where once Augusta traded the staple crop as the second-largest inland port in the world, second to Memphis—where then you walked block after block along Reynolds Street, treading atop baled cotton, from Fifth nearly to Hawk's Gully, and never touch the sidewalk with your shoe. Upon this primordial shore—where the watercourse made a bend and chose to run due east causing this sandbar, where the sediment and granite rocks made the most navigable point upriver, where foottrails converged and fur traders, Shawnee and French, made a camp, where by way of Charleston then the Lowcountry and across the Sandhills Woodward found them, and soon after Oglethorpe made a town on parchment, and Augustans eventually made a city—upriver two hundred miles from Tybee Island, the wild pigeons clung to the thick grown Virginia creeper and ate of the wine berries. And as they walked the floodwall Verdery said it again, weary and inward, as he had all of his adult life, *I cannot live here, but this is my home.*

They drank beer at a café named for cotton and the legacy of cotton and on the television watched the storms coming for the Southeast and Gulf Coasts. There came three storms, a pair named for men, the third for a woman, one tracking the next making paths westward across the Atlantic. Rhind checked the time, then he remembered it did not matter, and he drank more beer searching the window panes, watching the wild pigeons and the daylight go to dun.

Only two days before Verdery stood upon the Headmaster's verandah, and they spoke hard and angry telling each other's future. Verdery telling because he had known Catharine and because he had loved her, and not finished loving her, and because her mouth was soft and her breath uncluttered with worry or age or indecision. And the Headmaster telling because he believed Verdery did not belong at The Lake School or another place like it, and he had imagined tasting Catharine's mouth too.

Verdery, have you touched one of your girls?

You know I haven't. You know that.

We can't have even the rumor.

Then don't make a rumor.

We can't have it.

She told me she came to you, but she's lying.

Catharine is an amazing woman. The Lake School is fortunate to have her. She went to Princeton. You didn't go to Princeton, did you Verdery.

You know where I went. Richard, what would you like to know about Catharine. Because I know all of it.

I didn't hire you. That was somebody else, and he's gone, and we can't have stories about grown men touching students.

Verdery hit him, a succinct motion, with his foreknuckle precise to the jawline, and the Headmaster of The Lake School knelt to his painted porch boards, more frightened than hurt, though he was hurt for a month.

If the wife comes out, should I tell her why we disagree. And if you call someone should I tell them.

The Headmaster only wagged his head, a moan, a palm to bone of his jaw, his eyes watered and expression fixed, telling a fear and knowledge of men and women, and deceit. And he let Verdery go, a price for Catharine well paid, though he would never see or hold her in soft crimson bedroom light, as he wished more than anything.

And Verdery drove out of the circle of the overleaning elms, and from her room Catharine watched him and the road-worn truck and the white boat turned upside down make the turn to Nepaug, bearing right twice. And southbound somewhere in the Shenandoah Valley, where Sheridan one hundred and thirty years before had ravaged all the people and soil ahead of him, burning everything useless, Verdery reasoned he did not love Catharine after all, because then why would he abandon her, and why would she release him—because letting go cannot be love.

"And Emmy said?"

"She's alright," said Rhind. "Sure, she's fine with it. What would she say."

Outside a slow, heavy breeze moved a sycamore, the leaves deep viridian and tender, as large as dinner plates the way they grow nearby the river.

"We can use the Ouachita," said Rhind.

"We've never had much luck in that. The bottom's round. I have one."

"When did you get a boat?"

"I got it up north. A Cherokee sold it to me."

"A Cherokee up north."

"Yes."

"I'll ask my dad to come."

"I like your father."

"That's because you can get away from him."

Rhind stood and drank the last of his beer all at once. He had his father's shoulders—sloping and thick muscled. He could run full out with fifty pounds of antiquated video gear hanging from him ready to shoot with tape rolling. In his first professional year, on the canal road he dragged an old, filthy squatter from his burning shack. He carried the shabby man over a shoulder and his camera and gear over the other, and the old man vomited on him before Rhind could lay him down on the clay levee. Rhind went again to the fire and coughing through the vomit the old man bellowed, *what in the sumbitch you think you doing?* And Rhind told him, *Cooter, I'm shooting your goddam story.*

"You ready?"

"You go on. I'll stay downtown for awhile," said Verdery.

"You can get back okay?"

"I'll get a ride. I'll call someone."

"You going to call Ms. Eaves."

"I could call Ginny. I might call Ginny."

"How is she."

"I don't know how Ginny is."

"And you're not going back up north."

"I'm not going back."

"They know that?"

"Will, you know, you bust your ass for people and it comes to nothing."

"I know it. Sometimes it comes to nothing."

"I'm not going back."

"Annie says hey. She always says hey. I know she would."

"Hey to Annie." Verdery groped in his pocket and he pulled out a keychain with a medallion and the medallion was blue and gold and of the Lake School's seal. "You'll have to get her some keys to go with this."

"Alright," said Rhind lightly, and he sighed heavy and spun the keychain into his palm, and he left Verdery alone and went out into the dusk, whistling once, calling the wild pigeons, and the pigeons watched him whistle.

That night a sudden shower rained. Rhind sat on his porch steps alone, with the house empty of his wife and his little girl, and it rained and he moved not out of the rain. He drank whiskey, and he sat in the shower storm. When he was ready he got up and he left his drink glass where it sat, and went inside and lay wet in their bed.

CHAPTER TWO

Verdery breathed deep into his lungs the wet, solemn air, remembering the taste of it. On the levee the air changed to the color of night, and a deep saturate blue hung like water smoke. At the old drawbridge he searched the far shore lights. There a houseboat had become more a lean-to, with a vapor streetlamp for a porchlight. Above that on the bank and into the trees, more dim porchlights, where squatters were now community, and their nightlights peeked softened, gauzed in the summer haze. Across, a little village named Hamburg once lived, and from Hamburg to Charleston the first passenger rail line in America was built. In 1814 Henry Shultz dreamed his Hamburg would rival Augusta. He left Germany and boated an ocean and built a bridge across the Savannah and a decent wharf, to secure an inland port to trade cotton and tobacco, running round-trip steamboats to Charleston, ten days' travel. But the Augustans, and more than that, the river, would kill the dream, and when he died they buried him in the Carolina sand with his back to Georgia, as he asked. The floods and freshets washed Hamburg away, and now a few frame houses survived and the freight trains only sounded as they passed making restively for Augusta.

Verdery walked the tracks away from the river to Broad Street, and there he turned west, walking the store facades, some aged and unkept, some better. At a pay phone he dropped coins and spoke quietly, and in a moment he put back the handle and walked on. The streetlamps cast amber canopies in the thick night air, cones aligned, reduced in perspective by distance, and he went into them. In Connecticut the air had already turned to cool. Crisp, thin, the daytime sky cerulean, the nighttime sky all the stars ever created.

From a cross street and the dark, what seemed an old woman came to him, and he saw her when she spoke. "Sir," she said, and he stopped, and she offered out her palm. "Sir, I's wondering if you could help me with something."

She was brown, and her teeth shone yellow in a pained smile, and her eyes gleamed in the streetlamp's cast as if brushed with orange shellac.

"Sir, I wonder if you could tell me something. Sir, can you tell me how much I got here."

In her palm a single dime, a nickel, and four pennies. She raised her palm to show them better.

"It's nineteen cents. You have nineteen cents, ma'am."

"Well, good then. I wonder if I can ask you one more question."

"Yes ma'am."

"I's wondering if you have a little something to help me get some biscuits and gravy."

"Biscuits and gravy."

"Yes, sir. A little biscuits and gravy."

"Where you going to get biscuits and gravy, now."

"Right down yonderways. At missus what you call it."

"Which way."

She teased with her head without showing a direction.

"You know right over yonderway. Down at missus . . ." and she said a woman's name but Verdery did not know it. He felt into his pants pocket where he kept his bills and his coins, and he felt for the coins. She watched him finger the coins.

"Let me ask you something."

"Alright, sir."

"What is your name?"

"Why you want to know that."

"I just want to know who I'm giving my money to. Can't I know that?"

She searched the dark, into the falloff from where she had come.

"My name is Barbara."

"What's your other name."

"Rice. Barbara Rice."

"Barbara Rice, you ain't going to drink this money are you."

"No sir, un uh. No. I'm headed over yonder to get me some biscuits and gravy at missus . . ." and she said a woman's name like a secret and Verdery put the coins into her hand.

"Yes sir. I shore do thank you. Now I's wondering if you could tell me one more thing. How much I got now," and she offered her palm up, brown and small and unsteady, the coins oversized.

"Barbara, now you got ninety-four cents."

"Yes sir. I shore do appreciate it. Yes sir."

"Alright, Barbara Rice," said Verdery, then, "here," and he felt for paper and he fished a five-dollar bill, and rolled into the five two more single dollars, and he set the traded paper into her brown and white toy-sized palm.

"Oh, yes sir. I shore do appreciate it. That'll shore help Barbara. That'll shore help. Thank you for your good kindness."

She said it like his mother, grateful for painting half her house or telling he loved her.

"Alright, Barbara Rice, get you some biscuits and gravy," and he looked in her wet eyes, and they read thank you and damn you, and he turned to walk on.

"You have yourself a real good evening."

When Verdery looked back, she stood the same with her hand in a fist, counting by feel, lost in counting, as small as a puppet. She was called Anita by her grandmother. She raised her fist and spoke a secret, and eased again into the falloff.

He crossed Broad Street, and he walked toward scarlet lights, then into a club in one of the shotgun-style buildings, with the bar to one side and at the far end a jazz quartet on a small raised stage. The club seemed all of wood-work, with a heartpine plank floor that sagged when treaded upon, and the ceiling coffered tin. Verdery knew the steadies there. Born Augustans, some immensely gifted who traveled away and came home again, and some who never found the curiosity to leave at all. The club abundant of local genius and a place to trust for lack of change, even when a thousand miles absent.

He met the music walking then stopped to speak to a drunken woman giggling at him and a man shaking his hand. The woman bartender, dark-headed with dark pretty dark eyes, raised a glass flipping it upright, and Verdery nodded and she poured a beer. She said it had been awhile, and he said it was true but explained no more than that, smiling half, letting her eyes go.

The band played tight, and it was *In Walked Bud*, a tradition of the place, birthright the excellence of it, and he leaned to the bar and drank and let the sound and the good beer taste and the drunkenness overtake him.

She pinched him at his false ribs and put an arm around him, and he pulled her close and held her for a moment with his palms on the back of her hips, holding to remember her shape, and the memory returned all at once.

"Look at you," said Ginny Eaves, she searching him, taking him in, truly surprised that he could appear so handsome to her, and she said again, *look at you.*

He took her hand and held it carefully and tight and kissed it, and they sat. She was brown with her hair lightened from the summer, from yard work and weekends at Charleston, the beach at Sullivan's Island. Her bare arms slender and tanned and her eyes clear, healthy, and full blue. Younger than he had seen them last. She smelled the same as when they had first met years before, purposefully, but he had not bought her that fragrance for a long time now.

"I know you're ready for a break. How was it. You made it okay."

"Good. It was alright," said Verdery. "I came down through the Shenandoah Valley."

"Like we did. It's beautiful there. You're ready for a break. You need a drink and you need to relax."

"I have a drink."

"You need to think about very little for a couple of weeks. Was it too crazy?"

"Not so bad. Crazy. Not so bad."

"I remember. Too many shows. After seven weeks I had to run from that place, fast. It made me too crazy."

"It's not so bad. But summer school wears me down."

"It's more than school. You do good work for them. They don't know."

Ginny Eaves smiled and put her hand on his, and she looked at them joined. When they were together, when it was new, full of the rawness and thrill of sharing a breath, she told him she loved his hands the most, because of what they could do.

"The leaves were already turning."

"It's so beautiful there, but it's so far away."

"I need some summer. I need for it to last awhile."

"How is it. How is everyone?"

"They said they missed you."

"Good. I miss them. I miss them. But that place is too crazy. It makes me crazy."

"They care for you."

"I loved them."

"What they liked about us was you."

"You do such good work for them. They don't know."

"It made me tired. It made me tired this time."

8

Verdery pinched her softly in the ribs, and she feigned surprise, her way, though it was familiar all again.

"Hey. You're beautiful."

"No."

"Yes. The sun looks good on you."

"Augusta makes me too crazy. Sometimes I just need to go away from here."

"You've been to Charleston."

"No. No, not too much."

Verdery bowed his head, and he grinned, even simpered at himself, and he felt the drink and the music and her fragrance sweet and clean, so long absent, warm and loosen him.

They listened, and it was good. They listened in that attitude of expectancy, veneration, and they smiled at the music and the players, and the band played reverent too, playing *So What* as if it were the first song of all songs, smiling easy at one another sharing the private language spoken only in the moment of art.

"Sometimes I just need to get away."

"It's alright," said Verdery. "It's alright if you need to go to Charleston."

"I like to get away. It's so close, and it's so beautiful there."

"It's good for you. I can see that."

Ginny Eaves crossed her slender arms at her waist and shook her head. "I have no interest."

"There must be someone. There must have been someone in two years. I know there has been."

"No. I have no interest. It's not something I do."

"I know who you see in Charleston. It's alright."

"Him. I've known him for years. Longer than I've known you. He's concerned about himself. He always has been. Charleston is beautiful. I like to go there and forget. All anyone ever tells me here is this problem or that problem. Grown people do this to me. They're all one in the same. People talk and talk and talk to me, and I stand there like a board, and listen, and sometimes I just want to ask them how long they've been grown, and why am I the one who has to listen to all this."

"But you don't ask."

"Sometimes I just like to forget, and to get away. And I do that."

She quieted and she searched the stage through the silk of blue cigarette smoke. She knew the song, but not the song's name.

Verdery watched her, and she allowed him, her head posed tipped with her chin raised, her legs crossed, now with a glass of wine propped on her knee. In the soft light he knew the shape of her and he imagined her as they had been, and he remembered his palms on her hips and her stomach and thighs. He remembered too, as if a concomitant writ, that those hands let him go a dozen times to drive a thousand miles away, and he turned from her, casting the room where she searched, plying to release the image of memory—and this time he doubted strength.

"How is your friend in Nepaug?"

"My friend."

"Yes, your friend. The smart, beautiful one."

"I imagine she's just fine."

"She must love you to let you come home and see your old girl."

"I don't ask."

"Is she patient with you. Does she do a hundred little things that make you insane."

"It wasn't that way."

"No?"

"Ginny, it's been a long time since I moved. I spent a lot of time alone."

"I've spent a lot of time alone too."

"What would you like to know. I'll tell you anything you want to know."

"I don't want to know anything. Don't tell me anything."

Verdery put his palm to the back of her neck and his fingers underneath into her hair. She leaned back to his palm.

"I can't work here. I can't work here. I tried, and all I did was aggravate people. All I did was try to show them how much I know."

"You would go insane like the rest of us, if you were here."

"I see it better at a distance."

"You do such good work where you are."

The beer had made Verdery drunk, and now her hair was the same as seven years past, those nights of their first summer together, beneath the overreaching elms of The Lake School, and above the Berkshire hills all the stars ever created.

"I do alright."

It had rained a sudden shower, and in the warmth and wetness and the soft cast of a streetlamp she leaned to her car, and she did not mind it was wet. Seven years past, on a similar August night, they made love for the first time. They met that summer at The Lake School and for six weeks they taught professional theatre. And when it was over and the summer almost finished they traveled home separately and met again at the club, on a Sunday, and late that night he took her to the city ponds. They walked the paths circling the black water, and they drank blush wine on ice, and they made love out of doors in the warm summer night wind. For five years they survived as a couple, needful of each other, but Verdery restive for professional work and wander and change often left her alone, and somewhere in that long year she decided the aloneness was enough. She never said to him, *do not go*, she only said she loved him. But he was young and poor and underaccomplished, and The Lake School, because the Headmaster and more the Headmaster's wife were fond of him, offered him a position and a title. She only said she loved him, and he went, because she let him and because he had the strength to not stay.

She reached for him, and put her palm to his forearm.

"It's late," she said, and he smiled away from her, into the distance, the thick dark.

"Can you smell the air."

"Everybody here loves your work."

"But I aggravate them."

"You're dedicated."

"Aggravating."

"Intense. They know that. The Lake School is lucky to have you, but there are other places too."

"It's different there. There's distance. I can see for a thousand miles."

Verdery took a full slow breath tasting the heavy air in his lungs, and her.

"I'm glad you came. I'm glad you called me," said Ginny Eaves, and she gently drew him to her. "Are you going to keep me from going insane to-night."

"I didn't know I could do that."

"I just want to feel good. I just want to feel good again."

"There's no one to make you feel good?"

"They're all little boys. And they just want to talk about themselves, and I can't listen to them anymore."

"Who are little boys?"

"All of them. Every one of them."

"Even in Charleston they're little boys."

"I like to get away. It keeps me safe from the crazies. I listen until I can't anymore, then I go there and listen until I can't anymore, then I come home. I've known him longer than you."

She pulled him closer until her hips touched just below his.

"I just want to feel good. It's been bad for so long, I just want to feel good again."

He looked down the length of her, then to her eyes, then again the distance, the spires of the streetlamp's cast light templated through tree boughs, they as substantial as rumors and swords.

"You could have come to Nepaug."

She smiled only half, and lay a palm to his face. An intelligent, well-shaped hand of so many talents, fragrant of time gone.

"No, Thom. It's too far. I've been away. I've been there. It's too far anymore."

"But Charleston is not."

"No, Charleston is not."

She took his hands in hers and held them to her breasts. "You don't have to go to your empty house. I'll be up late if you want to come by. Or we don't have to go anywhere."

"I know it," said Verdery, and he kissed her on the forehead and took his hands away from her.

She said again she would be up late and he kissed her hands and only half-smiled, and stood from her car, and closed the door for her.

"Let me take you home. It's so late."

"I'll be alright. Nobody's going to trouble a big boy like me."

"I'll be up if you want to come. You can wake me too."

"Alright."

"You called me. I thought . . ."

"I know it. You're beautiful without me."

"Thom."

"I know it."

"Are you going down the river?"

"I am."

"Is Will going?"

"I don't know. But I am."

"You worry me. Are you going to be careful."

"Yes, probably."

"I'll be up late."

And he took her chin gently between his forefinger and thumb, and she tipped her head as if to gather in that single motion a memory of touch and time escaped from her.

He watched the brake lights glow, then dim, then vanish. He walked a different way than he had come, and in a half hour atop the floodwall he stood upon the benchmark at two hundred river miles. He breathed deep the wet air, musty hackberry and sycamore, the river too. More the river than all else. Alone he became almost giddy. A boy in the dark of the late summer night, and only the spill of starlight casting the shapes of the world. In soundless, lengthless minutes coursed the rest of his life. Nothing yet known. When he was a boy, outside his bedroom window, a dog he knew as gentle and proud came by hunting the summer night, and the puppy stopped and raised his nose to the air testing the dark before trotting on. And the boy and the dog pausing would share this, this to which no sleeping creature had a privy, with none a witness.

Giddy alone, sometime in the deep of the night at the bottom of the flood-wall upon a wooden dock he squatted, surveying where the surface gently boiled. Near upriver he heard a muskrat slip in, the water closing above it. He sat cross-legged conceding now that Nepaug could not have been a part of him. He granted too that in all the places he knew, they now carried on, yes, surely lived well, without him—Catharine too. This time in the dead of the night the distance was too great. He fought it for all the years he wandered from his home, and now it was beyond him, because heartless you cannot reach across a thousand miles, and then it is only vain memory, as weak as a clay pot.

He undressed and let the clothes lay where they fell. He knew it would be cold and probably fast too when he dove with his fists out.

The river shunted the air from him, and he came up coughing hard. He swam a crawl to warm his muscles until he tired, then he checked the silhouette of the shoreline to see how far he had drifted. His foot touched something and he knew it was watergrass, elodea, then soon later he touched something again, and he did not know what it was. From the South Carolina side the porchlights of the houseboats reflected as filaments, luminous threads upon the surface, thin, cool and reaching, and unsteady. He let the river's flow take him and the sting eased in his flesh and muscles, and he became giddy again.

In Lake Nepaug too he treaded water, and he searched the shoreline's circumference, full round. In the thin air with the wide sky above, and the good feeling of distance from the Deep South, in the unsilent hum of a thousand-miles' separation, he waited for her. She appeared at the sloping path out of the hemlocks and came to the grassy point with a book and a towel under an arm. Devoid of self-consciousness she waved to him and he watched her slip out of her shorts and pull her top away. She shook her head and her hair, running her hands through it, and the sun caused a fine backglow, a highlight shaping all her body.

He met Catharine the summer at The Lake School when he went alone. There was one night early on, a gathering of old friends met, and there was affection and drink. They escaped the crowd, sitting on the grassy tilt behind the boathouse amidst a stand of white birch, just beyond the porchlight's throw. They heard the others calling, but did not answer, and did not go back.

I want to kiss you right on your beautiful mouth, he said.

I know, she said the same way, her eyes brimming and dark. *Do.*

Her mouth was warm and soft, more than he had imagined, and her breath sweet and uncluttered by age and indecision, flavored by the scotch he had given her. She was tall and slender and her legs shapely from running, and only occasionally ungainly, and that too charmed Verdery. She held a quiet, winsome quality that seemed either granted of birth or well learned, and it was a lesson taken and unrelinquished, and as pure as the shamelessness within her eyes.

Verdery flinched in the shadow of the drawbridge piling. He rolled to one side swimming beneath the span for the shore at Sixth Street. The current took him on a diagonal and he swam hard for the marina and the slips. He took hold of the first he came to and rested regaining his breath with the current nudging all of him. In one motion he pressed himself up and he lay upon the dock boards searching the sky. *The air is warmer than the water,* and his breathing eased and evened. He heard voices of a man and a woman from a nearby houseboat. The woman laughed, tittering, it trailing away into silence, then they were quiet again. A hum, an attenuated conjoining of distant indesegregateable noises brought the giddiness of isolation again to Verdery, and, save the low distant chorus, there was only the creaking of rope and wood and boat hulls, where at work each mitigated the other's strength, each acquiesced, bound in equitable service. The voices came again, then it was only the woman's, but she was not speaking. He listened to her moan until she was quiet again, until a last time there remained only the hum, and the groan of boathulls and lanyard and wood.

He walked the dirt path under the drawbridge where the trains crossed from old Hamburg. Ahead he heard something slip into the river, then he heard something again. Just out of the bridge footing's shadow she sat upon a granite stone with her elbows to her knees and her head low. When she knew someone was there, she spoke.

"Ooh. I see you Ghostman. I see you, now."

"No, Barbara Rice, I ain't a ghost."

"Ghostman, you best get some clothes on. Them mens will get you and worry you to death."

She spoke thickly, her words tossed, and her head bobbed in slow rolls as if fighting sleeping, or dreams sleep causes.

"How were them biscuits, Barbara."

"Hey, Ghostman. I ain't done nothing to that man's store. I just went to look in that window. I can't help it if it's always on a Sunday when I needs me something. When I needs a little something, I needs a little something. But I ain't done nothing to that man's window. They know I ain't done nothing, they know Anna."

"Barbara, what you done gone and done."

"I ain't done it I'm telling you. That man, he give me some money. Look here." She looked up, her head bobbing up, and Verdery stepped back into a shadow. She held out something rolled into a ball in her small hand. "You see, I got some money. I ain't got no need to steal."

"You show them that when they come for you, Barbara."

"Hey, is you a ghost, Ghostman," she sang, tuneless, and rolled her shoulders in a laugh. "*Hey, Mr. Ghost-Man, hey, Mr. Ghost-Man.*"

"Barbara, you need to find you someplace to stay tonight."

"That's alright, they coming for me. They coming for me in a little while. They know where to come."

"Well, you need to find you someplace."

"You out here Ghostman. Can't I be out here too?"

"Alright, Barbara Rice. You watch out."

He heard them coming when he reached where the brickpath began at the riverwalk. The shaft of a flashlight beam spiraled in the air and they called to her, and it was a different name and as they neared he heard them slipping, summoning, more annoyed than angry, making their way down from the tracks along the levee wall. And then he heard her calling in return to someone or no one because she had been full of wine for three days. Crying out to the dark, the pitch of her voice sharpening when they found her.

He ran the brick, first a jog, then full out, until he could not determine the words, and he did not slow until distance had obscured them altogether. He went below the escarpment to the dock where he started, and he dressed in his moist clothes, and he knelt then sat in the escarpment's shadow until the pain in his legs and lungs eased. With the dew settling on him he lay to one side using his forearm against the planking as a pillow. With the river easing under him, he made arrangements in his head—water, something to eat, a bedroll, something to drink too, not water. He told himself to keep an order, remember properly, but before he knew, he slept.

His sleep made a lengthless dream of Lake Nepaug, and treading water. Once, in the memory, Ginny Eaves was with him, and together they were seven years younger. The air full of hemlock was foreign and unknown and fresh, and the Berkshires blushed, washed in a folded hue of gray and violet, all at once timeless and adolescent. In the memory too was Catharine, and buoyed weightless in the surround of the blue lake he watched her undress at the grassy peninsula, and despite the distance, he kissed her warm, soft mouth.

He wakened without moving to a noise in the air in the same position he lay. In that moment before he remembered where he was, it overcame him. A rush of solitude he had drawn upon himself, and it came at once, a bitter and familiar taste. A sudden squall traveled and aged, coursed by a stale tradewind. And then it was gone, and he lay alone, unmoved and only moist from the dew—and in that moment unsleeping and unwaking he doubted he ever had a home.

To the river's far shore, Carolina, the low sky tinted. A heron flew, unhurried, just above him to upriver, in and out of the reaching, bleached arms of the sycamores. He sat up cross-legged, as still as cast statuary or carved trinket, something forgotten, facing the east, the tinting low sky, and he remembered vividly only the last of his dream. The dock had let go from the escarpment, and he sat watching the floodwall go small in the distance. Some gathered on the bank but he could not collect the faces, and as they turned away from him he receded, taken by the insistent water, and he knew there was no remedy and no slowing. In the dream the sky's bottom tinted to roseamber, burning upward to hueless the night away. A single great blue heron called across the silvering water, and Verdery stood turning to downriver and left all of them at his back.

CHAPTER THREE

After two A.M., the fog was a rain. A fog that wets all things God grown and man built. The fog you breath into your lungs, and it comes off the river and takes all of downtown. With Rhind late, Verdery hauled half his gear, then waited drinking a beer that made him shake with cold and giddiness. Soon headlamps bounced and shone scattered by the body of the fog, and it was Rhind and they spoke tacitly and hoarse voiced and together hauled gear through the cut in the levee, each trip a hundred yards. Last they loosed the Ouachita and carried it, hull up, over their heads, and at the slip they flipped it and set it into the water and bound both painters to lashing cleats. It was seventeen foot of rugged aluminum craft, sewn by rivets, born in Texarkana, Arkansas, as old as the two men that carried it, scarred and paintworn from use but as good as the day it came whole into the world.

When the gear was loaded and the Ouachita heavy in the water, wagging slowly in the current, they spoke again.

"We'll pack it right, when we stop, in the morning."

"Sure," said Rhind, taking a beer, backbending, taking a long drink.

In the balance of the night, wrapped and hidden in the fog and the falloff of the halflight, they looked to one another, sharing the cold of the drink and the giddiness.

"Lord," said Rhind.

"Lord," said Verdery, the same, then as his father practiced saying, "and half the day's gone."

"Lord," said Rhind again, backleaning with the beer to his mouth, then asking, "we ready?"

"Go," said Verdery.

He let Rhind in first. The seats were already wet. Verdery stepped to the keel, and sat in the bowseat. As they worked the painters loose, she emerged from the escarpment's shadow, materializing in the thick air near to them, in the glow of the halflight.

"Jesus," said Rhind, as much an aspiration as anything, and Verdery twisted in the bowseat, and he told himself he already knew—even before he looked up to the canopy of the streetlamp backlighting where she scuffed to the dock, where he saw her for the third time.

"Y'all going on a trip."

"Jesus, woman," said Rhind, "where in the world you come from?"

"Hey, Barbara Rice," said Verdery, and Rhind said *Jesus* a second time.

"I knowed y'all was going off somewheres."

"Barbara, you in trouble?"

"No, Barbara ain't in no trouble. Everybody leaves Barbara alone, but that's alright. Them mens ain't bothered me none. Them mens know me. They know they can't bother me none. Ghostman left me alone, didn't he. Hey, y'all seen anything out there in that water."

"No ma'am, we ain't seen nothing yet."

"Well, y'all need to look out. They's things in that water. They's all kind of things. They's some people too. I seen them. I done seen them."

"We'll look out Barbara. And if we see some people, we'll tell them Barbara said hey."

"No, you ain't got to call me a fool. No, they can't hear nobody. Ain't no use in that. Ain't nobody in that water can hear none of me or you. That ain't what I'm saying to you."

Rhind tapped the Ouachita's gunnel with the blade of his oar to have Verdery loose his painter.

"Barbara, we got to go on here."

"I knowed you was going on a trip, Ghostman. But you ain't got to worry about Barbara Rice. Everybody leaves Barbara alone."

Rhind loosed his painter and the Ouachita swung about, and Verdery did the same and they eased from the dock with their oars in the water, and the Savannah began taking them.

"See that you don't fall in this water, Barbara Rice."

"I'm alright. I ain't going in no river. And you know what else? I got another name too. God gave Barbara another name, a long time back."

"I know," said Verdery. "I know it."

She stooped in the direction they had gone, reaching to see the last of the two white men and their longboat. Verdery watched her, twisted in the bow-seat, as the Ouachita came about again—she now only trinket-sized stooping on the dockboards as if a child or a child's toy awaiting another child. Then dissolved, overtaken by the mist.

She spoke a last time across the water, her voice clear again near to them. "You watch out for that man. You watch out for that Ghostman, now. Cause the Ghostman leaves you, then you alone."

Rhind waited to know she had finished, as her calling died in a single diminishing echo, returning from the far shore.

"That your new girl?"

"Sure. Sure, she is."

"And you found her where."

"Walking the street. She was alone."

"And you gave her all your money."

"I gave her some. I got more than I know what to do with."

"Alright, rich man. Alright, Ghostman, let's get our nose right."

They brought the Ouachita about once more, working their oars gently, not knowing their true speed, and they listened carefully for echoes to know if they were running over anything. They made the drawbridge as the halo of the city dimmed, and they cleared passing near to the concrete footings, and soon to their rightside the marina's low groans and whispers of lanyard and wood and boathull.

"We're at it now."

"Yes, we are."

"This is how you wanted it."

"Yes. This is it. This is good."

"Now, here," said Rhind, and Verdery set a beer on the blade of Rhind's oar, and he took one for himself, and when the drink made them shake with giddiness, they eased their oars again into the black water.

Soon they passed under the Fifth Street bridge, then the Highway 1 bridge, careful to clear the footings. The air lost its color and there persisted only the last of the city's glow at their backs, and soon that faded too, and all about them was only the constant palm of the fog, laying close, attentive. They rowed poised and steady, unhurried, working one gunnel then the other. They stroked how they learned, countering, guiding the bow to downstream, keeping Augusta behind. In the mid of the night's giddiness, nearly sightless, soundless, sleepless, they eased on, with none a witness. Ahead on the Georgia side something slipped in, the water closing with a gentle clap above it.

"Turtle."

"Muskrat."

"Beaver."

"Otter."

"Gator."

"Nessie."

"Grendel."

"Grendel's Mother," said Rhind, and he tapped the gunnel with his blade, and Verdery set a beer on it.

In four statute miles they made the Beech Island bridge. From Georgia they heard tires whine on the asphalt approaching then slap in rhythm at the expansion joints above them, and at the same time they cleared the footings. They listened until there was only the mild complaint again, now fading into Carolina, and they eased on into a stretch they had never made, and in half a mile they neared the C&WC railroad crossing.

Verdery reached, half-lunging with his oar, but the bow point had already struck, sending a deep, resonant shot across the water. It threw him hard against the bow and he slapped at the bascule's footing with the blade of his oar, and the shots came back to them in layered echoes from either treeline. Rhind cursed and fell forward in the hull, grasping either gunnel, and cursing he fought to keep them from going over. The flow shunted the Ouachita heavy into the rough footing, and it ground the full length of its gunnel, metal to concrete, until it cleared, spinning end for end in the persistent flow. Now end for end, torpid, slowing as the needle of a searching compass.

Rhind groaned cursing, then Verdery too. They sat with their asses to the hull, and neither oared to correct the boat, and each improved the other's cursing.

"Damn, you didn't see that."

"I saw it when we hit it."

"I lost my drink."

"Next goes your toothbrush, then your boyhood."

"We made Beech Island fast. This is Beech Island, isn't it?"

"We made it fast."

"Damn if we didn't."

"Have you done this part?"

"No. Here to the new lock, no."

"What else we going to hit."

"I don't know. I think we're about done with things to hit."

"Well, alright."

They listened and there was nothing in the air and the dark, save the distant verse of fathomless, conjoined noises. They sat up again and they put the Ouachita bow forward according to the river's speed against their blades, and caressing the river with all soundless save the reachless hum and the water's wash against the oar blade, they made for the new lock and dam.

CHAPTER FOUR

There is a time of the morning when all natural creatures sleep. Muskrat and great blue heron all silent, and the only worry something from a man. A car door slamming a chassis, wheels wearing the road, the drone of industry testament to work ethic, or simply a drunk not knowing to quit singing or crying. There is a time when all natural creatures sleep. Because it is necessary, because it is that time of the dark. Recovery. Pureness, and none a witness save two.

Just before daybreak called a heron. The air warmed and it moved, and the river wakened. Payne's Grey lightened the rim of the world, and in the gray the great blue heron flew to upriver. The fog opened and through its thinning gauze the shape of either treeline appeared. Verdery lay the oar across his lap, the water running its length to the top of his thighs. He slept only a moment without knowing it and dreamed a sudden, inconsequential dream, with a voice coming first in his dream then from behind.

"You with me?" said Rhind, and Verdery straightened and raised his oar for the first visible point. They made lines for one bend then the next, and when they cleared the second they could just see, then hear, the new lock and dam. They rowed purposefully now, in tandem counterpoint, and where the boat's riveted bow upturned and smiled, the keel lay a whitened, fluid crease of the Savannah to either side. Near to the dam they used their oars as rudders clearing the buoys, and Verdery twisted in the bowseat checking for the ball of the sun, and there was none yet. He spoke over the dam's rumble and spill, "Either way, I want to be on the other side before sunup."

"Alright," said Rhind, over the noise, as the Ouachita's bow tapped the lock's rung ladder.

The lockkeeper shouted down, "What the hell you people doing," and that was the first they heard of him and his bawling pitched voice, cracked and thin. Fowardbent, he was small, atrophied, withered by age and worry, his old face unshaven. He wore all white—the white off-color from wear and wash— canvas shoes, painter's dungarees, and a pullover shirt, oversized for his sorry frame.

"What the hell," he wailed again, though he had already seen them coming, cutting along the water, making the upriver bend.

"Sir," said Verdery upward, into the rising daybreak at the old man's back, "do you know what time it is?"

The lockkeeper blinked and searched over them in an amazed and petulant regard, telling himself: *forget they came here atall, forget they crazy, and now these people talking to me too?*

"William Rhind," said Rhind, and he waited for the shrunken old man and there was nothing save the undiminished, amazed look. "William Rhind. My father works in the D.A.'s office. Daniel Rhind. And we just came to get through."

The lockkeeper blinked at Rhind, then looked at Verdery and blinked the same, waiting to see if the other one also had something ridiculous to say. He blinked and overbent he put his palms to his hips and he wagged his head with the same surprise as when he had been told the same, that they would come. Told by the man in the unusual hat an hour earlier, smoking the tipped cigar, the man with the same name as the foolish one in the back of the boat.

"Where in the hell you people going?"

"We're headed for Savannah, and we'd like to go on before the sun gets too high up," said Verdery.

"Savannah."

"Or as far as we can get in the next few days," said Rhind.

"Savannah," said Verdery. "We want to make Savannah."

"Savannah."

"Yes sir. The law says you have to let us through, no matter what size," said Verdery, as if he knew the law, though he only knew what was told to him.

"The law. You going to tell me about the law now," said the lockkeeper, straightening the aged bent frame, wagging his head the same, holding a last moment's amazed regard at the two men and the longboat, before disappearing from above them and going into the control house.

"Well goddamit then. We'll portage around. We'll just do that," said Verdery, as he searched the rung ladder and stones in concrete above him, and he thought to climb it, standing with both feet centered at the Ouachita's keel and a fist wrapped to the third rung, and he only sat again and cursed again. "We'll just go around. Goddam gear and all." He raised his oar with the blade flat showing Rhind the direction he meant, and the pitched voice bawled again from above.

"You got to tell me why."

"What?"

"You got to tell me why. You know whatall I got to do to get this thing opened for a real boat, much less that piss pot y'all riding in?"

"Sir. My father works for the District Attorney's office in Augusta. Daniel Rhind."

The lockkeeper flattened his hand and shook his palm at Rhind.

"I ain't talking to you. I ain't worried about no damn district attorney. I'm damn civil service, dammit, and I ain't worried about no damn lawyers in Augusta or nowheres else, trying to tell me how to be. *He* got to tell me why y'all want to be coming through here. I done let a lot of boats through here. Damn if it ain't been fifty years' worth. I done seen the princess and the mary queen, and the robert lee. Hell, I done seen the tamaha, way back when. But I'll be damned if I ever seen such as this."

"Altamaha," said Verdery, then wishing he had not.

"What?"

"The Altamaha is what you meant to say."

"You ain't got to correct what I mean to say. I know what I mean to say. I seen all this for fifty years, and in two more weeks ain't nobody going through here, ever again. And I won't be here ever again. All you got to do is tell me why you want to go through here, right now. I'll be damned if I see the need for all this foolishness. Y'all know what time of day it is?"

"Thom," said Rhind.

"No, Will. It's alright," and Verdery checked the east treeline for the ball of the sun, and there was none yet. "He wants to know why."

"That's right. Fifty years. I done said it. I want to know."

"Thom," said Rhind, his voice gaining that terse quality caused by aggravations he had no imagination to suffer.

"No. He wants to know. You want to know? Well I can't go back, that's why. I can't go back, and I'm not going back. That's why."

"Well, why you running? And from what. If you got trouble with the law you need to talk to his daddy. Ain't that right, lawyer's boy."

"Hey, old dude. I want you to tell me something."

"Easy now, lawyer's boy. I ain't got to tell you nothing about nothing."

"Well, Moses, what if I just come up there and we have a prayer meeting, just the two of us. You been to church once, right?"

"Easy now. Watch all that. You know you ain't going to do that. I'm just asking him why, and he told me. Ain't that right."

The lockkeeper half-squatted, as low as he could, like an ancient, half-assed umpire, like picking blackberries, and he wagged his head at the longboat, then looked to upriver to where they had appeared. "Well now, why is it you don't want to go back to where you come from."

"There's no reason. I'm just tired of there, and if I'm here, then I'm not there. And I'm going to Savannah if I have to carry this thing down Tobacco Road to Butler Creek and put back in."

The lockkeeper laughed, the laugh cracking, then *sheeit*, he said, and he wagged his head. "Free," he said.

"What?"

"Free. That's what you want to be, ain't it. That's what you want. That's what you telling me."

"That's not what I said."

"Free," the lockkeeper said again, this time insisting, his gray eyes feral and soaked with petulance and imagination, searching again the last bend upriver where they had come from.

"Alright, old man. Free. That's what I want to be. You hear me this time? I said *free.*"

"I hear you. I hear you, freeman. That's all you had to say in the first place. You just got to know why you come, that's all." He wagged his head and, *sheeit*, he said again. "It's been fifty years, y'all see, and all I want to know, is why. That's all. There ain't been but one day in fifty years they saw me gone from this place. And that was when my gal left me, and I had to go sign a paper in some damn tourney's office. One day in fifty, and somebody's just got to tell me why."

"Well, maybe you can get another fifty years someplace else."

Sheeit, said the lockkeeper, and he hooted and he wagged his head to up-river not seeing another fifty years. Not seeing one more. "Well, I got to open the gate, then I got to flush, then I got to open the other gate. Then y'all will be free as hell from here on down to Savannah. How about that, freeman and lawyer's boy?"

He straightened a portion with effort and cursing, and went to the control house, all the while cackling and repeating it as if it were a song lacking a catchable tune: *sheeit, sheeit, sheeit . . .*

The gate closed behind them, and the lock was fifty-six feet across and three hundred and sixty feet long, and it pooled and drained fifteen vertical feet. They sank, and Rhind held tight to the gunnels, and the concrete and stones rose all about them as the pool flushed, and Verdery, holding his oar across his chest, waited for the bottom, for the lower gates to swing open and for the Savannah to rush upon them and to overtake them in all a white tumble, and the only thing he had against all of it was his oar, close to his chest held on the diagonal, like a bend sinister.

Then when the second gate swung out there came only a gentle stirring and a commingling of the lock and the river waters, and almost as an instinct, something half-wild let out of a pen, they slid the Ouachita clear and into where the fastwater began again. Behind, the diversion dam's spill crushed pure white, and behind them now too, half-crouched again, waving slow a single flat palm, as if judging a fastball, or carefully a pie, or taking a crap, was the old man atop the wall.

"Free," he said aloud. "Y'all free now. Y'all lucky you came when you did, cause next month we all shut down. Y'all come on back this way sometime and we'll talk somemore." He hooted at them—the Ouachita already going small in the distance—but the laugh weakened his lungs, and he straightened that portion coughing, and with his palms to his hips drawing air he watched them go until they and the boat upon the turgid water were truly only and less the size of a gazunder.

The fastwater carried them wide of the Carolina side, and Verdery checked the treeline for the ball of the sun. Full round upon the horizon there had come a low roseamber, and to the east above the Carolina sycamore there grew upward a tinted salient. Verdery twisted in the bowseat looking back, and high upon the structure he remained gesturing in the glare and the rising mist, soundless, no more than a bauble, more artifact now than disturbed old crier.

They rowed clean, their blades deep and steady, plying speed upon the river's new flow, and the Ouachita's bow cut the surface away in whitened burls. Verdery eased only once, again reaching backward. And there was no foolman or sack of dancing bones, and now even the low frost of the dam boiled soundless. *One last time*, he thought, then he turned to downriver and joined again in counterpoint to Rhind.

They made for the first bend holding a straight line against the flow, and when they rounded it, clearing snags then a small sandbar, they made for the next, a place called Twiggs Lower Bar, the same way. The air came mild against them, and now the first of the ball of the sun, it already cupreous, made rising the most distant treeline. On the Carolina bank a sandbar began at the point and wrapped and persisted for two hundred yards. In its pure white, fine grain, the water and less so the wind had carved shape—undulate ripples and smoothings. Near the old shoreline, half in an eddy there rested a ruined cotton barge, on end, three-quarters sunken. It endured captured, sculptured wailing muted, ruddy and ruined from exposure, posed obliquely. Frozen in time gone and time to come, surrendered, after some wild unwitnessed struggle—a remainder, too.

And in front of it all stood a man in shorts with his legs apart and firm in the sand, as if he might have grown, the same as the useless river barge, from that very spot. He wore a hat of an unusual style, and he was shirtless. Slope shouldered, with his fists to his hips and something in each hand, he watched them come to him, and Rhind knew first that it was his father—and the second thing he thought after *that is my father* was *now that he is here, how do we get back?*

CHAPTER FIVE

In Dan Rhind's left hand was a bottle of cherry rail beer, and in his right a black pistol. The copper ball of the sun rose just above his hatted head, and they made for him. He wore cutoffs and the hat was an outback hat—origins unknown, untold. He knew his boat and them coming in it, and he went to the eddy where half an hour earlier he had landed Verdery's Old Town, and stuck the pistol in his shorts and got three fresh beers. They put the Ouachita fast into the sand, and its bow gave a short hush before it quit, and they took only a moment to get their legs under them, as he came for them across the sculptured, barren field, holding to the three iced cherry rail beers.

"Goddam, I thought I'd missed you."

"No sir," said Rhind to his father, "we're right here. Just came through."

"Through."

"The new lock."

"The new lock? The hell. Two weeks time and it'll shut tighter than a tick's ass, and nobody's going through anymore."

"Well, we did."

"The hell, Danny."

Dan Rhind grinned, simpering at both of them, offering the beers, pleased that the asshole lockkeeper had done as he said he would, and the twenty dollars was enough to make a half-crazy, old bastard truthful. Offering the cold beers he was the least tallest, but with the widest shoulders, and he was not yet sixty years old.

"Morning, dad," said Rhind, and he put a palm to his father's bare shoulder and he began across the bar to urinate in the eddy backwater.

"I went and got that boat of yours."

"I see," said Verdery. "You found it alright."

"Sure, sure. I went to the back of the house and I was quiet and thought about your mama, but I was quiet anyways."

"It's been a year. Just a lot of emptiness. It don't matter how much racket you made, you didn't bother anybody."

"Well, I was quiet. I had that thing tied and was driving quicker than you could take a leak."

"Well, I'm glad you got it."

"She was a hell of a gal, Thomas."

"She was."

"People just seem to go on, no matter what. That's just the way we do. But she was a hell of a gal, what I knew of her."

"Yes sir. It's good you came on out."

"Oh, hell yes. Sure, sure. I told Danny there's not a thing keeping me, and y'all better watch out for me." Dan Rhind looked to upriver, to where they had come from across the water. "The new lock."

"Right on through."

He stood grinning with the river barge at his back and the sun just above his head, with the pistol and the beer at either side, and his arms jacked out from his ribs by his back muscles, the way they do in some men with thickness. He spoke with a tone of agreeable oppressive optimism, and often more so in company of others who were not his family, and again more so with those he had just met.

"Then where'd you put in?"

"At the benchmark. At two hundred," said Verdery, and Rhind said the same as he came again to them.

"At Eighth Street," Rhind said, speaking formally, even courteous, the way he did with his father.

"The hell, like you said. Sure, sure, then you've done come a good ways. And here I stand and not even pissing good yet."

"We're just getting started," said Verdery.

"Hell, I hear you. Through the new lock."

"Yes sir."

"The hell."

"Truth. They have to," said Rhind. "It's the law like you said."

"And he just let you on through."

"On through."

"The hell. Good then."

"Truly," said Verdery, this time looking to Rhind to see if he had anything more to tell of how they passed, or of the weathered, disagreeable old clown who had mocked them.

"In two weeks it's shut tighter than a tick's ass. Then nobody goes through, either way."

"Then I guess they go around."

"Hell, I guess."

In the morning sun's first warm cast, their bare feet in the pure sand of the bar, they drank the Door County cherry rail beer Verdery had given to Dan Rhind the Christmas before. The summer before that, he had designed a stock season of scenery and lighting for a friend's company in Fish Creek. A pair of overdone musicals, one straight play about hearts rending apart. For three weeks of his time there he was bedded by a young, frothy-haired actor who had been married for only a few months. She was bright spirited beyond good reason, and ambitious beyond her talent. In Door County Verdery bought the cherry beer for gifts, for Catharine cherry wine, and the same wine for Ginny Eaves. At Christmas cherry beer for Rhind and his father too, and wine to make them drunk and warm, though he only cheated on Catharine, and less so, Ginny Eaves.

At the playhouse he asked the young performer about her new husband, who also worked a summer stock job, making handprops, back East.

Oh, he's alright. He understands how things are, she said of her propmaster. *We have to work.*

Then maybe you will tell him. Maybe not.

Of course not, Thomas. We'll spend the rest of our lives together, and he'll never know about this, or any other one. Because in ten years will it matter?

When at the final dress rehearsal, when Verdery could abandon his lighting, he stood from the designer's table and went out of the theatre a last time, and she was tapping a big finish over the painted maple and singing in her head voice, selling her unreasonable optimism to an empty house. From the rear of the auditorium he raised a hand good-bye, but his front wash blinded her and she could not see him walk out. He drove with a good carload of the cherry rail beer and the wine the twenty hours to Connecticut, and somewhere crossing Pennsylvania near Erie it occurred to him that he had not left her a thing to keep. And again later burning up the Taconic Parkway, due south, he thought it just as well.

"Did you put in at the boat ramp, dad?"

"Sure, sure."

"We just didn't think about a ride back, is all."

"Well, I talked to the wife."

"The wife. You mean my wife? You mean Emmy?"

"Actually, a boy from work said to call him when we're ready, at Blue Springs."

"Work. Who from work?"

"Blue Springs," said Verdery.

"We just didn't think about a ride back, is all."

"Savannah," said Verdery.

"Alright then. We'll call somebody or another. They got phones down there. Hell, Emmy'll be home on Sunday, won't she?"

"Savannah," said Verdery, "not Blue Springs."

"Well, we won't bother her with all this."

"She can do something for you. It won't kill her to do something for you, for us. You just have to ask. It won't kill you to ask, and it won't kill her to do something."

"Savannah," said Verdery, "not Blue Springs."

"Savannah," said Dan Rhind. "Savannah's a long ways off. There's a boy at work, said just call him when we're ready on Sunday."

"Sunday," said Verdery.

"Well," said Rhind, "I can't bother Emmy with all this. This is our worry, our foolishness, not hers."

"How far is Blue Springs?" said Verdery.

"Blue Springs?"

"You been to Blue Springs."

"No, I've never been there. I mean I drove there once, but I've never been there in a boat. I've been down to the 301 bridge. Me and Danny's sister's boy came out here messing around for a couple of days. That's why I say come Sunday, you going to want to get near a telephone. Blue Springs is seventy-eight."

"Seventy-eight what," said Rhind.

"Seventy-eight miles on the map. You say you put in at two hundred, and back there at the new lock is one eighty-seven, and Blue Springs is seventy-eight."

"Well we don't have a map," said Rhind looking to Verdery.

Verdery shrugged, "No, we don't have a map."

"You don't have a river map."

"No sir."

"They sell *NOAA* maps at the marina."

"We don't have one."

"Well, alright, I got one."

"No sir, we didn't bring one," said Verdery, "but the river goes that way, right?"

Dan Rhind simpered and he wagged his head at them. "Alright," he said, and he lowered and wagged his head again, and Verdery crossed the sandbar to the warm eddy near his Old Town, and he urinated into the backwater, the same as Rhind. He closed his eyes tight and he steadied himself, and the beer and the quiet hummed in his ears, and all he heard was the quiet chorus and the sound of his pissing and the baritone voices behind him.

"I just don't want Emmy involved in all this."

"Danny, that's alright if you don't. I didn't call her. Hell, when would I have done that? Hell, we're grown men, we'll get back."

"Did you call mom?"

Dan Rhind drank of his beer and with the back of his hand that held the pistol wiped his mouth, and he tossed his head.

"But you called someone at work. Who's going to tend to your car, dad?"

Again Dan Rhind drank of his beer and wiped his mouth the same, and this time Rhind did not know what the motion of his father's head meant to say. "Who's going to tend to yours?"

"I just can't get Emmy involved in this thing, that's all."

"Alright," said Dan Rhind, then, "hell, we're grown men. Now y'all come on and let's go on down this river somewheres."

He went from his son crossing the sandbar meeting Verdery halfway, and he stopped and finished his beer, then raised a straightened arm and the pistol at the surviving quarter of the river barge.

"You shoot that thing?"

"Hell, I don't get to shoot it at home."

Dan Rhind closed his fist and the pistol cracked fire and smoke, and the bullet whined a furious pitch, singing off the barge's belly. Verdery ducked covering his ears, cursing, watching the ruddy vein of rustsmoke break loose from the old steel of the hull. Dan Rhind fired twice more, with the second round pocking the sand just short, and the next singing as the first, leaving only the trace of the rustsmoke. He lowered the black pistol regarding the scrap iron sculpture as if he half-expected it to retaliate, and when it did not he walked on saying, "Thank you for that northern beer, son. Now, let's you and me and that boy of mine go on down this goddam river somewheres."

CHAPTER SIX

With the morning light they repacked their gear into the Ouachita. They made it so to remember to pack it the same each time, and they made it so their drinks were easy to get at.

They backed the Ouachita off the sandbar and Rhind sat first, and they saw that Dan Rhind in the Katahdin was already to the river's far side, making for the next point, becoming small in the distance.

"My dad," said Rhind.

"Think we'll see him again?"

"If somebody doesn't get him first."

"Well if they get him, they get us."

"Who would want *us*."

They worked the Ouachita into the flow, and in only a few strokes they made the same, already extinct, pathway Dan Rhind had cut before them.

"Savannah," said Verdery aloud, as if he spoke the syllables for the first time. He tried out the sound of it again, and by the third time he sang it, separating the parts slowly, inventing scales and intonation, all of it inspired by cherry beer and sleeplessness, and the roseamber August morning—and by the distance still gauzed in the low morning atmosphere, and near to them the river's body turning to emerald in the sun.

Rhind said something in German, the way his mother taught him, and he tapped the gunnel with his oar and Verdery set a beer upon his blade, and he took one for himself. *One more*, he said to the open water, to the distant blue mist, *then we work*.

They rowed oppositely, concordantly, making for each point in a line as they cleared each bend. They spoke tacitly, short sentences. Eyes narrowed against the morning glare, groping the distance. They encouraged the Ouachita, it as ceaseless and faster thrice than the river itself, and each stroke and each quarter mile took them to where they had never been.

Sometime in the early morning they cleared the last spill canal of the soap and sawmills that politics and industry had situated on the Georgia side. They rowed hard until they were sure they had put it behind them, where the water and the air became pure again.

They followed Dan Rhind into what he believed a cutoff, where the river runs straight past an oxbow, and after a half hour it narrowed not to rejoin the channel, and they were another half hour getting back.

Soon they saw the first markings in a beach, and they guessed it was alligator, and soon it was true as they neared one, asleep in the sun on the trunk of a deadfallen gum. It was small, two and a half or three oars' worth, common so far upriver. When it sensed them it went not into the water but back again into the switchcane, into a tunnel path it had already pressed. They saw more tracks cut into the beaches and the sandbars, but despite the evidence all the morning they did not see another.

They stopped only once before lunch, sliding the Ouachita into a beach amidst a growth of white willows. They stood to feel their legs, and Dan Rhind, now kneeling as he rowed in the Katahdin, came close along the shore.

"Did you see anymore after that first one?"

"Just him."

"They're all the way up to Augusta now. All the way up to the goddam canal."

"We'll see some more."

"I imagine we will. Don't let one get you," said Dan Rhind, grinning and nodding, indicating the willows with a tip of his hat.

"We'll be alright."

"Y'all come on. We'll stop for lunch here in a little while."

"That'd be a story," said Rhind, watching his father's broad back working the boat, one gunnel then the other, making again for the channel, like a boy.

"Sure, and you without a camera."

"Tommy, when is cocktail hour?"

"Not for a little while yet. Miles to go before we drink."

"Miles to go before we drink."

They made places called Fritz Cut, Hungry Swamp Lodge, and Head of Stingy Venus, and Silver Bluff, but they did not know the names or that they were named. They made bend after bend putting one quarter mile then another and another behind them, and at mile one seventy-one they stopped for lunch on a beach opposite the landing at Jackson, South Carolina. They sat in the yellow sand and ate beans out of cans with crackers, with Rhind and his father drinking beer and Verdery drinking from a gallon jug of water. They studied Dan Rhind's rivermap and spoke of the alligator, and they watched across the river a young couple fishing from the rocks alongside the boat ramp. The pair had a small boy that played on the rocks and at the water's edge, and every so often they heard the mother speak loudly to the boy, though across the distance they could not determine the words.

The first people since the new lock, thought Verdery—*I know them, the same as the old man. Husband a laborer, short a year or two his high school. Wednesday off to fish, and I hope that he is kind to his wife and child, even though they are poor. Don't be at ease in your lack of school, and remember always to fear stupidity and contentment. There are too many of you already that do not.*

Verdery took a drink from the gallon jug, and then too, with his eyes fixed across the emerald water's tensile surface, he thought, *you are wrong about all of it. There is water in Lake Nepaug the same as the water here, and Catharine came from Princeton, and when you next blink, in the next beat of your eye or your heart, you will put all of it away from you. But I do know you people. I have always known you people. Where you come from, how you behave. I have always known these things, more than anything.*

Verdery stood and he sighed heavy and long, and in the next breath he was sure he was wrong about all of it.

"It's a old swingbridge," said Dan Rhind. "It's the damnedest thing you ever saw."

"Where is it?"

"It's the old 301 crossing. But now they got a new bridge."

"I mean, where is it on the map?"

"It's one nineteen. One hundred nineteen rivermiles."

"And where are we now," said Verdery.

"One seventy," said Dan Rhind. "That's Jackson, right across."

"And Blue Springs is seventy-eight," said Rhind.

"And how many is Savannah?" said Verdery.

"Savannah is fourteen. Fourteen upriver from the Tybee lighthouse, and that is zero. That's why I say, it's a long ways off."

"Fourteen," said Verdery, watching the couple and the child upon the rocks opposite the body of the emerald river.

Dan Rhind cleaned the beach after himself, and Rhind and Verdery did the same, and when Dan Rhind had lighted a tipped pantela, he went again upon the river in the smaller boat. He made for the channel and the fast water, leaving behind only a keelmark and footprints on the beach, and a thin line of blue smoke trailing in the air, and he did not look back upriver for half an hour.

In the afternoon's full sun Verdery leaned back upon the gear and he slept. Silently Rhind eased the Ouachita through the channel, working the blade gently into the river, keeping the oar off the gunnels. He grimaced and smiled together into the water's glare, and the sun made his face red and brown. Verdery slept lightly and wakened wetted from sweating, twice, then slept lightly again. When he wakened the third time he sat up, and he could not remember dreaming. He looked back to Rhind, and he did not know how much river had gone under them, and as the sweat cooled his skin the giddiness came again.

"Stay down, Thom. I got it."

Verdery searched in a full circle the jade and sungold water, and the darker opposite treelines of each state. The channel had straightened to an inestimable stretch, and at its greatest distance the air silked to blue, and into the heavy gauze the river dissolved the same. The water and the air's fragrances commingled and they conjured a memory, and the giddiness came full.

"Hang on."

"Where you going?"

"To see my baby."

"Easy," said Rhind, and he lay down his oar and took hold of both gunnels and Verdery rolled from the Ouachita into the cold Savannah. He surfaced, blowing, yelping, then crawled to catch the boat, and he took hold to the painter at the stern, and drew it into the water with him.

"Mr. T. C. Verdery?"

"Yes, Mr. W. D. Rhind," and Rhind rolled the same as Verdery nearly tipping the Ouachita completely, and Verdery steadied it with a hand to the gunnel, and Rhind surfaced and yelped, and he swam and caught the boat at the gunnel opposite Verdery. Rhind yelped, then Verdery, and they swam alongside the boat, letting it alone, letting the flow take the three of them. They crawled until they warmed, and they met at opposite gunnels, and Verdery took beer from the cooler and together they drank beer, wrapped in the cold, flowing Savannah.

"Do we feel good."

"We do feel good."

"Did we know . . ."

"We suspected."

"Do we . . ."

. . . and they sang in their way, less than bluesmen, back and forth across the boat and their gear trying out a rackety version of the greatest song ever made, trying the day and a proud man's song from Augusta—because singing is what you do in a cold river up to your neck—and who was not and what was not from that place, and leaving that place.

"It's good."

"Hey . . . you know you can't tell them about all this up north, if you don't go back."

"I'm not. I mean Augusta, too."

"Augusta too."

"Augusta too."

"Ever?"

"Ever."

"You've said that before."

"I'm saying it again."

"So he was right."

"Who."

"The crazy man, the old bitch."

"That's what he said. But he's just a crazy man, talking through bad teeth. Did you forget about getting back? We have two boats now."

"Two boats and no cars. No, I didn't forget."

"There's Emmy."

"Yes, there's Emylia Gray. But fuck her, and fuck me. Is it cocktail hour yet?"

Rhind pushed off from the Ouachita, and he swam a one-armed backstroke with his beer aloft, working the cold out of his bones.

CHAPTER SEVEN

Each ten miles came a marker, a sign on a creosote post set into the water, showing the river mileage. They made mile one eighty at Hungry Swamp

Lodge, one seventy at Eagle Point, and one sixty the last marker they would remember that day. At mile one sixty-four they passed into Burke County, and they found Dan Rhind as he stood on a beach with his back to them, urinating into the switchcane. Approaching mile one sixty-two they made the Shell Bluffs, cliffs rising fifty feet on the Georgia side, where the ancient clay held fast the remnant giant oysters, where in prehistory the ocean swam above them.

There too de Soto had been half a century before, with the six hundred men and horses, possessed with the vision of gold—and now at the cliffs, avaricious of the pearls too. They would take it all if they could. The ragged Spaniards milling about, footsore in the water, speaking low among themselves, where once they cursed their coming, now again their purpose crystalline—resolve and greed too restored. One of the six hundred breaks from the gathering, maybe de Soto himself, shouting in the rugged fevered new language, *estamos aqui*. Desire arcing, they slog on, upriver, finally crossing, and after all of it they find Chufitachiqui, the savage woman of beauty and grace, she adorned not in a single coin or shot of gold, and they find too the mounds of shells and burned and cracked pearls, because the Creek cared only for the meat of the oyster. Then, knee-deep in the cold water of an aimless watercourse, what is a lost Spanish soldier to think of the home he will never again see.

Rhind made cocktails early, and now they only meandered, and the gin brought the soft gauze of drunkenness over them. They talked the past, girlfriends and women and places lived, and they giggled like boys and bellylaughed like grown drunken men, and their laughter echoed off the treelines and joined again with them. They drew near to Dan Rhind and offered a cocktail, and he wagged his head and simpered at them and raised his beer to them. Shirtless, he had reddened, and he wore the outback hat with half the brim snapped up and the chin-tie loose.

Verdery asked if Rhind remembered the dark-headed girl named Mischel, and Rhind thought and asked, "was she a mean one," and Verdery said, "yes."

"Did she slap you once."

"Yes, twice."

"And did you deserve it."

"Yes, twice" said Verdery, and Rhind said, *yes*, he did remember the dark-headed girl named Mischel.

They had more gin, and with the drunkenness and the warm air over them, and the cold drinks in their bellies, they made riverbends, and the bends became miles. They made a point named Flowery Gap Bar where the river switched back and both shores became all sand, and through the shallow clear water they could see the river bed was sand too—and bent and waving in the flow beneath the surface grew full beards of elodea. Verdery did not see Dan Rhind ahead, and a moment later the small white boat crossed in front of the treeline, its profile low and reduced by distance to something alike a sliver of bone—master and vessel a mirage.

"He's making time."

"We'll get him after awhile."

"We'll get him."

Verdery asked if Rhind remembered the lake and the houseboat with the four girlfriends, and if he remembered it was May third, nineteen eighty-two.

"Was it a houseboat or a pontoon?"

"Yes. A pontoon."

"Was it May third?"

"Yes."

"How do you still know all that?"

"I don't know, I just do."

"Do you try?"

"I don't know. It won't leave me. Never will."

"That's Annie's birthday. May third."

"I know it is. I was there too."

They found Dan Rhind an hour later on a beach skipping shale into the river. Together they stood in the sand and studied his rivermap and they guessed at the rivermiles, how far they had gone.

"We knew Jackson. That was noon," said Verdery.

"Or one," said Rhind.

"I know it," said Dan Rhind, "but we just made one sixty. I believe we about here," and he put his finger to the map to show them his guess. "I imagine we got four hours of day left. We'll make a long ways before it gets dark on us."

"We might should quit before dark," said Verdery.

"Oh sure," said Dan Rhind. "Sure, we'll come along on someplace or another we like."

"You've been down this way before though," said Verdery.

"Down here? Not through here," said Dan Rhind, wagging his head, grinning, looking at his feet in the sand, then to downriver.

"You been to the 301 bridge," said his son.

"I've been in the car to the swingbridge," said Dan Rhind, looking downriver, admiring all of it unknown to him. "Me and your sister's boy came out one day and spent the night. But that was way back. Hell, since Jackson's been new water to me too."

"Dad," said Rhind, then, "hell. Well, alright," then, "hell," looking to the sand at his own feet, then to Verdery, wagging his head, his hands to his hips, his shoulders sloping the same as his father.

Verdery laughed and sputtered, and he went up the beach to the white willows, and Rhind then his father did the same and all together they urinated into the willows and the switchcane. They gathered again in the shallow, cold water, all three groping the distance downriver, all three bending, cupping the flawless cool water to their faces, wiping at the heat and the drunkenness. Dan Rhind lighted a tipped pantela and he spoke to the far treeline.

"They say it's six days, all the way down."

"But you don't know that."

"No, I don't know. I know what people say."

"Then how far to Blue Springs."

"I don't know. We're maybe . . . y'all in a hurry?"

"No sir," said Verdery, and Rhind looked to his feet in the clear water and the sand, and he wagged his head without answering. Golden sand, tiny shells there.

"Well, hell, come on here and let's all go somewhere we never been."

CHAPTER EIGHT

The river shaded with the cloud shadows passing. They made points and bends and switchbacks innumerable and alike and the miles slid under them. Late in the day when the sun cooled they saw a boy working a johnboat against the river with his hand to a motor throttle. He steered and he fished together beneath overhanging myrtle working eddies aiming for panfish. He jigged whipping his rod and his line, casting until the flow turned the johnboat, when he righted the bow to upstream. He caught redbreast snatching them into the boat, not stringing them, but flinging them to the boat's bottom. The myrtle obscured him, and it occurred to Verdery that he was the first person they had seen since the Jackson landing, and the johnboat and motor the first machine since the gears of the new lock, below Augusta.

Verdery washed his drink cup in the river and he took up his oar to work the Ouachita, and Rhind did the same. As they rounded the next bend they saw the old sea boat—a wooden cabin cruiser, sleek of line, a design meant for pleasure over work. It leaned tipped to the river nearly sunken to the deck railing, long ago suspended inanimate, frozen rising to the the crest of an unseen breaker. The bow sat high on the bank resting heavy in the sedge, tipped up in an attitude sentient denying its demise. Along the hull's full length ran eight portal windows, and the waterline began at the last four and overtook completely the last portal window nearest the stern. The pilot house stood mid-deck still intact, it large enough for a captain, a dinner table and chairs, with windows gone and a portion of the high roof gone too, showing the underplanking. There were two hatches, one just before the pilot house, and a large covered hatch astern, and it was yet a whole boat despite the rot, surviving and resistant to natural laws, let alone forgotten, partnered to the ceaseless river.

Behind the sea cruiser on a upward slope grew a stand of tall, grayed liveoak, their boughs hagged by Spanish moss. Beyond the liveoak at the hilltop stood a house of good size. Even at a distance it read large, with wrap around porches, one above, one below. An overgrown dirt and gravel driveway led from the house down the slope to the water, and in this drive-up, with the small boat pulled half-ashore, reddened and shirtless, hunched, his belly hanging over his long shorts, with the outback hat pushed back on his head, and a tipped cigar burning in his mouth, stood Dan Rhind. He had a hand to a hip and the rivermap in the other hand and his head wagging in its way. He seemed to curse at himself, but as they brought the Ouachita around they saw that he was actually speaking to someone. The other man was small and bent, sitting upon a riding mower with the motor running, and Dan Rhind did not curse but laughed, and each wagged and nodded his head to the other, alike and grinning, fatuous, enthusiastic.

In the longboat they maneuvered past piling stumps of a vanished dock and landed and they stood in the cold river. The old man shut the tractor off and he waved, thin limbed, his face sunned and creased with age. Drunk as they were, shin high in the river, they had no idea where they presently stood.

"Jesup," said the old man, raising his arm again when they came up out of the water. They spoke in turn, tasting the gin in their lungs, and the old man said *Jesup* again, and waited simpering. A little scab of a man, gaunt all of him and sun darkened. A sagging, worn and tired face, gray-eyed, eyes the color of an unpromising morning, teeth surviving unevenly in his head, remainders of long life and neglect. He coyed grinning, with that quality of near shame, as Southerners do, knowing strangers already understood him for what he was— suspicious possibly they knew more. *He is the same as the first one*, Verdery thought, standing near to him.

"How far big daddy?"

"I'm looking. A good ways I imagine. I just need to figure something here."

"Y'all need to stay with me tonight," said Jesup right away, his voice thin and pitched, and Verdery thought again, *yes, of course, he is the same.* "We was talking, me and Mister Rine here, and I said y'all can come on up and stay at the house."

"We got gear," said Verdery.

"I take care of this property here," said Jesup twisting in the tractor seat and nodding to the top of the hill. "I take care of the big house up yonder. This here is the Covington's plat. They ain't none of them here for awhile. The whole place is empty, with four rooms going to waste."

"Mr. Jesup invited us to stay the night," said Dan Rhind, picking tobacco from his lip, holding the pantela in the same hand as the river map. "I didn't say one way or the other. I wanted to see, there's still some daylight."

"We got gear," said Verdery again, "we came to camp."

"Well," said Rhind, almost as a question, rolling his shoulders, looking back to the river then up the hill to the house, and they all regarded one another in doubt, except Verdery who looked away at the longboat and the gear in the boat.

"Well," said Rhind again, and he sighed long and heavy tasting the used gin in his lungs, and he went to the nearest liveoak, and sat in the sedge propped to the tree.

"Danny," said Dan Rhind, asking after him.

"I'm alright. Do whichever, I'm alright."

In only a moment he might have become an antique discarded, left barren in wasteland soil, sibling to the ruined cruiser. He watched the river pass, it soft boiling and deep emerald in the late daylight, and he nodded once, then again, tasting the gin deep in his lungs, and Rhind slept before he knew he slept.

CHAPTER NINE

Verdery saw now it was bound at the bow by a chain heavy and darkened of hackberry, sagging taut to a near oak. He put a finger to the bumper and he took a chip of paint away, and the paint left a spot of chalk on his fingertip. Close now, Verdery admired it for its age and what he imagined to be its endurance, and for its lines. He ran a hand along the gunwale and arriving at the stern he read its name, drawn in brush with an artist's hand. The transom descended half into the river and the name sank with it, but he could yet read it rendered, *Caron Lee.*

"She's something, ain't she," called Jesup, coming along the path Verdery had made in the sedge. He moved, careful but quick, animation refuting age, afoot with the agility of knowing his terrain. Dan Rhind came too, and the three stood close, with two of them reading the transom, the name brushed with oils thirty years before in a Lazaretto Creek marina.

Verdery said it aloud, and "Oh sure," said Jesup, looking too at the lines and scribble, knowing the spoken name, remembering its shape of how it sounded in his hearing.

"Sure, she was a hell of a gal. Covington brought her up from the city. Not the boy, you know, or his brother, but the old man. See, he gave the boys the house back there, and the plat too, when the law got him."

"Got him," said Dan Rhind, through his teeth and his cigar. "What did they get him for."

"Hell, because he was against them, I reckon."

Verdery guessed and said it. "Covington stole the boat from Savannah— that's the city, right? And they found him and it here, and they got him for it."

"No, no. No sir, that ain't got nothing to do with the shooting."

"They shot him?"

"Shore."

"Why'd they do that?"

"Hell, I reckon because they needed to."

"This's Burke county, right?" said Dan Rhind.

"Shore it is."

"And they shoot you around here if they need to."

"No. Only if you against the law, I imagine."

Dan Rhind made a noise to himself and teethed the cigar's tip, taking a moment to taste it.

"But Covington brought the boat up from Savannah."

"Well, shore. But what I'm trying to tell you was he brought the gal first."

Verdery made another guess to himself and he looked the length of *Caron Lee*, as if in her lines and leaning and her endurance and her rot he would engage her past.

"She was a hell of a gal when he brung her here. Hell, that was fifteen, twenty years ago. Seems like a hundred. Hell, I was a young man then too. Younger."

And Jesup told some of it in the pitched, exalted voice, the sharp tone the mockery of a woman, and Verdery thought again too amidst his guessing, *yes he is the same as the other, of course they are the same.* Jesup coughed recollecting, surprised at even himself in the telling and the opportunity, the need. *Hell,* he aspirated in short bursts as if fallen against the earth with the air shunted of him, and Verdery nodded as if listening more than he were, more than he could as drunk as he was, and he surmised all of *Caron Lee*, and the places of his own ghosts abandoned tens and hundreds and thousands of miles away from where they presently stood. Jesup paused coughing and cursing, breathless a last time, and Verdery and Dan Rhind made noises to themselves and nodded, and Verdery started again back through the path in the sedge with Jesup following, and Dan Rhind following too with the blue smoke of the tipped pantela trailing and rising, vanishing a last forgotten spirit, the last and the fourth of them.

Verdery kicked his bare foot against Rhind's, and when Rhind did not waken he kicked a second time and spoke. With the attitude of his head unchanged, resting against the liveoak's gray trunk, Rhind opened his eyes in a suddenness and clarity and stillness, and he had wakened not like this in all his thirty-five years. He regarded not Verdery or the others standing above him but only the river's gentle, deep emerald boiling. And with the Ouachita's motion persisting in his blood and bones and his face rendered expressionless by fatigue and the gin, he closed his eyes again, and Verdery spoke a third time, then let him alone.

"We're staying."

"It's a bed and a shower," said Dan Rhind.

"Like I said, y'all come on up to the big house."

"We right behind you," said Dan Rhind.

"Y'all come on, we'll get us some supper," and Jesup climbed, clinging and sudden upon the tractor, and he drove clattering and grinding the slope to the house.

"He'll be alright," said Verdery. "I'll get what we need, and I'll get him up."

"You been drinking some."

"We have."

"I'm fairly beat to hell myself. That boat of yours."

"We'll swap and you can ride with this one here."

"I'm alright. Hell."

"Was that his boy fishing?"

"Grandson. A youngun."

"Dinner and a bed. And the middle of nowhere."

"Hell, I'll take it."

The upper porch surrounded the house and met the slope at the front door on the side away from the river. There was a brown peafield, and past that another field grown full of broomsedge, and past the meadow in the west sky the sun had just made the treeline. Above the porch hung a sign, a plank excised from *Caron Lee*, hand lettered to read *Cliff's Folly*.

"Who was Cliff," said Verdery.

"Hell if I know," said Jesup, and Verdery nodded. *Why would you know.*

It was a well-made cabin, grand-sized, purposefully rustic, board and battened, cedar screen doors, rugged beams and cedar porch posts, and bench furniture in the style of bentwood, for sitting and viewing the west. A large kitchen, then the great room. Off the great room the back porch, and from it they scanned the broomcorn and undervine of the slope, the oaks, the dimming river. Within three bedrooms and baths, and all of it mephitic of redwood and cedar, and the must of disuse. Jesup told that the older Covington boy came infrequently, and then only with liquor and women, since his wife let him go. And the younger Covington boy anymore did not hardly come at all.

Verdery guided Rhind into a bedroom, and Rhind stood saying only *no*, and scuffed to the great room and lay on the sofa, with his head toward the cold stones of the fireplace. Above him, mounted, hung the head taken of a wild boar. Tusked and black glassy eyed it stared feral blind in still rage. It was hunted across the river at the government reserve, where they made tritium gas for nuclear weapons. The animals were protected and the sows and boars grew large, wild and fearless, and only by license were they culled.

On the west porch the daylight was nearly gone, and Verdery and Dan Rhind stood hunched, weary, polite and as attentive as the wear of the long hours allowed. Reddened by the sun, and empty with hunger too, they nodded, fatigued and gentle smiling, and listened as Jesup told it this way, of the boar.

CHAPTER TEN

How it was, you see, was he, Jesup, and his grandson, the same boy who was bringing the fish for supper and the youngest Covington boy, had tracked the pig with the help of a hunter named Toombs. The youngest Covington boy had a reputation for being a good shot, though it wasn't true. The one time he was just awfully lucky, it turns out. Now this Toombs for real held a license from the government, and they for real paid Toombs to cull them hogs.

"You using a rifle, not a crossbow."

"That's right."

"You ain't afraid to scare them off with the noise of it?"

"I don't aim to scare them, I aim to murder them."

They hunted for a good long day, and they finally found the pig at the same time they realized the boy was gone, and they heard the boy wailing and crying like the rapture visited. And when they got to the boy at the foot of the tree, there was that great big hog waiting for the rest of them. And it rushed them, Toombs and the Covington boy, and Jesup himself. Jesup climbed the first stump he found, and the Covington boy lay into the weeds, he crying now too, and Toombs, he leveled the rifle steady and put a single shot right center of that pig's head, like a third eye. And that pig, even after that bullet went into its bone, came on, until its brain told it, let it, quit, and it lay down right at Toombs's feet, like a dog, or anything other than a wild proud creature.

Then Toombs, he helped first the wailing grandson out the pine tree, then he stood the praying Covington boy back to his feet out of the sedge, then he let Jesup down from the pitch stump, and he asked if they wanted anything left over from the pig seeing as how it had a bullet through its skull now. The Covington boy could not talk to answer him, and he couldn't even look at the hateful creature laying so close to them all, so Jesup spoke for him, saying *hell yes* he wanted *the damn thing*, and he even knew someone, a fellow named Todd over in Barnwell, who could fix that hole in that pig's head, to make it look like the thing died naturally.

And the result of it was when the *oldest* Covington boy saw it fixed up, he had Jesup put the damn thing over the fireplace, and the other result was his grandson took to fishing, and the last result was that the youngest Covington boy didn't come around, even on weekends—and when he did he didn't mess around in the front room or stay in the house atall; and can't nobody understand such behavior.

And what about Toombs. Oh he got killed awhile back, and *no it wasn't no pig that got him.* No, it was his wife that shot him when she caught him fooling around. And no, *it weren't even another woman,* but *that taxidermist named Todd.* Reckon *he* knew him too. Yes, and that's why when it's all said and done, he, Jesup, *don't mess around with either of them anymore: wild hogs or grown women. And, of course, I never was a queer.*

The sun sank into in the pines now, and they sat on the porch with their feet in the grass, all but silent, patient with hunger and weariness, watching the peafield and the western sky shading to roseamber dusk. Jesup leaned and spat tobacco juice into the grass, and spat a little upon himself, and chewed, pleased with himself, in that fatuous manner of people who believe in God and tobacco. Pleased with the day how he had found company coming off the river. Dan Rhind chewed too sharing what Jesup had, and they spat into the grass on either side of Verdery.

Passing the days Jesup pecked around the property traveling with the small tractor under him. He seldom went into the cabin, and he kept the windows shut. And in the days and the nights of *Cliff's Folly* it was only the cedar and the must, and the soundless, raging, captured boar within the redwood walls, with Jesup traversing the property, full of animation and restive purposelessness, crawling amidst the cornbroom and liveoak, and him, and all of it too, overviewing the ceaseless, impenetrable river.

"Yessir, this is what I look after."

"Sure, sure. It's some fine land."

"Y'all from Augusta."

"Sure."

"Way over Augusta."

"Sure."

When it darkened and the treeline blackened to silhouette, the boy came toting a stringer of fish. He appeared from below, making the rise, walking with his head down, somber and inward, holding the redbreast proud. At the water he saw the two boats tugged high into the sedge, and he remembered seeing the one man, then the two men on the channel. He was a thin and tanned teenager with muscled lean legs of an athlete, a ballplayer. He came barefooted with the stringer swaying heavy full of fish. Nearing them he nodded once, diffident, and he raised the stringer high to the old man, showing an arm lean and muscular and not yet full grown, and he waited for his Grandfather to speak.

Jesup spat, simpering to the dusk, and not looking to the boy he spoke to the failing light.

"Seems like you did some good, Jase."

"Yessir."

"Well, we about starved to death waiting on you."

"Yessir."

"You see it done got about dark here, and we still got groceries to fix."

"Yessir."

"You got the boat pulled up good?"

"Yessir."

"It going to be there in the morning?"

"Yessir, tied good too."

"Good then. We got company, and I imagine they about starved to death.

Run to the house and get them things cleaned so we can get some groceries going. We coming right down."

"Yessir."

"Good boy. And Jase, you know I love you boy."

"Yessir," and he bowed his head again and went on for the top of the rise, with the stringer wrapped to a fist, heavy alongside, grounding him and his reduced silhouette.

Jesup coyed, grinning, and with the dusk upon his aged, grayed eyes, he did not look at the boy fisherman, even when he crossed in front of him, even when the boy's thin, diffused shadow fell across him. He only lowered his head and spat the dark renderings, nodding up again only when the boy had passed. He waited until his grandson made the rise and descended again, then he stood and patted at his thighs in dirty cotton slacks as if cleaning himself of dust.

"Let me go on and get these groceries started. Y'all come on here in a minute and get you some good supper," and he went on making the path and the rise as the boy had, he shrunken against the deep lavender, altogether a trifle and remnant, the sky dimming even as he moved through it, bobbing once, then again, a toy against the dun, then too vanishing.

Inside, Verdery wakened Rhind, and he saw Verdery first, then in the quarterlight, his father, then the boar, and then in the next moment he knew again where he was, and he sat and stood from the sofa all at once.

"Alright."

"It's supper time soon," said Verdery.

"There's fish," said Rhind, his arms loose by his side, his face drawn from sleep and lack of it, he searching the dim portal of the screendoor.

"Sure."

"The boy. The boy in the johnboat caught some fish, and the old man told us to come to dinner," said Rhind.

"Did you dream that?" said Verdery.

"Is it not true?"

"Sure, it's true. You up now?"

"I'm up now."

"Then we can go on and eat some fish."

In the great room's fust and disuse, with the suspended, feral head above, with only their breathing and a mild hum of silence and a faint fragrance of spent gin airborne in the dusk graying room, they stood barefooted upon the plank floor, and the wear of the long day had come to them. It had been a good long while and they had made miles of river, and in their weariness came the small comfort of knowing one small thing—they had come far.

In the portal of the doorframe his shape might have been anyone, anything, but Dan Rhind knew the round shoulders as his own, and he knew then too that long ago his son had outgrown him by a head. Rhind sighed heavy and he shrugged once putting his hands to his hips, and in the motion the silhouette became again familiar, a child and friend.

"Hey, Ghostman, hey, big daddy, let's go eat some fish."

"Sure, Danny."

They waited a moment longer, then Rhind went off the porch stepping first into the finish of the dusk and they walked the dark rise where the gifted boy fisherman and the tottering old storyteller had led.

CHAPTER ELEVEN

Jesup abided in a pull trailer for a home—a moldy camper set up on blocks, with airless tires still nutted to the axles, and the door opened with the warm incandescent interior light spilling outward and across a stack of cut floor joists, sleepers, used for steps up. Even the pine woods were fragrant of the peanut oil and the potatoes and the cornbread and the fish. He tended to three cast-iron pans over a gas stove, arms above the cookers, testing the rising heat, settling a blessing or a spell. Just cooking up groceries for all he was worth.

They sat within an arm's reach of Jesup and the stove, and they watched him at work, hovering above the smoking oil, conjuring the dinner. Laid out on the small tabletop were paper plates and tarnished silverware of various designs, and beneath this a board game, with pawns and dice at the center. An accordion door shutting off the back half of the trailer opened, and the boy came through it and joined the men, and sat silent alongside Rhind at the table, staring at his own hands, his hands just washed of fish blood and scales and a day's worth of soil and balled together upon the tabletop. Coming with the boy trailed a fragrance of soap and something else, and Verdery raised his head slightly to it, but, consumed in the smoke and the boiling and heat of Jesup's work, it in a moment was gone.

"He likes to play," said Jesup, nodding, grinning at the gameboard and pawns. "Hell, I don't mind myself. It keeps your mind active."

Rhind offered his hand to the boy, as he might to a colleague or an interview, saying "William D. Rhind," and the boy took it lightly and did not say his name.

"Jase," said Jesup. "That's Jase, ain't that right boy. Tell them who you are."

The boy grinned and nodded, the same as his grandfather, and he reached for the dice, rolling them in his fist, tumbling them on the board.

"That boy likes to fish. He don't care nearly as much about anything as he does fishing. Hell, if I allowed it he'd stay here and not even bother with nothing else. His school starts up again on Monday, and you see him right here, don't you."

"Where do you go to school, young man," said Rhind, leaning to the table, speaking the same as to his daughter, with respect and a gentle challenge of intellect.

"North Augusta," said Jesup. "He's one of them Yellow Jackets."

"Well, I live over that way. I work for Channel Two news. You know where Channel Two is?"

"Yes sir," said the boy, tilting his head to Rhind. "We seen it from the street."

"We cover the football games at North Augusta. I shoot some of them myself. I shoot videotape."

"Now that's what I like," said Jesup, spooning fried potatoes and cornmeal out of the oil with a basket ladle. "I like that football. We'll go see us a game or two this year. But the boy, he don't play football. He plays that baseball."

"Baseball? Sure. I played years ago. And you see that one over there? We played together. And that one, he was good. He could play."

The boy looked to Verdery, and Verdery looked away to the worn and dirty trailer floor. Uneven and dogged vinyl tile, lost in the corner against the pitted base trim a tiny earring of false gemstone.

"You played?"

"I played."

"You look like a baseball player."

"I'm not much of a ballplayer."

"But you were? I mean one time?"

"No, not much, ever. Mr. Rhind just isn't remembering it right."

"I remember," said Rhind, letting Verdery alone because it had been twenty years. "But you have to be in school to play ball."

"That's alright," said the boy in a near whisper. "I ain't so good, either. I fish better."

Jesup shut off the stove and with his gaunt hands straining against the weight of the food and oil set the fried potatoes and cornbread to the table.

"Where are his folks?" said Dan Rhind.

"Well, I'm one of 'em," said Jesup, "but I know what you mean," and he turned again to the stove for the fish. "His mama's something. Even after that girl lost her husband, she kept on moving."

"Moving?"

"No, I'm saying traveling. She likes to go places. You know what I mean? She can't sit still for long, before she's off to someplace or another."

Jesup finished at the stove, and with the food done he stood above them, bent and sweating and simpering, wiping at himself with a cotton shop rag he kept in his pants pocket.

"No, hell, that girl went and lost her other husband too—saying he couldn't keep up with her. That boy just wanted to relax, and maybe just hunt once in awhile. But she kept on. Hell, she's off somewhere's right now, doing whatall. She ought to be back here in a little while, coming to get these younguns. But hell, I don't mind. They give me some company when she runs off."

He took a billfold from his slacks pocket, then without searching he took a photograph from the billfold, and he gave the photograph to Verdery. In the snapshot her hair was lightened unnaturally, but captured within the paper she smiled effortlessly, and in the print she was young and her eyes unashamed. *This was before the boy and the husbands*, thought Verdery, and he passed the photo to Dan Rhind and in polite admiration he made a noise to himself, and he passed the print to his son.

Jesup went to the trailer door checking that it was full open for air, saying, "Y'all go on and get you some of these groceries," then he went in the back from where the boy had come and he spoke into the dark. Outside in the pines the cicada had started chanting, and their first crescendo shrilled the night air, and Jesup came again with a hunter's chair under each arm, now too with the clean fragrance trailing him, and he worked to fold out the seats and crowded them into place. He called a name, then he shook his head and clucked, and he served two plates. Rhind lay the photograph on the gameboard, and when Jesup saw his daughter in the print, he quit chewing and called the woman's name again. He waited until he heard the trailer's floor sigh, then creak with movement, then he went again to eating.

I heard it right the first time, thought Verdery, and, *it is the same*, thought Dan Rhind too, remembering how the name had been drawn upon the deceased cruiser's backboard.

All but the boy quit eating when she came with her arms crossed, searching the floor, and her dark hair falling half into her face. The boy slowed eating only momentarily to put the print of his mother into his shirt pocket and he started right again.

It is the same name, thought Verdery looking to Dan Rhind then again to her, thinking too, *she is darker, but she is the same as the photograph.*

"Kerrenle. Girl, come on here and sit down and get you something."

She stirred the heat of the trailer bringing a faint wash of cool with the soft clean fragrance, and it opposed the oil and smoke and odors of the men, and it caused Verdery to remember they had not bathed that day. She sat with her head lowered and a rich, dark veil of hair about her face, and Jesup reached with his starved fingers to arrange her hair and she leaned from him and tossed her head, settling only when he took his hand away and he went again to eating.

"Hello, young lady," said Rhind in the same voice he had used with the boy. He said his name, then his father's and Verdery's, and they waited but she did not raise her head, then shallow-breathed and less purposeful, actually now polite, the canoeists went again to their dinner.

"Come on now gal. Come on here, now," said Jesup, and with the cicada's shrill growing, all surrounding them, hand to mouth they ate, the three visitors picking and chewing silently.

CHAPTER TWELVE

"Caron Lee," said Verdery.

"Shore. That's this one here. And that one's, Jason. Jase. You see that's your fisherman over there. They pretty ain't they."

"They favor their mother. The picture."

"Shore, their mother's always been a good-looking gal. All of them pretty. Their grandmother, she give it to *all* them to start with. Now, she was a good-looking gal, but that cancer got her. It'll get them pretty ones, like that. God help me." Jesup clucked his tongue, because what could he do against God but curse and gesture. "Then it was just me and *their* mother. And she was pretty like *her* mama. Even somebody's daddy could see that, if you know what I'm saying. It don't take no stranger to see all them good looks. But when she growed up, she couldn't keep no man. That one over there is from *one* daddy, and this one right here is from the *second* daddy. And that gal couldn't keep *neither* of them men."

"But they're the same. The same age. They're not twins," said Verdery.

"Seems like it, don't it. They shore do favor one another, ain't no doubt about that. But their mama couldn't keep *none* of them men around."

"Her name is the same."

"The same as what."

"The boat. The same as the boat."

"The boat."

"Down at the—"

"Oh, I know what you mean, but that ain't got nothing to do with it. That ain't the same at all. You see, their mama she's gone one place or another. She'll get settled awhile, then run off somewheres again. You know, she says she's running from that cancer of her mama's, but I ain't seen no cancer. I say she ought not talk no such a way about her mama. God help me. She'll come on back here and settle awhile, but I ain't seen no cancer. Hell, you got to die from one thing or another anyhow. Ain't no amount of running going to solve none of that."

"It's not the same name?"

"Name? No, see, that never was none of mine. See, you talking about somebody else's property there. That was Covington, and all his doing."

"Covington's boat."

"Shore, he used to call her kerrenle."

"He used to call the boat that."

"Her too. He called her and the boat the same."

"This child here. He called this child here after the boat."

"No, hell no. They got him before this child came to be. No, that girl was from the city, and he went crazy over her. That's the one with the same name as that old boat you been looking at. You see, that's another pack of dogs, them Covingtons. They ain't the same as all us setting here."

Verdery blinked at his plate and the designs the cooking oil had imbued into the paper, and he read nothing of the stains. Jesup stood, using his arms for strength, making a noise to himself, and he cleared all the table but the girl's plate, where she had not touched the heavy food.

"That boy's going to want to play that game with you men," he said standing above them, hunched, his palms turned backward to his hips.

"That's alright," said Dan Rhind smiling gently at the boy. "We got nowhere to be this evening, but in the bed. And it's not too late yet."

The boy rolled the dice once against the board, and he gave a pawn to each player and one to his sister. His hands were tanned, but not with the depth of his grandfather's, and his fingers were slender like his sister's. He explained the game, instructing them almost formally, in his woodsy drawl mimicking the kind voice Rhind had used, saying there were cards and questions, and saying the rules. The men nodded, all but Verdery. With his head full of the girl and her fragrance he digressed lost in another game and task exploring the women's names and the boat come upriver a time ago from Savannah. She turned to him, almost accidentally, and in that lengthless moment he saw her eyes and he saw a color he would not remember, and he looked again down to the gameboard. He rolled the dice at his turn, and he let the girl move the pawn.

"You said Covington named the boat from Savannah after the woman from Savannah."

Jesup rattled the dice in a fist and, troubled, regarded the entire board, as if he might evidence something in the frame of its maze wheel that had eluded him. "Damn a deuce," he said, then, "what now?" and with his legs crossed at the knees like a woman and an elbow on the table, he rested his chin on a fist looking hard at the board and the slow marching pawns. "Hell, that's why they shot him. They shot him because of that kerrenle."

"The woman, or the boat."

"No, hell, no. Well, yes, alright. Because of both of them, I reckon."

"And that was the sheriff. The Burke County sheriff."

"Yes sir."

"Then, why?"

"Well, I reckon he figured he needed to, with the old man high up on the tower like he was. And toting a moll too."

"Where was he?"

"Back over yonder. At the plant."

"The plant?"

"You're talking about the Sardis Plant," said Dan Rhind.

"I am. Now I ain't talking about the government property right across the river. This one right back over yonder is the power company's doing. They made the first one, great big tall thing, you know, then they made the next one. And you could see both of them, from right up there in the field. It was dark when y'all come over."

"Sure. We saw the lights. Didn't know that was it."

Said Rhind, "Nuclear. Two reactors."

"Great big old cooling towers," said Dan Rhind. "Right on the water."

"That's right, and that shore as hell is where they shot him."

"So because of Caron Lee, Covington climbed the cooling tower at the Sardis Plant."

"Near as anybody can figure."

"And they shot him for it?"

"Like I say, I expect they figured they needed to."

"That must've been about in seventy-seven," said Dan Rhind.

"Coulda been. They was building them things for years. You know, my girl saw all of it with me. I weren't the only one to see it."

"You mean their mother?"

"Shore, my girl. And I hated like hell for that to happen. But you couldn't a done anything about it. Hell, it's all done now anyhow. God help me."

Jesup sowed the dice out of his brown fist, and he squinted expecting the cubes might tell more than the numbers. The boy read a card aloud and Jesup coyed with his mouth hanging open and wagged his head in submission, giving the dice away to Verdery. They played passing the dice counterclockwise, skipping the girl, with the boy reading the cards until it was his turn, when Dan Rhind read aloud. They played amidst the cicada's shrill, it arising from the dark, spilling into the open windows and door. Verdery coaxed Jesup, and Jesup squinted and grimaced to retrieve the past, and out of his near-toothless open mouth came clouded tellings shrouded in distance and disuse. He spoke it as it was said to him or as he imagined it said or as he had misremembered it, but for him it was all the same: grayed, nearly irretrievable, only resurrected and surviving now because it had been asked after. Twice.

CHAPTER THIRTEEN

Covington, the Father, built houses, with his hands, until he became successful. He met a woman from Augusta, and both young and bright they married. They raised two boys and built the place above the river for the weekends to relieve the sameness of the city. She became sick when the boys were in high school, and it overtook her and she died in the big house, leaving the three of them alone. The doctor then the law had to come and collect her from him, and as they drove away crossing the peafield he sat into the furrows and he wept cursing until it got dark, and on until it got light again.

Covington soon lived full time at the big cabin, and, restless, he worked days outside where he became strong again, sun darkened and his hands roughened again, as when he started out. He and Jesup finished the house as it should have been when his wife lived, and at the dusk of the last day, when they lay aside the hammers and spirit levels, Covington sat again into the sedge, and he wept cursing until it got dark and until the next day.

The next spring and summer Covington and Jesup worked side by side setting pilings for a boat dock. Covington's boys came home from college and stayed and worked too, rising the dock out of the river. Each day Jesup's girl brought cool drinks for them, down from the cabin house, down the slope through the undervine pathway and the sedge. Cast in the relentless summer-heat they watched her descend the slope, stepping careless and featherlight against the gradient. On a tray she brought sweating drinks, and they took them overlooking their work, and she overlooking the river itself, searching the greatest distance viewable with the heat beading her face and neck, her cotton dress drawing to her skin. Returning to the cabin house, winding weightless, unhurried, upward along the path, Jesup boasted of how she favored her mother, taken also too early by a callous God. And shirtless, his sweat running off him, Covington said "Goddam Jesup, they're gone. Can't you just leave them alone," and Jesup nodded, relenting.

In the dead still of an early summer morning Jesup found Covington and his two sons halfway along the rise. He heard first the low cursing and grunting, and then he saw the father against the older son, and the younger son failing to keep them apart. Nearing them Jesup heard the breathlessness, but not clearly the words. The younger boy said, *he's here now*, just like that, nothing more, and the father and son broke apart, sieving for good air in the strawdust and the heat that had never cooled from the night before and the day before. And none of the four of them spoke, cast in an array of expectation and disgust and ignorance, the father and son—their torsos swelling, emptying, sullen hateful, each seeking surrender.

The older son turned and took the rise past the cabin house, and none of them would see him again until a week after they buried his father with a bullet hole through him, in the Georgia dirt. Covington walked the rise too, but he went inside the cabin house, and there he found Jesup's girl. He explained, his breath uneven, that he and his sons fought and why, and when he got to the matter her eyes fell off him and she groped the cabin's wide floorboards, not looking up until Covington went out again. Descending not slowing, he went past Jesup and his younger son—the boy posed in half-disbelief; and Jesup too tethered in that state of suspended exasperation in which invariably he endured alongside Covington—to the creosote pilings, and he started with the hammer and the walkboards, the shots cracking throughout the liveoak and to the Carolina treeline and back again.

Jesup and the younger son joined laying the planks, no one speaking—the younger son knowing and not knowing and fighting the fear that causes weakness, and Jesup simply unsure and lacking the imagination to query.

Two days after they finished the dike, where no words had passed among the three remaining men, and at the last of the day's light with the cicada's shrill rising in the dun, Covington lay down his hammer and he made the rise in long strides. He went into the cabin house again and he found her there again, standing nearly the same upon the floorboards as he had left her, as if in the must she might have by inanition hardened to statuary or salt. With the dusk spilling through the doorframe landing softly upon her face—and the face flawless in youth and carelessness—he asked for the answer from two days before. She saw nothing of him but his darkened shape, he hulking in the doorframe, weighted and bent with a full life lived, and the nascent imaginings of another life just begun—he searching the near dark, groping in anticipation and suffused feral expectation, a day and a life gone and another life begun already running through him.

They stood apart—she still as a glass ornament, he bent and weighted, upholding the clinging debris of all the lives he had drawn to his own—and at the finish of that lengthless moment, she said *No.* The breath of her word traveled as pure as a shot, dissolving even as it was spoken, and he waited, vestigial and relict in his purpose, that he might hear it again, listening not for the sound but for the shape of her breath. And sure it would not come again, she spoke, and the shape of her breath washed him, stirring all the must and the dun and dousing his smoldering fantasy—and again it was *No.* The word alone dissolved, and Covington made a noise to himself, and she saw the hulk move, not for her but into the dimmed portal and out of the doorframe, and again he descended the slope in a plundering rush crushing yet a new pathway through the undervine and broomsedge.

As he passed Jesup and his younger son they spoke in turn and Covington spoke in return saying only *Savannah,* or it might have been *Tybee,* or both names said and something different altogether, and he marched on for the dike. Neither saw it clearly when he dove into the river. They heard the noise of the water splitting apart, and lapping closed again. Jesup went first, and the son came after to take hold of Jesup, and upon the narrow dike they fought in a stumbling duet, with Jesup searching the dark water, and the son talking all the while close into his ear, saying all the while as they scuffled upon the walking boards: *you don't want to go in there. Don't help him undo the both of you. All of us.*

In the moonless twilight, with the cicada's call rising, they clenched a last time and Covington's son spoke again, his breath nearly gone, a curse.

She said no.

Godamit, he can't swim all that way.

He'll come back again, then, *she said no,* and still Jesup could not see to understand. *He's not swimming anywhere.*

After a day and another day Jesup did call the law, though the younger son would have none of it. And out of uniform the Burke County sheriff stood with him on the dike.

He just jumped in.

He just jumped in. Said he was heading for Savannah. And went on.

Hell. You think he's swimming from Girard to Savannah? Did you see him go in.

Naw. Naw, but we heard him.

We.

Me and the boy.

Boy.

Covington's boy. Up yonder in the big house.

And nobody pushed him in the river.

Naw. Hell naw. We was up in the scrub.

But you couldn't see him.

It was about like it is now.

Why didn't the boy call?

Hell. I can't understand it neither.

They dragged the river when it got light again. They dragged all day, working the first bend just below, at Clearwater Creek, in the six olive-colored johnboats the sheriff could muster. And after fourteen hours, the twelve men in the six boats straightened from their work and listened to the cruiser's engines steady groaning against the flow, as it came wide around the bend. From the pilot house, through an opening where a window might have been, the captain leaned into the open air and raised an arm at the twelve, never trimming his engines a single nick. In the near dusk, what the men actually witnessed to make their mouths fall open—nevermind the drowned captain and the full-bore sea cruiser—was the woman sitting cross-legged the deck above the pilot house. She sat cross-legged with her palms to her knees facing the cruiser's bow, and she wore denim shorts and a cotton blouse of a certain tailored style with nothing under, and the only thing of her that moved was the blouse and her sunned hair, the wind seaflagging the both of them out behind her, they trailing her posed torso in the lilac air.

The johnboats, nearly swamped, fell in behind Covington, in the flatwater between his wake, and they trailed the cruiser and the woman, upriver. At the dike the sheriff waited with his hands to his hips, his head wagging, already guessing and knowing. Jesup looked at the sheriff, then downriver, then at the sheriff again. *What is it,* he said, and the sheriff only wagged his head once and spat into the river and wagged his head once more. Jesup took the tieline from the woman, where she had come down—she a captain herself because she had been born on Lazaretto Creek and learned watercraft on the Bull and the Wilmington Rivers and on Tybee's Back River—and the sheriff stepped right onto the cruiser's bow, and he went right for Covington, even before he could shut the engines down.

When the engines quit there was nothing for a moment, then the one voice started, then the other voice contested, its pitch a little deeper yet, and for a little while the fuss they made was the only noise along the river. The captain leaned from the pilot house first, with the sheriff shadowing him repeating, *listen here, Covington*, then they all heard,

Is it a crime to disappear, then come back?

That's not what I'm saying.

Then you'll leave me be.

Listen, Covington.

Even when Covington stepped heavy from the cruiser to the dike, even then, Jesup did not know him. Covington went past him with the sheriff trailing still going on with, *listen now, Covington*, and then Covington spoke his name, once, *Jesup*, almost as a question, then Jesup like the rest of them knew.

Covington took the woman's hand in his and they made for the land, then the rise. Jesup followed scrubbing the disbelief from his eyes, and the sheriff filed in too right along behind Jesup, low cursing, still wagging his head, spitting into the river until he made the path. And too in an ant line followed his twelve men, they gossiping in the near dark—all at once stammering when the sheriff halted and cut into them with a scattershot look of futility and exhaustion, and incredulity, they all stumbling to pause with their heads down—and when he quit, they all shuffling again, stretched in clumsy single file, one following the last nearly to the top of the rise and the cabin house.

Covington slowed none even when he passed his younger boy, speaking again a half-question, *son*. With the woman palm in palm he crushed a path to the cabin house and shut one door then the next, with all of them gathering in his wake, milling about open mouthed in the grass and the dusk, and no one saw them for two more days.

Wearing the same expression of incredulity the sheriff looked one direction in the near dark, at nothing, then opposite at his twelve men, cutting into them again, and he called out once, *Covington*, shouting only to himself.

Said Jesup, *it's a hell of a thing ain't it*, and he wandered on, and in a little while he had a fire going in a clearing by the water. A few of the sheriff's men came to help the fire grow, and then in awhile they all had gathered, with the sheriff standing just at the falloff of the cast light—not partaking, but still too simmering to leave it all alone—and the younger son further off yet, in the sourweed where his father discarded him.

Some took a knee and some squatted like bean pickers and the rest stood, all entranced by Jesup's fire, eager for the speculation and the telling, as if somehow by sheer proximity there might pass in woodsmoke this oracle's disease, despite where truly not a single one of them held the knowledge of a separate simple fact; save that Covington had come again: *with a boat and a woman.*

The sheriff drew no closer to his men, saying because he had to, *you boys know it's against the law to burn down the forest, and somebody's property.*

Yes, sir. Shore, said one then another, each agreeable to the last.

Then I do expect Covington will have to look after you all. But hell, I wouldn't come out if I was him.

Yes sir, they said, some chuckling now too, as the sheriff turned then vanished, ascending the rise into the dark.

Huddled, sharing the very same breath and heat, they cursed in short giddy bursts, in hyperbolic disbelief and speculation over the man who had drawn them together—first upon the river, then the narrow dike, then, in the pitch of a moonless, warm summer night washed in clumsy firelight. In their stories they invented where he had journeyed for the four days—how he swam for it, how by wits he acquired the cruiser and won the woman and possessed her—some groping the dark in the direction of the cabin house, full of awe and wondering, others warming to a low restive craving of occurances in Savannah, at immediate intrigue within the redwood walls of the cabin house.

They quieted to a man when Jesup spoke, reverent for the words of this telling voice who had partnered Covington for as long as anybody knew. They nodded searching the bastard flames for his meaning and they groped again where the cabin house should have been, imagining full how good was this life for this man Covington, and seeping jaundiced envy over the possibilities with a woman like his woman.

He swam clear to Savannah.

The hell.

Then how?

Ain't no other way.

How can that be.

Some men we just don't know about, and Jesup sat cross-legged upon the pinestraw, insensate to the fire's heat, wagging and nodding his head at all of it and now letting them speak.

I'll tell you it don't matter how. We all know he got there, and he come again, and that's what we know.

He walked right up and gave somebody or another cash for that boat, and he drove right off, right out the slip with it.

Where'd he get the cash.

It don't matter how or where the money come from. You see the damn thing right over yonder. Gamblin, winnin.

You reckon she come with it?

Hell, I imagine she found him.

Hell, she was sitting up on that top deck when he found her. He walked right up and give a man the money, and drove right out the Lazaretto Creek docks with her sitting just like that. And just like that they come a hunnert and something rivermiles with him driving, and her setting on that top deck all the way, just like he found her.

Lazaretto Creek.

That's right.

Well, who in the hell is she.

I'll tell you who, said a stooped, pea-headed one, taking an arm of pine from the fire and plundering throughout the sedge to the water's edge, then in knee deep, arching the flaming limb to the cruiser's transom, calling back the twenty yards to them. *This is who she is. Who in God's name did you think she was?*

They nodded and cursed in short, exaggerated bursts, and wagged their grimy heads as a flock, some changing knees, some standing and jamming their fists into their pants pockets, as if they had forgotten it was the dead of summer and already unbearably warm. And Jesup let them giggle and whisper and curse, and he let them wonder, he searching the crimson of the fire, speaking the name to himself as he had a moment before heard it, as he would from then know it—*kerrenle.*

Standing then kneeling, then to his feet again, just past the firelight's fall-off, in the same weeds where his father had mislaid him hours before with the woman in tow, the youngest Covington watched and listened. He studied, regarding this separate race of men, they not discomforted by proximity and closeness to one another, bold and sharing in their simple ways—learned in the manners of a creed inscrutable. In the dead mid of this summer night, in the spun firelight and the pinesmoke, the thirteen wagging and nodding and shuffling restive and peripatetic, might have been smearings of pigment upon a cavewall come alive: ghost of Cheraw, revenant Braves of Chufitachiqui, stooped and shrugging amidst so many jaundiced flame-ruined pearls.

He watched upward too, to the cabin house the window of each room—his father's bedroom. He sat again with his back to a hackberry in the reaches of the fire's falloff, and he searched above where within the redwood walls his father lay with the woman claimed from Savannah. He closed his eyes to what he took as the truth and opened them again, and behind him and below the campfire spat unevenly a small patch upon the river and into the mossed woods and broomcorn. They had quieted now, save Jesup's telling of him and Covington: of his sons and the land, the big house and the dike, their wives who had been claimed by some obdurate jurisprudence and damn bad luck, gone from them, where in the stories' very soundings he persuaded himself and the other twelve of their inviolable truth. A cackle broke, then settled, then faded as the telling began again—some of it swallowed by the Carolina treeline, most of it by the near woods and the unwashed men themselves, and some rising, lofted by the flame heat high into the dark of the treetops and the reaches of the starlight beyond.

Days later the sheriff came again and stood again upon the dike with his hands to his hips, spitting into the river. *What the hell does he expect me to do,* he said, speaking pitched and strained in suffering half-disbelief, to the same woman who had lighted upon them like something burning out of the sky.

I called for you. He did not.

Well, where in the hell is he, if his boy's missing.

He won't come from the house.

Does he expect me to go up there, so he can shut the door in my face, one more time.

I called for you, he did not.

He spat into the river, making a noise to himself, wagging his head, slow.

Well you know what miss. Sometimes boys just go away. This ain't the first time. That's what boys do, especially around here.

So you're just going to stand there and tell me that, and spit into this river.

He turned on her in a single motion.

You know what I think miss. I think part of his trouble is he can't even worry himself enough to remember when we came for his wife. And he can't take a minute to recall how everybody looked after all of them after all that mess. Hell, she was better than anyone in this pack of dogs, and you see what she got out of it. I tell you what, I think you and him ought to go down to Savannah and look in the same place where he found you. I'm sure there is another one just like you, and I'm also sure that sons are like their fathers.

She had not wavered until just then. Then she looked down and away from him to the cruiser, where it waddled, gently contesting the river. The sheriff cursed himself beneath his breath and wagged his head downward to his worn shoes. He cursed himself once more then looked to her. She stood with her arms crossed wearing the same cotton blouse and cutoff shorts and canvas shoes she had first appeared in. He saw that she was no child, and he saw clearly now in the mid of the day what he had suspected in that lilac dusk when she came to them—that she was truly beautiful with courage, and uncommon.

Miss, can I ask you something.

Yes.

Why did you come here with that man.

Because he asked me, and he was kind. The sheriff looked to the cruiser where he had first seen her atop the pilot house, sitting cross-legged and straight-backed, something alike a carved prowed figurehead. *And because sheriff, sometimes you see that there is nothing in this life beyond kindness. No money or gifts, or words.*

Yes ma'am, he said, the same as saying good-bye, and he crossed the walking boards to the weeds and Georgia earth. *Miss, I don't know what to do right now, but you can call me again if you need to. I might not know then too, but you're welcome to call.*

When he made the rise he thought not even to look at the cabin house. That day, in late August of that year, seen from the high ground, an exoskeleton of scaffolding encircled the cooling towers of the Sardis Plant. In the distance, tradesmen and laborers, small as nits, swarmed the structure and the wind bore the faint noise of their efforts. The sheriff bowed his head not the last time for that day, as he sat into his lawman's car.

That same early evening, when the air turned bruised and dim and slowly disembraced the heat of the day and the day before, Caron Chapplear sat upon the dike. She drew her knees close facing downriver and waited that he might come from the cabin house. An hour before, amidst the fust of the redwood walls she had asked *why.*

What?

Why did you come.

Because Savannah is downriver.

And if Augusta were downriver you would have gone there.

But it isn't.

I thought you were something different.

I am.

She waited nearby the cold stones of the fireplace, but he said nothing more and she went from the cabin house. She waited a last time, because there are some that do, and all around the visible earth the long day gave to dusk, and she loosed the tieline from the lashing cleat. From the cruiser's bow she watched the dike become small, and when the bow came about again, across the distance and through the dim moist air she descried a shape upon the pier. As if in demonstration, a single point of fire flared and fell to the walking boards, and the bow rounded again to downstream as the cruiser ferried wide in the bend.

He heard the engines turn over, and across the water their droning eased and he knew she went as fast with the flow as the dusk would allow. The creosote grew slowly the flame, and he waited amidst the heat and the pitch smoke until beyond the treelines of the riverbends the noise of the engines were gone.

CHAPTER FOURTEEN

"You said he was *shot*."

"Who."

"Covington. You said Covington was *shot* and killed, not burned."

"No sir, I ain't said he was burned. I got him off the dock, and the dock brand new and on fire. He woulda burned, but I got him. He was looking where that gal had done gone in his boat, and he ain't cared one way or another."

"About the woman."

"About the fire."

"And the fire didn't kill him."

"He was burned some, but he shore enough was shot. Seemed like it was a few days after. That fire set him down for a day or two, mighta been a week. But he shore enough was shot. Me and my gal took care of him up in the big house. I stayed with him and stayed with him, and she told me to go on and she was going to look after him. She was good that way, looking after somebody else before herself. When I come again they was there, just like I left them. By then she didn't want nobody near to him. She was sitting right on the bed watching him, and you could see he had himself a bad morning."

"And they came to look at him?"

"Who."

"A doctor, or someone from Girard. Or the sheriff."

"Damn a doctor. Damn the law too."

"But he was burned."

"No, he weren't burned. Not too much. It was the smoke. Just the smoke and the weakness. That city gal had done gone off and left him, and she set the fire to his work before she let it all alone. Damnation, we worked hard setting that thing in the river. And there she went, burning it out from under his feet. And plus, stole his boat too."

"Covington said that."

"Didn't have to. We knew it."

"It was Covington's boat."

"Hell yes it was his boat. And I'll tell you why everybody knowed it. Because, did you ever hear tell of somebody naming a boat after hisself."

"Caron Lee."

That's right. Kerrenle. And it musta been true. It just makes sense. Sheriff's boys figured that one out."

"But it came back. They found her."

"That weren't none of my doing. And they ain't found her. As far as I ever heard, ain't nobody found her."

"But they found her, Caron Lee. I mean the boat."

"Boat was left in Port Wentworth. Right beside the 17 bridge. They call it Hooleehan. They found the papers with his name on them, and they called the big house for him. But we tried to explain that he was already shot, so he didn't much care that his dock was burned up, or where they found that boat. Our sheriff talked to their sheriff, and nobody said that they much cared which way that girl went—damn sure least of all me—because he had done been shot."

"Now, why?"

"Why what."

"Why was he shot."

"I done told you. Because I reckon they figured he needed it."

"What did Covington do, to cause himself, to be shot, Mr. Jesup."

"Well, you just can't go and climb on somebody else's property and expect not to get shot. Especially toting a moll, and working at it like you was trying to take the whole thing down."

"What was he taking the moll to."

"Them towers. One of 'em, anyway."

"Towers."

"Shore, over yonder ways, like we said."

"You're saying the cooling towers. Sardis Plant."

"I am. That next day, you see, he made us all leave him be. You see, what I was trying to say was, he wouldn't let any of us call for the doctor, and when the doctor did come, he told him, he said, *Amp, I appreciate all you did for Louisa, and I knowed you for a long while, but if you lay one of them sweaty horse doctoring hands on me, I swear the last thing I will do in this life is crack your neck.* I swear that's what he said. So we let him be. I had to about drag my girl out of that house. She was good that way about people, caring for them. And as soon as we let him alone, I reckon he took off."

"To the cooling towers."

"It was a Sunday—hell. Hell, I remember that part now. Ain't that something? Like it was this morning. Hell, ain't it something that I remember it that way. And weren't nobody working, naturally. They said once he got through the fences, weren't no problem for him to go on up them platforms, just like them everyday workers."

"The scaffolding."

"That's right. Scaffoldin'."

"And he carried a hammer."

"Hell, it was a moll. One of them with the long handle, you know. And he went to work on that concrete. Hell, you could hear him all the way back over here. Some folks said you could hear him all the way back to Sardis. Otherwise, wouldn't nobody come. He coulda been sleeping or camping up there, and nobody woulda cared until they found him come Monday."

"And the sheriff came."

"Shore he came. I went up the hill at the big house, and that boy was standing there like a damn ghost, watching his daddy just a-working on them pipes. Like he was banging a church bell. Hell, that's a hell of a way to say it, ain't it. Well, it was only the one tower, and you couldn't tell for sure who in the hell it was. But he was gone. "

"Covington was gone."

"Shore. He weren't in the big house."

"And his son came back."

"The boy did. The second one that run off."

"The younger one."

"I don't know where in the hell that boy had been, but he shore enough looked like hell."

"So the sheriff comes, and he shoots him down."

"Well, no. That ain't all there was to it. The sheriff, he comes here first. He says we all best try to talk some sense into the old man, because he done tried and he couldn't do no good with him. And hell, I'll never forget this, he looked at the boy and said, *I reckon you done come back too,* and the boy said, *yeah,* and the sheriff said, *you know you look like hell don't you,* and the boy said, *yeah, I know it.* Just like that."

"So, he took all of you over to the plant."

"It was, me, my girl and that boy. He said somebody needed to get him down off there. He said he was shore the power company won't appreciate somebody trying to take apart their work."

"What was he doing to a six-hundred-foot reinforced concrete tower."

"Hell, I reckon the point of it was it was somebody else's. You can look at thing today and see he ain't even scratched it, much. But I reckon that weren't the point of it."

"The point was he got shot for it."

"Sheriff said, which one of us was going to go up there and try to talk sense to him. I looked at him like he was crazy as hell, and I said, *ain't that what you people do?* He looking at the three of us, and I said, don't even think about *her.* And the boy ain't said a thing. He's just setting on the county car watching his daddy way high up in the air, like he weren't no part of it. Like what was going to happen was bound to. Like anyways you cut it, it was all baitfish. So the sheriff sends up one of his boys, and johnnylaw gets halfway and is shaking so bad that he had to send up another one just to get the first one down.

And it was the damnedest thing too. The old man would beat on that pipe for awhile, then he'd quit for awhile, then he'd shout down something or another that nobody knew what it was—then he'd go back to working on that concrete. When the sheriff got his men back on the ground, he figured he'd just let the old man wear himself out. Then the boy comes over, like a damn earthly walking ghost, and he starts telling the sheriff what he ought to do. Just like that. He ain't said *two* words since I found him standing right up yonder at the big house, like he come out of the woods, then he just comes out telling the law what he ought to do. And damn if he weren't right too."

"What did he say to do?"

"It ain't obvious to you?"

"No, not to me."

"Hell, he says to go and get one of them workers, and let them do the talking. The sheriff says then, that they was already on the way, and the boy says *good.* He figured we was all too smart not to think of such a thing beforehand."

"But the sheriff shot him anyways."

"Them workers never had a chance to do any good. They got about half-way up, about where the sheriff's boys had to quit, and *wham.* That rifle let go, and here comes the old man, flying like a bird and falling like a rock, both. It scared the hobble hell out of all of us. The sheriff, when he figured out what all had happened, went right over to that boy and took that rifle right out of his hands, and he put it back in the county car, and shut all the doors this time, so the next time couldn't nobody get to no weapons without him saying so."

"The boy? The sheriff's boy?"

"No. No sir. The old man's boy."

"Covington's son shot him."

"Well, he pulled the trigger. Least we all figured that. Nobody for real saw him do it. But he was standing right there holding the rifle, with the barrel hot, and one of them long-distance sights on it, you know. And they was a mark on the car where he had propped himself up—powder or something or another. Hell, he was doing the sheriff's work anyhow. Sheriff said he reckoned it saved him from having to shoot a man, and the boy said weren't nobody going to shoot his daddy, but hisself."

"You're going to tell me next that the son didn't go to jail."

"Yes sir. Yes sir. Not even for a day. Like I said, nobody for real saw him shoot. We all reckoned the sheriff figured it was bound to happen anyhow. And if the sheriff had to do it, was he going to take himself to jail? No sir. But I'll tell you who was worried about it more than any of them, law or not, was my girl. It seemed like she was trying to catch him when he was coming down. When he hit the earth she went right on top of him. Right into the dust he raised when he hit, and on top of him. And they had to take her away from there, from him. I shore do wish it she had never seen such a thing atall. But like I said, she was good that way, she was good about people that way. Something or another like that was hard on her. It made her different from what she was naturally. It made her like she is to this day today."

"She cared for him."

"Like I said, she was good that way."

"And she changed. It changed her?"

"She went off from here and married a fellow back up in Augusta, where y'all from, and come back the next spring with a new baby—that boy right yonder—showing him off like he was the only child ever born to a earthly woman. She showed them Covington boys too. You know, they was back up in the big house by then. She showed them like we was all from the same family, like they ought to care about somebody or another's child."

"But the boat came back too."

"Not by itself it ain't. That youngest boy went and got it. We was up in the big house and they called, said they found that boat just setting at the Wentworth dock, and weren't nobody tending to it. I told them it don't matter anyhow because the old man's been shot, and weren't nobody here that needed a boat. Then the boy wants to know did they find *her, and was it paid for,* and says he's coming to get that boat. And he does it too. Puts it right yonder where it sets now. Right where our work was before it burned up. And when that boy drove it against the bank, that was the last time it moved. The only thing that boy did to it was to take one of them planks from her and write that new name on it and tack it up over the porch."

"Cliff's Folly."

"That's right. And it ain't gone nowhere since. And it ain't going nowheres until it gets washed away or decides itself to fall apart. And maybe then, that'll be the end of it. End of me too."

Jesup tapped a finger to the gameboard to waken his grandson. "Jase," he said, and the boy whined once, more childlike than young man. The girl, an hour before, without instruction, had cleared the table of drink glasses and she had cleaned and gone, closing the accordion door behind her. And now, with Rhind and his father gone to the cabin house, it was only the two of them, and the boy sleeping with his head to the gameboard.

"I imagine you all'll be getting it early in the morning."

"I imagine. I like it early."

"Can't see too much in the dark, though."

"That's alright. There ought to be some moon. I like it that way."

"You got a ways to go to make the City. Hell, it's a ways to Blue Springs."

"Savannah's where we're going. And we got time. I do anyway."

"Jase," said Jesup, and the boy raised his head. "You sleeping out here to-night, or back yonder with your sister, or you going in the woods like them Covingtons?"

The boy's eyes, without seeing, fixed upon the gameboard and the dice and the pawns—where they had not answered the cards nor finished the game.

"Where you headed, Jase," said Jesup, insistent now, and the boy stood and went clumsy, half in a child's dream, to the bedroom with his twin sister.

Upon the pinestraw Verdery stopped and turned to where Jesup stood, bent, a size reduced by age and wear and expectancy of decrepitude, in the doorway's amber spill.

"Those kids need to be in school, Mr. Jesup."

Jesup nodded, "They something, ain't they. Y'all rest good. Leave the house open, I'll tend to it."

He nodded once more, and Verdery could not see if now he grinned or coyed, as he tugged closed the trailer's door.

Along the rise Verdery stopped, listening for the river. The cicada slept now and the whitening moon cleared the treeline. To the south its cast shaped the dead concrete towers, they reduced in the distance and dimness as something unknowable, indwelling at one of innumerable riverbends as something allowed to walk the earth at moondark, and it occurred to Verdery a last question unasked. The wear of the long day had caught him and he could not remember when it began, and he went on along the straw path where likely all of them had gone before. For sure Rhind and Dan Rhind, likely the same as all of them, de Soto and his lost European heart, Chufitachiqui's minions too, and before those, some also known of prehistory surviving in ancient mistellings. At the top of the rise Verdery stopped again and he searched each direction in the godsent mooncast—a place and a time already gone—and he held fast to what had already become his memory.

"I was about to go get in one of those beds," said Dan Rhind.

He smoked, sitting on the porch, watching the moonfall across the peafield, the red fire of his tobacco flaring, a single point alike a failing star. "You know, I like to stay up late. Feel like I don't want to miss anymore than I have to."

"I know, it's late. You alright?"

"It's just fine. Just want to be in it, you know. I mean, the night, you know. Here, now."

"Sure, I know."

"It don't matter. We'll be gone from here in a few hours anyhow."

"I want to get out early. We'll have some light."

"You got a shower in there. Last chance."

"I can wash in the river."

"Alright. If you can get that boy up in there, then we can go on right now. It don't matter to me, but I bet you can't."

Dan Rhind stubbed out his cigar on the porchboards and together they went inside. There was one light on in the house and it was poor and it shone the color of must and Dan Rhind's son sleeping on the sofa.

"Is he dead?"

"Yes sir, this is how your son looks when he's dead."

"He drank somemore."

"Seems like it."

"The two of you drank a good bit today."

"We did."

"The two of you have always drank a good bit."

"We have."

"Well, I'm going to get in one of them beds. We'll be up and gone early. Him too."

"Alright, Dan."

The moon cast a luminous path upon the river. Verdery took a beer from the Ouachita and nearby the cruiser he watched the ceaseless watercourse gently boil. He took his bedroll and another beer, and he went along the rise equidistant between the river and the cabin house and lay the bedroll in a clearing amidst the sedge, and he lay and drank the beer. He lay with half the bedroll under him and he pulled half over him, and he finished the beer and he closed his eyes to the endless spray of heaven, and for the first time in two days and two nights he slept deeply.

He dreamed of Catharine and Ginny Eaves as the same woman, and he dreamed of the many places he had been with them, but in the dream he did not know any of the places. He dreamed of Jesup's telling, and in the dream he tried to restore it as told, but already he had folded and blended it into another thing—a halved recollection told half again, then offered as a changeling, swapped at last for involute truth.

CHAPTER FIFTEEN

Verdery wakened lying on his back in the same position he had fallen asleep. The moon had traveled high and over, reducing and blanching to pure white. She had been kneeling with her palms to her thighs, only a short while in the broomsedge in the moonlight watching him sleep, waiting for when he would know to waken. He saw her shape as a void, something empty of form, a shadow, and in the first moment he could not descry what had come for him.

"It's only just me. Don't worry, I'm not a wild animal."

"Jesus," he said, his voice thickened and rough with sleeplessness and the three hours of sleep, then, "why are you here?"

"Everybody's dead asleep. Everybody's dead this time of the night."

"Jesus, what are you doing out here. What are you doing out here in the woods."

"Woods are over there."

"What?"

"Where you going?"

"What? Jesus . . . what?"

"Where you going in your boat?"

"Jesus, girl . . . do they know you came here?"

"It's alright. Everybody's dead asleep this time of the morning. Always are. Where you going in your boat?"

"My boat."

"Yes sir. Where you going?"

"Jesus," said Verdery a last time in his ragged cursing voice, leaning up to an elbow. "We came from Augusta, last morning."

"I know, my mama lives there."

Verdery cursed to himself and coughed once, and what he spoke might have been anything, "Is she there now?"

"She's coming back soon. She's coming to get us. But where you going in your boat?"

"When's your mama coming?"

"She's coming soon. When she finishes."

"Finishes what."

"What she's doing. But where you going in your boat?"

"What she's doing . . . we're going down the river."

"But where you *headed*."

Verdery sat up cross-legged with his elbows to his knees. In the distance at the shore, with its attitude tipped to the river, the moonlight glanced off the cruiser's deck and hull. In the blanched cast frozen caught, suspended, in the mid of a yaw and a roll.

"I know you're going that way, but where you *headed*."

"I think my friends are quitting at Blue Springs. But I'm going on from there. You know where Blue Springs is?"

"I know how to drive there. Grandaddy took us before. He knows a man there. Mister Small. There's some houses, and a store, and a boat ramp. Nothing much else."

"That's all we need."

"You going to Savannah?"

"Savannah?"

"Is that where?"

"I don't know. Maybe. Yes. I'm going to Savannah. Yes."

"That's where the boat came from."

"I know it. He told us. He told me."

"We have the same name, me and that boat. But he don't understand it."

"He says it the same."

"But he don't understand it."

"No. I don't think he does."

She quieted with her head lowered, then stood going near to Verdery, kneeling at his feet, at the edge of his bedroll in the weeds, in the same posture as before, with her palms to her thighs. Her hair fell about her face, it gleaming dark in the mooncast, and she put it behind her ears, and despite Jesup's cooking oil her fragrance was the same as when she first appeared to them at the supper table, an uncomplicated cleanliness of soap.

"You need to be back in your house, not out here in the middle of the night."

"I like it out here. I like it at four in the morning. It's not the morning at three, but it seems like the morning at four."

"I like it too, but you don't need to be out here."

"It's the first hour, and everything is dead asleep. Can you hear anything?"

"No. Just you."

"That's what I mean. And I can walk and listen, and I'm the only one here, or anywhere."

She quieted and in the morning's first hour they observed the mute world. When he was restive and almost finished with The Lake School he walked often down the steep meadow to the hemlock, then Lake Nepaug, and he waited in the morning's cold for the light and the wind to come over the water. When it was not so bitter cold he waited at the peninsula for the ball of the sun. He thought to say again that she needed to be at her house, not in the woods, and he remembered that it was a trailer, and that he was her grandfather, and the boy her half brother.

"Is this why you came out on the river?"

"What?"

"For the mornings? For now?"

"Sure. Yes. Sure."

"And you found us."

"We did."

"He didn't tell you right."

"When?"

"About me and Jase being twins."

"He didn't?"

"He don't like the idea of twins. He says it's bad luck to have two younguns born at the same time in the same place."

"Bad luck."

"Yes sir. But it wasn't the same time. I'm eight minutes ahead. I'm eight minutes older."

"When your mother came back from Augusta, there were two of you, not one."

"I guess, I can't remember. But he never says it any other way than how he told you."

Together they quieted, she kneeling, and while they did not speak she did not raise her head to him.

"You need to go on back in the house," he said a last time, now only suggestive. He knew he would not sleep again, and he knew that soon he wanted Rhind and his father and himself to be on the river. "Here. Sit here." He lay his bedroll open, and he patted his palm where he meant. She sat alongside him, cross-legged too, and together they searched past the ghost-armed live-oak to the river, where it shimmered silver and bone.

"I can go if you want me to."

"Alright. You can stay for a minute, then you can go and get some sleep."

"Do you have a job?"

"Yes."

"But you're not going back to your job."

"How do you know that?"

"If you don't know for sure where you're going, then you don't know if you're going back."

"I said I was going to Savannah."

"You said you guessed." She quieted, waiting for him.

"My job is teaching. I teach at a prep school."

"Prep school?"

"It's a high school. I teach kids your age."

"You teach girls too?"

"Most of my students are girls. About like you."

"Are they smart?"

"As smart as they want to be."

"Do you teach English?"

"No. Why do you say that?"

"Because you talk so good. You don't sound like anybody from around here."

"I talk this way because I'm old, and I've had lots of practice talking. I'm from Augusta, like anybody else."

"You don't look old."

"Well, thank you. I just mean I'm not a youngun, like you."

"We're all from Augusta. My mother too. But none of us talk like you."

"Well, there are plenty of places I go where they don't think I talk so good."

"Is your school in Augusta?"

"No, it's up north."

"You mean like North Carolina, or the other north?"

"No. No, I mean like in Connecticut."

She quieted and drew her knees close, wrapping her legs with her arms. "Do you know where Connecticut is?"

"No sir. I've never been there."

"It's in the Northeast. A thousand miles from here."

"A thousand miles."

"Yes."

"How did you get a thousand miles from Augusta?"

"I don't know. I've been all over, mostly in the North, for miles and miles. That's where my work is."

"Your work ain't in the South?"

"No. No, it took me north. From home. Away."

"Grandaddy doesn't talk good about the North. He says the stupid people come from the North."

"There are stupid people all over, not just in the North. There are stupid people in the West, East, and South too. The South has plenty. But there are very smart and good and kind people all over too."

"Are there good people at your school?"

"Yes. Many."

"Are there stupid people?"

"Yes, some."

"And which one are you?"

Verdery made half a laugh to himself and searched the distance, the yawing, disused cruiser frozen of time and purpose in the bleached mooncast. The air moved already warm through the liveoak, less than a breeze, bringing off the water the first fragrance of the morning—odor and taste of an inscrutable promise, the imaginings of a world turned, a beginning day.

"Well, Caron, I suppose you'd have to ask somebody else about that."

"And if I asked somebody, what would they say?"

"I don't know."

"Well, I don't think you're a stupid one. I didn't mean to say that."

"Well, thank you Caron. I appreciate that."

"I didn't mean to say the wrong thing."

"I know it. It's alright. But you should go on into the house. The morning's coming."

They quieted, still, sitting alike amidst the sedge, and Verdery resisted letting the fatigue of the night and the day and the morning before come again.

"Do you think I could go to your school. What I mean is, do you think I'm smart enough?"

"Yes. I think you are as smart as anyone. I think you would do well there, at Lake."

"Lake, is that what you call it?"

"Yes, The Lake School. Given by Mr. O and Mrs. C. Lake of Nepaug, Connecticut, and other parts unknown."

"Those are funny names to say."

"You have to say them often enough, so that they sound just like anything else. Like Mr. Jesup, and Mr. Jason, and Ms. Caron Lee of Girard, Georgia."

She covered her mouth with both her smooth, small hands backward and she laughed, tittering at him in a breath as insouciant, as rapid and fragile, as tempera. "You like the water, don't you?"

"The water?" and he smiled and grimaced together. "Yes, I suppose I do. Yes, I do."

"I like it too. I like it here, most times, but I would trade it for something different."

Verdery sighed as if she were not there. He closed his eyes tight and opened them again, and the dark morning and the world were the same.

"What you and your brother need to do is go back to your school, before you get too far behind. That's where you need to be. You both go to North Augusta?"

"Yes sir, but it don't start until Monday."

Verdery began to arrange the days and nights in his head, but he could not remember that it was Thursday morning.

"Monday. Good then. Monday, that's where you need to be. And your granddad needs to know that too."

"But what about your school."

"What about it."

"Maybe I can go to your school. Lake School. I like how you say it. It seems good just from the sound of it."

Verdery took a slow breath of the nearing morning, and the tile and the bricks of formal learning, the round hills and the smooth lakewater a thousand miles distant, came again to him. There came too all at once the high old elms, the walnut paneled halls taken from trees extinct, the stricture of a dozen fortunate generations—all of it gathered cloistered: sentinel, promise, secrets of doors open and doors barred, upon a gentle Berkshire mound.

"But it is so far away. And it costs so much."

"Does it cost money to go there?"

"Yes. It costs, very much."

"How much?"

"More than you can imagine."

"But how much?"

"Twelve thousand dollars a year."

"I don't have that. And my mama doesn't, and my granddaddy either."

"I know you don't."

"It must be an awfully good school to cost that much."

"It is a wonderful school."

"Are you rich because you teach there?"

"Rich. No. Oh no, I'm not rich. I'm from Augusta, just like you. I went to a regular high school, and I went to the College, and I went to another school in Illinois, almost in Iowa, that nobody ever heard of, except us who went there. No, I'm from Augusta just like you. No, I'm just older, and tired, and poor, and from Augusta, just like anybody."

"Well, you're not *old.*"

He smiled and grimaced, and he looked to her and he looked again to the river.

"Caron Lee, girl, you need to go in the house now. The day's coming in a little while, and we'll be going on from here."

"If you don't teach English, then what do you teach?"

Verdery stood to try his legs and back. He panned the sky in a full circle, then the Carolina treeline to the river's far side for the gray light, but he knew it was too soon for the day coming.

"I teach theatre."

"You mean like play acting?"

"Yes, like that. But I do my part of it. I do the scenery and lighting, and I teach my kids how to do that too."

"You draw pictures?"

"Yes, sometimes."

"I bet you draw good."

"I scribble."

"And you get paid money to draw pictures."

"Yes. Yes I do."

"See, I like the idea of that. Do you like it that you draw and show other people, and get money for it?"

"Yes ma'am, I like it. I like it very much. Just sometimes I have to make myself remember that."

74

"But it made you poor and old and tired."

"I'm not poor either. I'm alright. I'm luckier than my father was."

"But that leaves you old and tired."

"You said I'm not old."

"That leaves you tired."

"Yes ma'am, it does."

She quieted and waited for him to tell her to go to the house again, and he let a heavy breath, and sat again upon the bedroll.

"Caron, I think I will sleep some more until it gets light. You need to go on and do the same for yourself."

"I know it. I was just thinking it's too bad you're not going back to your school. Your Lake School."

"You don't know that."

"You said it. You supposed you was going to Savannah, and that means you'll spend the next week out here on the river. And if you don't know where you're headed, then probably you're not headed back to that prep school, Lake School. And if my school starts on Monday, then your school must start pretty soon here too. Unless you teach less up north than they teach over in North Augusta. And I don't think that can be. Why else would someone give twelve thousand dollars, when they could get the same treatment over in North Augusta, or South Augusta, or East, or West?"

"You got it worked out, don't you."

"It's not so hard to figure."

In Nepaug, in mid-August the maples and sumac turn, colored vermilion and scarlet, and the summer air thins and dries, so lifeless, so desiccate and stilled, it seems it might crack bones. A week before, treading the Headmaster's porch boards, Verdery quit The Lake School and Catharine. Only once while driving the Shenandoah Valley near Hagerstown, crossing into the Old South, did he flush with the realization of irreversible choice. But this suddenness and precipice emotion he had tried times before, and he already knew the feel of it, even as it came upon him. Another place gone from him, work and time abandoned, and he knew then, like he knew the shape of her face and body, that he would see none of it again—and that the memory of Catharine warm against him, and how she laughed, would fade too, he and recollection exiled the same.

"Did you tell them?"

"Tell who."

"Them, up north."

"I did."

"Were they sad?"

"I don't think . . . I don't know."

"I'm sorry it made you so tired. It makes me sad, for them, for that Lake School."

"I'm sorry too, miss. But it's a thousand miles away. Now, are you going to let me get an hour's worth of sleep?"

"Yes, sir. But what I meant to say before was, I could go with you."

"No, Caron. I can't go back. If I wanted to, I can't, and if I could, you—"

"No sir. What I mean is, I can go with you down the river, to wherever it is you suppose you're going."

Verdery spoke it to himself, saying it the same as she said it.

"Well, young lady, I don't think that will look too good. Three old rough men and a nice girl like you."

"But I can do it."

"I'm sure you can. But you know, we have a rule about strangers in the boat."

"But you can trust me. I'm more like you and your friends than my Grandaddy."

He looked at her, and she at him, and she the true likeness of the photograph Jesup kept in his billfold.

"No. Caron, no. That is not a possible . . . that's not something, that . . . no."

"Why not. You got two boats, and there's three of you. I thought about this."

"Caron, no. What you're saying isn't a good . . . No, what you're saying . . . no, no."

"But I know what to do out there. I know what the river does and I don't need much sleep."

"Caron, we're . . . we have our ways, the three of us. And it's not something for somebody like you to see."

"Why not."

"Why not. Dear, because you're fourteen, aren't you."

"I was fifteen in May."

"And because Monday morning you need to be in school, and not out with three old, smelly men on a river somewhere."

"I'm almost sixteen. And I'm not going with your friends, I'm going with you."

"With me."

"You're the one I like."

"Well, I like you too, for what I know about you. But not enough to steal you from your Granddad and take off downriver."

"It isn't stealing."

"I imagine everyone else will see it the way I see it. Especially the sheriff. The law tends to do that."

"But what if it wasn't stealing?"

Verdery stood from the bedroll and put his palms to his hips, and groped toward the river, to the moonmade patches of silver and bone.

"You think I'm just messing around, don't you. You don't think I mean it."

Days before in the Berkshire foothills, his lungs full of thin, lifeless air, his frame same weighted in a heaving lost posture, it was two grown men telling each other how each future would arrive. And each telling Catharine's future, and only one or none of them believing what he said about any of it.

"Caron Lee. What you're going to do now is go back to your house and go to bed. And I'm going to get forty-five minutes of sleep, before the daylight wakes me up again. Now go on. Go on."

"But what if it wasn't stealing."

"Caron, please."

"What if it wasn't."

"How can't it be."

"What if, when I said the same thing to Grandaddy, he just laughed a little and went on to bed."

In the slant of the moonshade she sat gathered, a surviving remnant of the foul hope of possession and the somatic promise of everything good and worthwhile. He saw that her head moved as she spoke, her hair gleaming in the blanched spill. He saw that she spoke not to him but to another place, to the void of the woods and beyond that too, as if trying her voice, testing it against the open space, the incalculable, fantastic distance.

"Did he send you out here?"

"No."

"Tell me."

"No."

"Caron."

"No."

"I swear I'll walk back over there and settle this right now."

"No. No. I told you. I like it when it's dark and quiet. I like to walk. I said the wrong thing again. It's not like I made it sound. It's me, not him. I come on my own."

Verdery cursed to himself, then spoke aloud to the same space as she, and to the east and the coming morning.

"No. Listen. I am thirty-five years old, and tired, and can't see beyond tomorrow, and what I choose to do is go down that river. And no, I have no plans beyond Blue Springs, but what you must do with your brother come Monday is go to school. This is what you must do. If I have to walk to that trailer and sit that old man upright out of his sleep and tell him so, I will do that. Everything I do is the result of something. All that I do is caused by something that has come before. It may be from ten years or one, or a month or week or minute ago. But everything I do now is because of what I've already done. This is what I've become. No, I cannot see tomorrow, like I could ten years ago. I can't even try. It's all just nothing, and I have no plans, and all I want to do is this one thing. And it doesn't involve a fourteen- or fifteen-year-old or her grandaddy or the law."

From sitting she knelt, the same as when she wakened him, as if she would stand, but she did not. She knelt, then settled, unmoving, as inanimate as decoration of carved or windworked stone or mineral. "But I need someplace to go."

"I know you do. You'll find it."

"I don't know how to get anywhere."

"I know it. But Caron, everything is in front of you. It's all coming to you, and you can make it what you want it to be. You can make your own way. It's like a story. You can make your own story. You just have to want it to be. You have to know, and not forget that you want it. You have to keep your eyes open, when even the seeing is hard, because when you see, you know. When you see, you understand, and you must tell yourself to never forget the truth. Because forgetting is easy, forgetting is failing, and remembering all of it is necessary. As necessary . . . as necessary as breathing."

"Is that what you tell them up north?"

"Maybe, some of it."

"Do they see?"

"Maybe, some of them. Maybe."

"I want someone to tell me all of that, that way. I want someone to show me how to keep my eyes open, and to tell me when they close the wrong way. I want someone to tell me not to forget."

"You'll find it. You'll find them."

"What is the truth."

"The truth is, everything is possible if you don't give it away."

"But I don't know what to do."

"I know it. I know it. But Caron, you are young and smart, and beautiful."

"Is that important?"

"Which."

"Beautiful."

"I don't know. Probably not. But it is what you are. The rest of what you are is how you make it. It's coming to you."

"But I don't know how to do it."

"But you will know. You will see. If more than anything you want to find your way, then you will."

She bobbed her head, as if nodding, once. "But you're tired, and you're not going back. And you can't help me."

"Caron, yes. No."

"That's alright. That's alright."

"Caron."

"That's alright."

"Caron, tomorrow's coming."

"That's alright."

She knelt silent, motionless, expectant as sculptor's raw stone set aside, and Verdery let her alone and he walked downward the slope not looking back. He took a beer from the Ouachita and drank half all at once. Near the cruiser he drank the rest of it. The river slowed only in an eddy pool at the transom, at her name.

He raised his beer to the boat, to the river, to the coming August morning. "Welcome, goddam welcome. Welcome home."

At the clearing she was gone and remaining only the trail she had pressed in the weeds, and he gathered his bedroll and put it away into the Ouachita. The treeline on the Carolina shore, as ragged and random as torn parchment, grayed to the edge of visibility. He sat into the broomsedge with his back to an oak, facing due east, and he closed his eyes, and in the first bluegray of the morning he slept without knowing it.

CHAPTER SIXTEEN

"Hey, Ghostman. There were beds up in the house," said Rhind, hoarse and giddy from sleep and lacking sleep, kicking at Verdery, and Verdery wakened sitting the same as when he had fallen asleep.

"What."

"You didn't come home last night."

"Well, hell."

"You going to sleep all day?"

Verdery stood, groaning against the stiffness in his bones, cursing without intention. At the Ouachita they drank a beer together. Dan Rhind came down along the driveway carrying all he had taken up the evening before. He loaded the Old Town, hoarsened too, cursing at no one, and he slipped on a smooth root and he caught himself against the gunnel, and then he cursed at the tree and at the gunnel. His face was drawn with sleep, and he lighted a pantela, saying, "morning boys," nodding to the East, and he slid the Katahdin full into the water and sat to the stern seat and started downriver with his head held up to the daybreak and a spiral tail of blue smoke behind.

"I got it all in the boat," said Rhind.

"Alright, good."

"Did you see the old man this morning?"

"I didn't see him."

"Did you come in the house at all?"

"I did. It was late. You were out."

"What did he call himself?"

"Jesup."

"There was the boy, and a girl too."

"There was."

"You think that was his first or last name?"

"Jesup? I don't know."

Upon the fast water Verdery watched Cliff's Folly become small. They made the first bend and the point obscured the hill, and he looked a last time, and it was only the treeline.

To the southwest they viewed the power plant's cooling towers, steam clouds mushrooming at the top, and even across the distance they could see to know that men had made and left to endure an inestimable thing—and amidst the persistence of industry and water and wind and time, Verdery could not determine that Covington and his moll had mattered. He made a small, unheard noise of adjudication, and he squared himself to downstream, and he cut his blade into the smooth enduring river.

The Savannah curled ahead of them at Clearwater Creek, then straightened, showing an everlong stretch. Two miles ahead the channel dissolved into bluegray morning mist, and now the sun had lightened above the treeline, and fresh and giddy for a short while they plied speed over the fast water.

The late afternoon before, they had passed into Barnwell County and the tract for the federal government site, on the Carolina side. They saw now the signage posted, obsessively close one to the next, black on yellow succinct warnings against trespassing—warnings to stay off the reserved land, where hidden amidst the scrub pine and the sand pastures the government processed tritium gas for atomic weapons, warshield poised against a hundred million invaders.

The small town of Ellenton, South Carolina, had been taken for the site. Another small town had been built as a replacement for the workers, and this proxy they named New Ellenton. Mornings early for fifty years, a single lane of cars and trucks, headlamps burning, crawled to manmade work along the once gentle sandhills in a line long and thin and bucked as a the tail of a Serpentgod—nose to end a dedicated temple procession—promise of economy, fuller of secrets. But with fifty years gone, in one season the world had changed, so terribly much and so suddenly, and sullen, sepia nations' partition walls had fallen to rubble, and so too in the artificial town of New Ellenton, they had witnessed the end of their government's invented purpose. In the old world those who yet breathed Lenin's rusted words could not break as many heads untold, and amidst the pine and scruboak Mom and Pop found they sold short on cake and beer and vodka to men with no good work, and Mom and Pop shut down too. Now at the government site there loitered only the cleaners, those left behind collecting the mess of the poison-soaked and -saturated earth, picking the septic bones of an industrial skeleton, mopping and maiding after the brilliant men, at an untold cost, because the brilliant men had moved on.

Once in the morning, they slid close to the Carolina shore, and they heard a feeding in the crisp fallen ground cover, amidst a tangle of wild grape, but they did not see the grandchild of Toombs's boar or its mate, and they did not slow upon the river.

In a half hour they cleared the government site, making Allendale County on the Carolina side. With Dan Rhind far ahead, his vessel only a bone splinter in the distance, they made odd and well-named places called High Low Jack and the Game Point, and Jack of Clubs Point, and Devil's Elbow. One after another came numbered erosion dikes, odds on starboard even on port, and every ten miles a rivermile marker. The Ouachita cut well into the river's back, its smiling bow laying aside fluid burls of white, and they steady doubled the water's natural speed, making long stretches and countless bends.

They put out at a narrow beach and at lunch they ate purposefully, and Dan Rhind searched the rivermap for their mileage and soon they all agreed to where they likely sat.

"301 bridge. We ought to make that."

"Sure."

"This ought to be Sweetwater Creek, about one thirty-five now. 301 bridge is one nineteen. Hell if we can't make that."

"We did thirty-five miles yesterday," said Verdery. "We do that again, and we're easy there."

"Hell yes, we are," said Dan Rhind, half-grinning, more surprised.

"We might not make it too," said his son.

"Might not?"

"I'm just saying we might not make as much today."

"We might not," said Dan Rhind, "but I don't see it."

"I'm just saying, maybe we shouldn't worry about this mile and that mile, and making one place or another by tonight."

"Well, that's alright too, but the river's only going one way. And it runs good down through here, and we just as well go with it. It's only sixteen miles to the swingbridge. You can float here on, and be there today."

"Well, that's alright. We'll get to the bridge. It's not going anywhere."

"We quit early yesterday."

"I didn't vote to quit," said Verdery.

"Nobody voted to quit," said Rhind. "I'm just saying we only just left Augusta, and why did we come out here if we're going to break our necks getting back."

"Son, I don't have to get back. You got to get back Tommy?"

"No sir, I don't need to get back."

"Nobody voted to quit."

"Son, that's alright. It was a bed and a shower."

"I might want to do the same today, as yesterday."

"That's alright, but I doubt we going to find another house to take us in."

"I'm not worried about a house. I got a house in Augusta."

"You boys drank a good bit yesterday."

"We did. We might drink a good bit again."

"Alright. At the swingbridge, there's a store a mile up the road. Used to be."

"We got everything we need," said Verdery.

"I mean there's a phone too. More than likely."

"Who you going to call?"

"That little boat's about wore me out. I been thinking all morning."

"We can trade out, Dan."

"But who you going to call, anyways?"

"Hell, I'll call a cab. How's that?" said Dan Rhind, simpering, standing, cleaning the beach after himself. He repacked the small boat, silent, as if he had come sixty rivermiles alone, and he put the Katahdin and himself again into the eddy. He lighted a fresh pantela and adjusted the outback hat and went on for the fast water, leaving only the thinnest trail of tobacco smoke.

Rhind stood too from the beach, watching his father go.

"He's going to lose us, again."

"He likes making time."

"Who's he going to call in an empty house."

"Maybe he's done. That's alright if he is."

"Tommy, when is cocktail hour?"

"In awhile, Fitzgerald. In awhile."

In the afternoon the first rain came—the remains of the leading Atlantic storm, called a man's name. It squalled warm and heavy, but with a stillness, and the air and the water blended all bluegray, and they could not see clearly the treeline of either shore. Above the hiss and the spatter and white noise they shouted to speak, awed and giddy and half-amazed at what the day had become. They put out at a tipped and mossy dock on the Carolina side, and they bailed the Ouachita and waited for the squall to ease, and when it did not they went again upon the river looking for Dan Rhind, and though neither thought it possible, it rained yet harder.

Verdery stripped and he rolled into the river and he swam in the bluegray rain. Rhind made a drink pouring the gin over ice, taking the squallwater also into his cocktail. He drank fast and he rested the finished cup in his shoe and he stripped and rolled into the river. They let the Ouachita go, its points compassing slowly end for end, and they swam along with it in the cold river and in the warmer visiting squall come an ocean, carrying the ocean's body from the earth across.

They made a poorly kept dock on the Georgia side and bailed again, but the Ouachita remained low in the water, and nothing of their goods or the viewable world survived dry. Rhind made another drink, and now Verdery made one too against his law, and as suddenly as it started, the squall quit. They bailed with cooking pots and they wrung their heavy clothes choking the stormwater and the ocean from them, and they did not see or hear her behind them until she spoke aloud.

There rested a homely cinderblock cottage at the top of the stairway that led down to the dock, and she stood on the second tread, and she cradled the shotgun in both arms—a hand to the stock, the barrel laying across an elbow—a violent asleep child in her cold care.

"What did we lose," she said, at the kneeling naked men and their work, saying it as a riddle answerable and unanswerable.

They looked at one another before they turned, as if the other had spoken and not a third.

"It rained on us," said Rhind, standing to face her, remembering then he held his shorts in a hand. He stood hunched, slope shouldered, the way he was made, with his arms and his wet clothes at his side.

Her hair grew long and thickly, blossoms of a smoke tree, grayheaded, but not an old woman. Plain cotton clothed, a pleated skirt to her midshin, wash faded, and a style of popular walking sandal, biblical or Roman, clumsy in appearance.

"It rained good," she said, bemused now at the sky. "It's all them storms coming. There's two more after."

"That's a lot of rain. We saw it was coming."

"It is," she said, looking down the length of Verdery, then Rhind, then again Verdery.

"Ma'am is this your property?" said Verdery. "This was the only dry place, and it rained hard, and everything we have is wet."

"Yes it did. Yes it is," she said, looking over all of him making a noise to herself. "Yes it did," again more to herself, cradling the shotgun, yet nothing more than half-bemused, the same as when she found them wringing their heavy clothes, all backs and asses to her.

She spoke Southern, but with the flat accent, taken to the language to harm it. Her first words, Verdery thought, spoken like actors wrecking with their tongues the charm and the nature—mocking the truth of it, themselves too.

The air moved less than a breeze, now that the rain had quit, and it cooled their skin.

"Ma'am," said Verdery, thinking too, *they're not good legs. And here I stand . . .*

"Yes sir."

"We can go on from here, just like we came, and leave you alone. We intend to. We couldn't even see the stairs for the rain, let alone the house." He cupped his hands over his dick to keep the cool air off, thinking, *bad legs and flat feet.*

"You sure?" and she wiggled the barrel of the shotgun at him, at his hands over his dick.

He cursed to himself and he watched the steel shotgun, and not her or her eyes.

"William D. Rhind," said Rhind.

"What? What now?"

"William Danforth Rhind, miss. Channel Two News."

"What?"

"Channel Two News."

"What? Where you nekkid people from?"

"We're from Augusta, miss. Channel Two News."

"Why you keep saying that, nekkid man?"

"I work for Channel Two News. Photographer. My father works in the D.A.'s office. Daniel Rhind."

"She don't care, Will."

"In the who's office?"

"District Attorney, miss. Augusta."

"She don't care Will," said Verdery, hushed and short. "Don't tell her all that. She don't care."

"You nekkid people come all this way from Augusta? You come all this way in that boat?"

"We did. Yes ma'am."

"Well let me ask you this—do any of you all wear clothes up there?"

"Yes, miss. These are mine here," said Rhind, and he bent and lay the wet bundle to the dock boards to show he spoke the whole truth.

"Stand up straight."

"Sorry?"

"Will, stand up straight like the woman says."

"That's right nekkid man," and now she wiggled the gun barrel at the sky, demonstrative to the sky. "Stand up straight, Channel Two." She rubbed her nose with her trigger hand, sniffed, checked for only a moment the air and the storm clouds scolded. "So you two been floating nekkid since you left Augusta."

"No ma'am."

"Then you decided just now to strip at my house."

"It's just the rain, ma'am," said Verdery. "Everything got wet, and didn't seem much use in wearing wet clothes in the rain."

"I bet you can see the use in it now though, can't you."

"Yes ma'am, yes I can. And if you let me bend down here, I can get my shorts on, and we'll all be decent again. And we can go on."

"You need to, don't you."

"Yes ma'am, I do. I do."

"Miss," said Rhind.

"Easy, Channel Two."

"Miss, I just fixed a drink."

"Take care, Channel Two," and she leveled the weapon.

"Will, god—just stand up straight for a minute."

She may have grinned at him, watching him take the cheap gin and squall water, and she cradled the gun again across her arm, but now she wrapped her palm to the narrow of the stock and her forefinger inside the trigger ring.

"He likes his drinks, ma'am. It's rained hard on us."

"I can see. I can see he likes them more than a decent man," she said, nodding slowly, quitting what might have been the grin. "But Channel Two, you ain't taking me serious, and if you move again, I'm going to shoot a hole right through your bare white ass."

"Sure. Yes, miss," said Rhind, drinking again, closing his eyes when he put his head back.

She looked to her feet, rocked on her heels, snapped her head up all at once to Verdery as if he had spoken. She held the shotgun better now and shut her eyes tight and squeezed her forefinger to the trigger. In the explosion Rhind coughed gin and Verdery bent at the knees to kneel but went not full down. She wailed to Verdery, her sound pitched as if it came out of another head altogether, and he stood half-collapsed, his palms cupped to his crotch, his erection declining in a moment.

"Now, Channel Two here works for the television, and you his running mate. So you must work for the television too."

"No ma'am. Lord no."

"You his friend, aren't you? Or did the two of you just meet up on the river, all nekkid, and join up. You all ain't funny are you?"

Verdery watched Rhind wipe the gin from himself—from his chest and stomach, and below that his dick too.

"No ma'am, we're regular. He and I are friends, but I don't work for any television."

"He and I."

"Yes ma'am, me and him."

"Then tell me what is it you do when you aren't nekkid, if there is such a time, and you aren't invading somebody else's property."

"I used to . . . I'm a teacher."

"Goodness then. What we got is nekkid man Channel Two, and nekkid man Teacher. Now, who is it you teaching, Teacher?"

"I teach high school."

"Goodness. That must be some kind of high school back up yonder in Augusta. Do they at least make you wear some pants when you teaching back up there?"

"Ma'am, I teach at a prep . . . at a . . . up north."

"At where?"

"Up north."

"You mean like in Atlanta.

"No ma'am."

"How far, then."

"How far?"

"How far north."

"Connecticut."

"Connecticut. That's up north."

"Yes ma'am, that's way up north."

"I know where it is. I've been places."

"Alright."

"You think this shack and this river is the only place I've been?"

"No, ma'am. Course not."

"What I'm saying is, how'd you get way up there?"

"Yes, ma'am. I don't know, they weren't thinking clear."

"You say it's a high school."

"Ma'am, if you'll just let me get decent here."

"I said, is it a high school?"

"Yes, ma'am. A prep school."

"Prep school."

"A preparatory school."

"Yeah, I know what it means, Teacher. I just didn't hear you the first time."

"Yes, ma'am. If you'll just let me get these wet clothes on, then I'll tell you everything you need to know."

While they spoke, Rhind sipped his drink, still wiping himself of the spilled gin, rocking heel to toe with his eyes closed, waiting for when she would finish with Verdery.

"What do you reckon you preparing for?"

"I don't know, ma'am. More school, I suppose."

"Sure you are. Now Teacher man, when you go on back up north to that preparing school, you think you going to tell them how you was bare-ass nek-kid, way down on this river, trespassing on somebody else's property?"

"No ma'am. I don't imagine so."

"No, I don't imagine so either."

She looked Verdery up and down as she had in the beginning, as if there were now more to see.

"You teaching teenagers, aren't you."

"Yes ma'am. High school age."

"You teaching boy and girl teenagers too."

"I am."

"Goodness, I imagine they enjoying that."

"I don't know . . . ma'am, I'm going to put—"

"I imagine so. I imagine I would."

"I imagine you are," said Rhind.

She turned to him, remembering now that there were two of them found. Two of them come to her, stitchless, from an ocean's squall on a Thursday afternoon, of all days.

"Say it again, Channel Two?"

He opened his eyes when he said it next. "I said, I imagine you are enjoying this. Right here and right now."

"Talk to me, Channel Two—but easy, now."

"William Danforth Rhind."

"I heard you the first time."

"You can shut up again, Will."

"You're the one with the gun, and we're the ones standing here with our peckers hanging out."

"Channel Two, give me one good reason why I ought not shoot your sorry white ass."

"It don't matter, there's nothing I can tell you."

"You don't have a wife and some younguns back up in Augusta?" She grinned at him while he drank, because this shotgun fitted her hands well, better than the others, and her arms were not tiring, and she did not believe they would. "I said, Channel Two—"

"Now this time, I heard you. And I do. I have a wife and a little girl."

"And here you stand like somebody just let out of prison. I don't imagine them you left behind would appreciate seeing all this."

"There's nobody looking but you."

"Well then, it's a good thing you done run off and left them and come out here in the woods with the Teacher. That way don't any of them have to see this shame."

She quit and she waited for him, and he only stood silent in the slow sway with his eyes closed to her again, and the drink held close to his mouth, blowing the icemist with his breath.

"I don't imagine you love that wife and child too much, to leave them all alone, and come out here in that boat with this here Teacher."

"I love them. I love them, and I love this Teacher too."

"I see. I see it now. So you all funny, and you come to be alone. To hell with everybody else. And I see something else too."

"Ma'am," said Verdery, "we've been friends a long time. A long time."

"He's my best friend in this world. He's my best and only friend in this world."

"Like I said, to hell with everybody else, and everything else too, but that drink." She clucked, "Looks like you got two friends, and one of them's in that cup."

"Ma'am," said Verdery, "I'm going to get my clothes on now, and all this—"

"You going to dress when I say it. And stop calling me ma'am. I ain't your mama. You call me who I am—Alice Mays. I think you ought to know who it is who's fixing to shoot your bare asses. I think it's right you know who I am. You say Alice Mays."

"Yes ma'am, alright," said Verdery.

"Alice Mays, what my best friend, who I love, means to say is, if you can just send your husband down here, we can get this thing straightened out, and we can be on our way, and there's no harm to anyone."

"Husband."

For the first time that day she felt the shotgun's weight, and she shifted the weapon and held it oppositely, with her opposite forefinger inside the trigger ring.

"Husband," she said again at the tall, slope-shouldered, barenaked man, who had left his wife and child far behind in a place she knew only by name since the day she were abandoned. "Anybody say anything about a husband?"

"No ma'am, Alice, Alice Mays. What we mean to say . . ." and Verdery quit.

"Husband," she said the third time, looking to Verdery, then again to Rhind, but looking past him too. "I see. You think some man's going to come down here and make everything alright between all us? You think I'm going to run up to some man, all worried, and drag him down here to the river, so he can work everything out for everybody. Well, you know what, like you said, I'm the one holding the rifle. There's no man holding this gun. It's Alice Mays, and nobody else. There *ain't* no man."

"He said it wrong, Miss Mays."

"Is that how you got it worked back up in Augusta. Is her hair and her clothes just right for you. Does she go to just the right places toting that baby, and she's just a small version of her mama? Just right too?"

Rhind swayed, the movement almost indiscernible. He closed his eyes to her, and spoke half in his drink cup. "I don't know miss, you'll have to find and ask my wife about all that."

"I'm asking you. A baby doll can't tell why she's in the window for sale. A dog can't tell why it's been kicked."

"Maybe you can tell me what's true about me. Then I can tell you what's true about you."

"I can tell you there's no man, because men don't stay. A man is nothing but what you wipe off the window to see better."

"And you see better. And we're sorry about all that."

"You sorry because you a man."

"Well, you know for sure, and we can't help it."

"No, a man can't help it, and a dog can't help it neither." She waited for him, but only to blink, twice. "What you can't help is you despise that wife of yours."

"No, you got it wrong. I don't hate my wife, I love her."

Alice Mays laughed and coughed together. It was a hard laugh, tasting of remnant emotion, and a cough of the unwell, a cough of memory too. With her eyes rimmed, soaked of a frenzy, she yet looked past Rhind to the river channel, the channel vacant of hue in the overcast, and shifted the shotgun in her arms, so that she held it properly, left handed, again.

"Channel Two, tell me this, true. When you got her fixed up just like you wanted her, and you saw it, how much then did you hate her? After all the fixing you did, what was it she didn't do for you? When you saw all it was you caused, from head to toe, how much did you despise her?"

Rhind took a long last drink, and he tossed the spit of the gin and squall water and the cup into the Ouachita, and that was when he saw his father, ferrying the small boat out of the near channel's fast water.

"If you're going to shoot me, you better go on and do it, because I'm going to get my wet clothes, and get in this boat, and take my white ass and my woodypecker away from this place."

She wiggled the shotgun and spoke to where she had been searching past them, and she leveled the barrel and followed Dan Rhind as he made the upriver side of the worn dock.

"You nekkid too?"

Dan Rhind worked the small boat against the current to the boards, and he took hold of a lashing cleat, then tied off without halfhitching, two succinct figure eights. He was shirtless with his shirt in his lap, but wearing the outback hat. The flow nudged the small boat to the pilings, and he looked the three of them over. He would remember later thinking just then, that he had not seen his son bare naked since he was a child. He stayed seated, and he put his palms together as a fist in his lap above the shirt, and he made a half smile out of courtesy, and he worried and estimated her and the steel and the stock of the shotgun altogether.

"You nekkid too in there?"

"Y'all alright," asked Dan Rhind, asking in a way that allowed only one answer, and he saw that they were standing, and that more than likely the round had been fired into the sky, the same as it sounded, and he looked again to the woman. "These boys are with me. We come on the river together."

"I say though, you nekkid in there?"

"No ma'am. I'm wearing everything I have in this world that's dry, and you can't count my shoes and my hat."

"You with these ones here?"

"Yes ma'am, we all together. We lost each other in that big rain." He thought to tell her that he hunted with the same gun, thinking too, *you have to shoot straight with that thing, it gets heavy,* and *we are bigger than a bobwhite, and slower too.*

"You come from Augusta too, then."

"Yes ma'am. This one here's my son."

"I can see that. I seen more than I thought I'd see today. Your mama must be tall then," she said to Rhind, and when his eyes remained shut to her she coughed once and wiggled the gun at Verdery. "You claim this one too?"

"Yes ma'am. He just as well be my other son."

"How you figure that?"

"They're just close, that's all."

"Close."

"Yes ma'am, close."

"I believe they funny."

"Funny."

"Yeah, funny. Oddlike."

"No, I don't believe so. They're just close, like good friends are close."

"You reckon."

"Yes ma'am, I do. You know what, I bet they want to get some clothes on. That ain't a problem is it?"

"They the ones showed up here nekkid as jaybirds. Close like jaybirds, you know."

Dan Rhind looked over his son and Verdery, then he looked to the woman again, and now he guessed her purpose and her ability according to how she gripped the weapon, and this second time he was less sure. "Ma'am, I wish I had someone in this world like these boys have each other. They're just out having some fun, meaning no harm. We all come from good parts of Augusta, and nobody's causing trouble."

"This one's from way up north."

"Yes ma'am, but he just as well be my son too. Nobody meant any harm to you. It rained hard."

"Harm. This one here ran off and left his wife and child, and this other one ran off way up north for some teenagers, and left everybody. And here come you, wishing for a man for yourself. Who you done left behind? Who you done let out a marriage?"

Rhind swayed and he made a noise to himself that might have been cursing, and he decided and sat to the dock.

"Danny. Hold still for a minute. You hear me? Hold still."

"That's right, you tell him that again, because I got one more in here, and maybe somemore after that. And he's determined to defy me, and I'm not going to tell him again."

Rhind lay to the boards on his back, and he covered his eyes with an arm.

"You see? He's trying me to no end. You see? I told him I ain't no pretty wife. I can't tell him again."

"Danny. I want you to sit up for me, alright? I want you to sit up, while we settle this."

They waited for him, with Alice Mays chewing the inside of her mouth, and he sat up, cross-legged with his elbows to his knees, and he looked at each of them, and slumped he wagged his head with his head down, cursing.

"Ma'am they just need to get some clothes on."

"You see? You see what I'm trying to tell you? Tell this boy here how men are with their women."

"That's alot to tell," said Dan Rhind, guessing when he would stand up in the boat, knowing, hoping, he bet right, that it was too soon yet.

"It ain't so much. All you got to do is tell the truth."

"Yes ma'am. I expect we can talk about all that on down the river. We going to be out a few days together."

"That's right. You all need to talk. You need to do the talking, while somebody else does the listening."

"They just need to get some clothes on, then nobody's seeing what they don't want to see."

There came a noise from downriver, a noise of wind in the trees, or another thing, and she quieted, searching past the three of them—likely to the far treeline, likely further on—the muscles and structure of her face fallen, expressionless, at once empty of the worry and the bemusement too.

Dan Rhind waited for her, half-heartened that his son and Verdery would know to wait too. He looked to them aware to show patience, then again to her. He sat straight-backed, motionless, with his hands in his lap, forbearing, almost confessional in his entreaty, with the river nudging Verdery's boat against the pilings. "Well ma'am, we can go on now, and quit bothering you. We got a good ways to go today."

"He said you work for the law." She spoke spelled by the vacant distance. The clouds had come heavy again, and it darkened and rained, and in just a moment it rained steady. Heavy drops flattened against the dock boards, and the drops pocked the river's surface, sizzling upward and out, filling the gray air with the same white noise they had heard coming.

"Ma'am," said Dan Rhind, now with effort against the rain.

"Your boy here, he said you work for the law back up there."

"I work for the District Attorney's office."

"District Attorney."

"Yes, ma'am. I'm an investigator for the D.A.'s office."

"Investigator."

"Yes, ma'am."

"Then you know about the law."

"I know a good part of it."

"Yes, sir. Then you understand why I have to shoot one of you."

"No, ma'am," said Dan Rhind, less petitionary now, near commanding, careful to be heard without mistake, knowing her ears were full of the noise of the shotgun and the squall come again.

The rain had matted her hair to her head, and it clung to her shoulders and back, a thick heavy veil, clumsily worn. Her face darkened, worried eyes darker, without focus, and she aged in the storm come from the ocean. Her blouse flattened against her torso, and she became smaller, reduced, and as Verdery watched the squall transform her he knew then that Alice Mays was insane, and that truly she was pitiable—and that doubtless, too, she was given to shoot one of them.

"Well, you said you know about the law. Then you know about trespassing too. That's the law."

"Ma'am, there's no need for all this."

"Need? There's a need. These men come here without permission, leaving everything and everybody behind, like it don't matter. Now, what am I going to do to set things right, but shoot one of them."

"No, ma'am. That is not your business."

"She wants us to be afraid," said Rhind, looking up.

Her eyes came half-alive again and she gripped the shotgun, and waist high she leveled at him.

"Say it again, Channel Two."

Verdery spoke before Rhind could. "We understand, Miss Mays. We understand we did something wrong here, but we can't change what we did. We can't change it, but we can fix it."

She spoke to Verdery, but she did not waver from Rhind. "We going to fix it now. All you got to do is decide which one of you is getting shot."

"You don't have to be this way," said Dan Rhind, shouting above the rain pocking the boards and the water, making that frying sound that tried to consume them. "It don't have to be this way."

She took a heavy, sorry breath, but she did not waver from Rhind, and she spoke to the three of them, and to the river's impenetrable surface, and to the squall that had come for them from half across the Earth. She spoke what she had come to tell when she had seen them first from her cottage window— then, exhaling his name, saying it not even aloud, *he done come, he done come back for somemore,* and reaching for the shotgun and stuffing two shells into it, hurried and wanton. "I used to say that too. I used to say that all the time, about every Friday and Saturday night. I used to talk about how he didn't have to be one way or another. About how he didn't have to take that drink all the time, and about how he didn't have to run off up the road to find some fun. About how we could be interested in one another, how we could sit out here in the evenings and look up in the good dark sky, and try to imagine it all. Try to see it all, past what we know for sure, and not be scared to imagine right up to the point where we can't see anymore, for fearing we lose ourself. Right up to where we lose everything we know, because there is a new way to know. I used to say it can be this way and that way, because there's nothing set in the stone. There's nothing already told about our living, because we do the telling. We can tell the story anyway we want to. You put the stone under your house to keep it straight and true, and to just keep it."

"Ma'am, let's get out of this rain."

"But there's no stone around our living, until we get buried in it, and then ain't nothing more you can do. You see that's why there is the stone under the house in the first place. There is some people let themselves get buried, while they still got the life in them, and there's nothing more you can say to these ones. You have to go on and let them live the death while they're still breathing and not seeing, and you best see you can't do a thing for them. Some people, they can't look up at the good dark sky and say it's amazing to them. Say it's beyond something they know. And you can't save a man like that. They already buried. Buried themselves."

"Ma'am. Miss Mays."

"See, I used to say things don't have to be one way or another. True, I used to explain it that way. But it don't matter. It seems things is the way they are, and that's all there is to it. And that's all you can do, and you don't need to know anymore than that. A man don't have to go off and look for some drink and some fun, when all he's got to do is look at the good dark sky, and don't fear the knowledge of it. All he's got to do is look past all his imagining, and know I loved him, and know there won't ever be any stones until he dies."

Rhind clucked his tongue at her and he reached for his shorts and shirt, and sitting he took the small heavy bundle in his arms.

"Channel Two," she said, strained and aloud and pitiful, adjuratory and suppliant together.

Rhind stood with the bundle to his chest, and he turned from her.

"Danny," said Dan Rhind. "Son, William," he said in a full shout, "be still. Be still, son. Be still a minute."

Rhind stood in place, slump shouldered, facing the river, with the bundle to his chest. The squall beat down heavy upon him, and he lowered his head, and closed his eyes, and listened only to the rain upon the river. With the taste of the gin in his lungs it returned the noise of his own painted porch boards, aloneness, a well-kept, empty, childless house.

"Things are the way they are," said Alice Mays. "So all you got to do is choose."

"No ma'am," said Dan Rhind.

"It don't matter. We all know who it is anyways."

"No ma'am."

"We all know what the choice has to be. We all knew it from the start."

Dan Rhind felt the pistol from his lap beneath his shirt, into his right hand. He gripped the stock and trigger ring, then the trigger, gripping it low, his arm hanging straight, his fist and the pearl and the steel of it altogether. He watched unblinking her hand on the shotgun's walnut stock, unblinking in the squall as it sluiced from the sagging brim of his hat. Later he would remember then thinking too, *she is left-handed. She shoots wrong-handed. But some do.*

The rain bottomed suddenly heaviest, with no sound save it beating the earth, the boards and water and their flesh, and there was no color, save the ocean's bluegray that had consumed them.

Her hand slid along the forestock for aiming and Dan Rhind, straight armed, trained the pistol on her. She turned to him tilting her head at last questioning *why* they had come for her, and slowly she pivoted with only her torso and the gun barrel leveling to him. But still he did not take her. *I will be the first, only if I have to be*, doubting it even as he reasoned, endured. They beheld one another suspended inanimate and destined amidst the squall's roil and hiss. They beheld one another suspended in the bluegray, nearness immeasurable, and he thought too, *if I shoot her, I won't even know her first name.*

From above the deputy called out her full name as he knew to say it, "Alicia Mays." He had paused only for a moment at the top of the stairs unable to determine there were four of them, and he came quickly descending, scattering the water upon the treads beneath his heavy dark shoes.

He called, "Alicia," stern and sharp, practiced, commanding, it dissolving into the squall. On the dock the deputy in long strides was upon her all at once, taking her in his arms, beside her then behind like a dance partner. He raised her arms and the shotgun in her arms to the sky all in a single motion, and the shotgun flamed its second round into the bluegray of the storm. Scolding, he spoke her first name again, and she allowed him the smoking weapon, and he held her and he lay the shotgun away from them. *Alicia Mays*, said the deputy this time most gently, more a query and assurance, and he helped her to sit on the dock boards into the shallow collected rainwater.

Dan Rhind's gun was gone from sight and he was already standing from the boat, and the deputy could see it was a man and two more, all standing.

"Anybody shot here?" and Dan Rhind answered saying *no*, and the deputy gripped the shotgun by the warm barrel and he slung it end for end to the river, and it disappeared soundlessly into the mist where the fast, deep water commenced. He knelt again to Alice Mays, and now Dan Rhind had come too.

"I'm sorry that boy don't love his wife," and she might have been weeping, but he could not know. "I'm sorry he don't love you neither."

"I don't know where she gets the damn things," said the deputy searching her rimmed crimson eyes, searching for recognition, taking all of the others in too—the apparently naked men now dressing in the soaked clothes, and the shirtless man close to him in the sagging hat and the cutoffs smelling of acrid tobacco, squatting like a baseball catcher, where he grimaced to the walking boards, to the shallow, pocking rain water. "At least she called. At least she did that. But I swear I don't know where she gets them. Tell me where you're from, and what's your business here."

"Augusta. Daniel Rhind, District Attorney's Office, Tenth. Those are my boys."

"And if I asked you for some I.D. you going to be able to show it to me, right?"

Dan Rhind said the name of the District Attorney, and he said the address on Telfair Street, the phone number, and then he described succintly by name the most recent case he worked, where the first man had killed the second man, because one of them could not quit loving the other. He didn't tell how the murdered man was salvaged in the chifforobe then later the Little Pee Dee River.

The deputy watched Dan Rhind's mouth while he spoke, careful to gain all of what the other said over the gun noise in his ears. "Mr. Rhine, you know what?"

"What, sir."

"I don't even want to know what you might've been holding in your boat."

"Alright."

"Because you got all the papers, right?"

"Yes sir, I do."

"And that other one's in the river now, and we didn't see either of them, right?"

"Yes, sir."

"And nobody's shot, right?"

"No, sir."

"Lord, Alicia."

"I had no choice. She wouldn't let us go from here. She had it on my boy."

"Y'all should know it's going to rain on you."

"We just stopped for a minute. Nobody meant any harm."

"You know you trespassing."

"We're just messing around on the river. We'd been gone from here a half hour ago."

"I wish you'd been gone a half hour."

"Yes sir."

"Damn, you come all this way from Augusta?"

"We did."

"Damn," said the deputy again, taking all of them in again, and finishing at Alice Mays, searching close the vacant, crimson eyes. He was uniformed in khaki, an arm patch reading Screven County, a rain shield wrapping his hat.

He wore good polished shoes, and his shoes and his holster creaked when he shifted his weight. "Y'all alright, for sure?"

"We alright. She shot it once in the air. Well, twice."

"Alicia Mays."

"We alright. We just need to go on."

"Where you trying to get to?"

"Blue Springs. We're looking for the 301 bridge today."

"You got a little ways to go."

"Sure. We figured in a little while."

"I'm going to take Miss Alicia up to the house, and get her out of this rain. I think your boys ought to go on, but can you come up for just a minute? I believe I'll feel better if you come on up for just a minute."

"I can do it."

"Good then. Did she make you all undress too?"

"She did."

"Damn if I've ever seen anything like it. I don't know where she gets them."

Rhind then Verdery sat into the Ouachita, and the squall quit. Dan Rhind stood against the pain in his legs and he went near the longboat.

"We're alright here," said Rhind to his father without looking up.

"Go on, and I'll be there soon as I can."

"We're alright here," said Rhind again, louder, formally, his way with people he did not know, his way with his father and all his family, his way when a mistake committed could not have been his.

"We'll pull up and look for you after awhile," said Verdery.

Dan Rhind watched them slip into the rising steam, where the fast water took the Ouachita, then he went for the stairs and the cottage where the deputy had taken the insane woman.

They spoke quietly, politely, because it was not their home, and because she was in the same room. She sat in a primitive ladderback chair and the deputy had dressed her in a cotton robe, but her hair still clung, soaked and mossy, about her shoulders. She sipped a warm drink, and she did not look up from the drink and the steam as the men spoke.

"Everybody around here looks after her. But I'll be damned if I know where she gets them guns. She don't mean harm to anybody. She'll call us every so often and we'll come on out and look after her. And most of the time it's nothing at all."

"You think she meant to hit someone?"

"I doubt it like hell. I don't know."

"Well, she just about did."

"She don't mean harm to anybody. It's just been hard on her."

"She called you out here today?"

"They got me on the radio. I guess it was when those boys came onto her dock."

"They didn't mean any harm either."

"I'm sure they didn't. I know they didn't. But what I wanted to take a minute and tell you, is this—I just as soon let it rest here. You know what I'm saying to you, Mr. Rhine? You both got something to forget about, and let alone. And as soon as I threw that weapon in the water, it was three of us. And I just as soon let it alone right here. We can do that much. There are some things we can't do much about, but we can do this much."

Dan Rhind nodded to the cottage floorboards. "You think she's going to let it alone?"

"I'll see to it. I'll say it again, I know she doesn't mean any harm. I've used better judgment than today. But here we sit. It's just aggravating, is all."

"Alright," said Dan Rhind, looking to her quickly then looking out the cottage window. The dust on the windowpane showed the rubbing of her hand and the summer rain. A dingy spiral galaxy smeared and spied through. "Alright then."

"I just want to say one more thing, though. I want you all to do something from now on—I want you and your boys to be careful. Did she make them undress, or did they come that way? Well, either way they need to keep their clothes on. I promise there are some people might appreciate it."

"Sure. Sure."

"You said you were headed for Blue Springs?"

"Yes sir. We looking to make the 301 bridge today."

"That's what I'm saying. If you going to just put out somewhere, you need to be careful about the property. Hell most people don't care, but you just need to be careful."

"I see that."

"You got a little ways to go, to make Blue Springs. But you all need to be careful. And think about whose property you're stepping onto. Hell, Mr. Rhine, I'm not telling you a thing you don't know. You probably know it better than me, to tell the truth. But I got to say it anyways. So there I go."

"Sure, sure."

They nodded to one another as if in contract, and Dan Rhind nodded again and made a noise to himself, and said, "thank you, sir," and went out of the cottage without looking to the woman called Alicia—the woman he was a twitch from shooting through the heart.

The deputy knelt before her without touching her, and he looked up to her.

"Alicia, what am I going to do with you, gal."

Behind the rising steam of her drink she remembered her name and that she was alone each day when the day got dark.

"Scaring people off your property is one thing, but I don't want you ever thinking it's alright to shoot somebody. You shoot somebody and they'll put you away, then what do I tell your sister? I don't want you getting anymore of them guns. You hear me?"

"He didn't have to go off looking somewhere else."

"I know he didn't, gal. But he's gone, and you got to stop worrying about all that, now."

"But he didn't have to go nowhere."

"I know he didn't. You going to tell me if you got more?"

She nodded with her eyes wide, fixed somewhere short of the floorboards, and it made the sheriff's deputy think of his girl, when she was small.

"And do you have some more?"

She wagged her head slowly without blinking, searching the space wherein nothing material was contained, and it made him think again of his daughter. And now she was a different age.

The deputy put her to bed, and he did not leave her until dusk that day. He went out of the cottage with his shoes and holster, creaking again now that they were almost dry of the rainwater. He drove along the dirt and sand road to the highway, not thinking properly of his speed, and when it occurred to him that it was about dark and he was too fast, he pulled his headlamps on and slowed, and he drove carefully the way to his home and his wife, and Thursday's late supper.

When she went again to the dock for that first hour going into the night, the rain started. She searched southeast into the rising steam, into the fog where the river must have taken them, and under an arm she held a rolled dishtowel. She stood attentive, patient for a coming, until her sight failed in the evening. With the flesh and muscles of her arm tight against the bulge where the un-tried pistol rested between the dry fiber, she waited until the charcoal gray had gone to black, but they did not return against the water, and he did not come again.

CHAPTER SEVENTEEN

The oxbow at Big Randall Point ran due south, then north for half a mile, before turning again to southeast. On the Carolina shore at rivermile one twenty-seven, Dan Rhind found them. They had already unloaded their goods and tipped and drained the Ouachita, and when Dan Rhind came Verdery helped him do the same.

Shirtless, apart from one another, they chose to stand in the sun warming through the cloud breaks, looking across to the Georgia side, gaining relief from the sitting and the rowing and the sameness of the river. Soon Verdery went to the water and stood in it, and bent and washed his face, and went again to them and stood between them, he now facing the treeline.

"She just wanted us to be afraid."

Dan Rhind bowed his head.

"What?" said Rhind.

"It's all done," said Dan Rhind, speaking down. "It's all, done."

"Were you afraid?" said Rhind.

"Everything's fine. We talked it out back there. It's all done."

"All we did was stop a minute," said Verdery, "get out of the boat."

"I know it. It's all fine. I can't see what you could've done to cause all that."

"You tell me this," said Rhind. "You tell me she wasn't a crazyass bitch."

"Like I said, it's all done. We worked it out."

"You tell me she's not a crazyass, gun-toting bitch."

"He said he looks after her, like he knew all about it. So I let them alone, and he let me alone. Us alone."

"You can't tell me that, can you?"

"Tell you what son. No. I don't know."

"You can't tell me."

"I don't know. We're all standing here now. And we leave it, if we want to."

"Leave *us* alone?"

"She had the thing on me too, son. But it don't matter now."

"It don't?"

"It's in the river, and we here."

"She can't be too much trouble," said Verdery.

"She can't?"

"They would have done something."

"They."

"Him."

"Well, tell me this then, Thom, were you afraid?"

Verdery wagged his head slowly, not even answering Rhind's question to himself.

"You just can't understand it sometimes," said Dan Rhind.

"She just wanted something from us, that's all," said Verdery.

"Right, and that's not a crazyass, shotgun-carrying bitch back there either, is it. She's just a little bothered, right? Honestly bitter. Isn't she, dad?"

Dan Rhind wagged his head the same as Verdery, and he took off the limp outback hat and put it on again.

"Son, it's like I said, we can leave it and go on."

"Don't tell me. I intended to leave it. *She* wouldn't leave it alone."

"Nobody meant any—"

"Nobody meant what. Nobody meant harm? She was holding a goddam shotgun on me. What do you think she was wanting to do with that thing? What do you think?"

"Son, I don't—"

"And where were *you* going to put *your* bullet?"

"Son," said Dan Rhind and he took his hat off and put it on again, and he went to the small boat, and he took the rivermap and a pantela. "We're only eight miles to the swingbridge." He lighted, unsmiling, even when he teethed it, and not even aware that he was pleased the cigars had somehow survived dry.

"You already said that."

"I imagine there's still a phone there. I can walk up and call."

"We already heard you about that."

"That little boat's just wearing me down, that's all. I didn't expect to stay out here all week anyway."

"Sure, dad. And you going to send this work friend back for us too, right?"

Dan Rhind gave the rivermap to Verdery, then took the cigar from his mouth and he spat and took his time to speak, because he knew what he was going to say next. "Son, I'll come back for you, when you're ready. Is that so hard?"

"No, not hard. But you don't have to worry about that either."

"You call from wherever you finish, and I will come for your ass. And now, that's done too."

Dan Rhind bit the cigar again, and he wagged his head, and he took the pantela from his mouth to curse. "No, I will not call my wife. Danny knows that, and Thomas would you like also to know why I cannot call my wife?"

"No sir," said Verdery, "I don't think I need to."

"Well, alright then. You'll know the swingbridge when you get to it. The fucker's turned the wrong way. Try to keep your pants on."

Verdery offered the rivermap, and Dan Rhind wagged his head and grimaced, and Verdery saw that it was more than anger, more than shame. "No son, y'all going to need that damn thing."

Dan Rhind set his bow to downstream, and soon the fast water took him equidistant to either treeline, small as a thumbnail.

In the broken sun wading shin deep, Rhind made a drink heavy with gin.

"She just wanted something from us," said Verdery.

"You said it already."

"There's more to it than we know."

"Right. Some of them are difficult to understand. Daniel Rhind says some of them are difficult to understand. Those are the ones that run off and leave your ass alone. Alone to preach, somewhere on a piss-wet river, to sons and sons' acquaintances, how much you know them, by virtue of how little you profess to know. Some of them are difficult. The difficult ones you'll know by their loneliness, their hatefulness, and their insanity. And they'll be the ones holding the goddam shotgun on your goddam woody."

They made a bend called White Woman's Landing, then soon Ring Jaw Point, then soon a place named on the rivermap as Fat Meat Point, and from the map Verdery remembered only the first name, and one other. They went wide at bends where the water ran fast, and the clouds and the bluegray rain came again, and quit again, and left all they possessed wetted and heavy as before. Rhind drank the rainwater with his gin, and he made another fresh drink heavy with gin, and he spoke aloud to himself. Rhind smiled a heartless smile wide beneath the veil of his drunkenness, and he held his drink high as a toast to Verdery, and to his father, and his mother and his wife—women who had left their homes for different succinct reasons, rather than stay with men they could love but not suffer and forbear—because time only turns everything living and inanimate old, and time cannot be endured, because it is the last of all things. Soon Verdery heard Rhind slurring, and Rhind's eyes narrowed and his face grew the broad careless smile of a drunkard. He toasted Verdery and his disappeared wife and child, his belly and lungs and brain full of drink that now witnessed the pall true, the softness true. His oar slipped into the water and Verdery slowed to retrieve it, and Rhind shouted something aloud and held his drink high to no one and wagged his head knowing that the shroud of the gauze was ever the only one true embracing and flawless thing.

A mile from the swingbridge they stopped, and Verdery urinated into the fallow sand of Allendale County, South Carolina. Rhind stood in the Ouachita's stern and urinated into the river and all over the boat's gunnels. He swayed and tipped, deadfalling heavy into the shallow water and hard yellow sand. The boat righted yawing crazy and Rhind lay fallen, coughing belly-laughing, shoulders tossing in wild laughter. He finished pissing lying sideways in the sand and water, pissing on himself. Verdery cursed and tried to lift him and Rhind slapped his arm away, warning him off in a drunkard's slurring oratory. Rhind cursed and belly-laughed, kneeling with the river to his waist. He coughed hard, sudden, then he lay back into the river and swam torpidly dipping his head once.

Verdery cursed him aloud, and Rhind spat riverwater and laughed and coughed from his torso and his gut the same heavy laugh. "Tell me about them Doubting Thomas. Tell me about all the ones you loved and lost, and tell me why."

"Drunkard. Goddam drunkard."

"Tell me why and how, and how many times, and how many times does it take, before it takes."

"You need to be in the front, now."

"Damn that."

"Get in and get in the front."

"Fuck that shit. No."

In half a mile Verdery heard the first traffic crossing the 301 bridge. The rattle and groan of a lumber truck burdened with fresh-cut loblolly bounced echoing against the treeline and over the water.

His father drove a truck and he taught him to know a truck's engine by sound. This one hauled too much, it was gas not diesel, and it stroked like a poor man's. Half of it belonged to the lender and the other half maybe to the driver, who, after fuel and repairs, regards the pulpmill's check in his hand with a weariness, a stubborn inanition, and climbs right again into the cab rattling the door shut, clutching and shifting to retrieve more tall bodies of fast-grown pine trees. It groaned and whined against the river basin's gradient, and it downshifted once and changed its pitch, and the pitch faded as the truck climbed moaning, running like hell and wear with desperate purpose and unfailing direction.

They cleared the bend wide at Stave Lodge and ahead through the quarter mile's faint haze he could see both bridges now. Verdery told Rhind to keep the boat straight and Rhind slurred senselessly.

Nearest stood the fixed bridge with highway 301 crossing, clearing forty feet above. And after the new bridge rested the swingbridge, abandoned now and pivoted open for passage. Massive and complicated creosote timber trestles guarded the center piers of both bridges forming a slip for river traffic. Numbers stenciled on metal plates marked the water height, and on other plates were printed warnings against trespassing and for horn soundings.

This is her, damn if we didn't get here.

The old truss swing bridge, designed and built equiweighted, flawlessly balanced, pivoted on a single massive center brick and concrete pier. It had been stored permanently open, aligned with the channel—a marvelous and useless thing. Reddened sumac grew from the mortar and brick, and hog apple too from the decayed landings at each bank. The steel was once painted a vibrant green but the hue and chroma had faded long ago from its skeleton, and it endured only a chalky tint, and going to rust. The great old cog underneath that spun it—flat, teethed and splined, an anonymous sculpture of industry and ubercraft, still greased in impuissance—a remainder the same as the greater remainder abandoned.

When the fixed bridge was ready to set aside the oldtimey world, the swingman pivoted the swingbridge a final turn. That day, a time ago, he swung it full round, just to see, as its parents and builders said it proudly would on its first day, with the paint rich saturated, the brick and mortar fresh, pure binding strong as stone. Piloting from the tender house he swung it one last time round, matching twice the landings at Georgia and South Carolina. He swung it full round, *three hundred and sixty galdarn, back to where we galdarn started, around she goes and where she stops . . .* And when he came around aligned with the channel, he shut it down. In the shadow of the new bridge, and the summer wind already seeding the veins of the aged mortar, the first manbuilt span at Burton's Ferry was finished. And beyond its very own gentle groaning in the wind, it never again accomplished any measurable movement.

He turned to say it aloud and he saw that Rhind's face had collapsed, his skin bruised beneath his eyes, his mouth hanging, fallen sick, in the last fifteen minutes consumed by the alcohol. The rain started, this time slowly, at first only a light spattering, weighting the air heavy warm and moist and the sky darkened, and daylight would not come again.

"Will," said Verdery as a question and a test, then thought it, then said it, "oh goddamit," and Rhind's eyes remained unchanged, depthless and glazed, and he lowered his slow-dumb wagging head, his mouth open but soundless, manipulated and the master unseen but in his blood and brain. The oar slipped from his lap and he moved none to regain it, and Verdery struggled this time to slow and spin the boat to retrieve it, and now he lay it to the keel, beneath his bowseat.

"Goddamit, what did I say to you?" and Verdery cursed forward to the massive trestle, plying hard to realign the Ouachita. They passed the upriver legs, black timber rising high and complicated and wafting of the tar-fragrant creosote.

Behind a single car passed over the fixed bridge, tires whipping the expansion joints, and as they cleared the swingbridge to the right side Verdery saw the landing on the Georgia side where Dan Rhind had pulled the small boat high out of the water, where he stood hunched, hands to his hips, upon the grass of a small mound. Verdery ferried hard against the flow, but alone and with his arms tight and tired, the current took him below the ramp. Nearly broaching, he landed the Ouachita as fast and as hard as he could, then made Rhind sit ass to the hull with his legs over the rear thwart, and Rhind cursed something senseless, then shut his eyes again. By the painter Verdery walked the boat and Rhind back upstream along the shore to the ramp, and he tugged the boat a quarter clear of the water, and he and Dan Rhind stood with their hands to their hips, overlooking the Ouachita and the mess it carried—a son and a friend—their feet in the sand and mud, hunched in the gray, spattering rain.

"How long you been alone," said Dan Rhind.

"A little while."

Dan Rhind looked over his paralyzed son, and he looked down to his own canvas shoes in the mud of Screven County, and he looked again to his son.

"Did you find the phone?"

"No, I was waiting. I thought maybe I shouldn't leave your boat here untended."

"I got it if you want to go walking."

"What you going to do with this one?"

"I'm letting him stay right there."

"Hell, son," said Dan Rhind, to Verdery.

On the highway a single car passed heading into South Carolina, tires whining in rhythm on the concrete, and soon again all returned quiet save the gray rain's persistent spattering. Dan Rhind looked across blinking beneath the soaked hat's brim. "You ever put that tent together?"

"No."

"You ever seen one of them put together?"

"Not for awhile."

"It ain't too much to it."

"I'm sure it's something I can figure out in just a minute."

Hell, said Dan Rhind, once to himself, then aloud. "Hell, it's only about six now. You want to go on for awhile or stay here?"

"You go on and find the phone, then we'll see about it. I think this rain's done. After today, I think it's done."

"You think?"

"I don't know."

"There's a flat spot back up behind us here. We can put the tent out up there or we can go on, and make a few more miles. Either way there ain't a dry spot in the goddam county."

"I can take my boat for awhile. Well. I could've. I should've . . . well . . ."

"It don't matter. I just get aggravated, that's all. I'm alright, I just get aggravated."

"You think he's looking after her?"

"Who? Sure, I imagine he is."

"He seemed good to her, like she was . . . we didn't mean to get you . . ."

"Tommy, we can leave it back there. If we want to, that's all I'm saying. Sometimes things just happen, and it doesn't matter. It's just leaving it, and going on."

Verdery nodded and Dan Rhind blinked, searching across the mile of distance, the rising meadow, where the highway disappeared into the mist and the treeline.

"They're cold, you know, when it's like this."

Verdery nodded, looking to where Dan Rhind looked.

"I mean the phones, you know."

Verdery nodded, and he made a little smile lacking heart.

"And you never know who's been on them. People don't appreciate what they're given. And they don't leave something for the next person. You just don't know what people are going to do with breaking shit and leaving it broken."

"We can wait if you want to try to find one. I'm already wet, and we're going nowhere fast."

"Hell, this ain't the place I was thinking about. Hell, I done forgot so much of what I thought I knew, and what I never knew, it scares me. Hell. Tommy, my boy's got no quitting sense, has he?"

"Sometimes."

"You always drank a good bit together."

"We have."

"But you don't get like this."

"I've had my times, and he's looked after me."

"Hell, everybody's had one time or another. Most everybody."

Rhind said something senseless aloud, and after a moment Dan Rhind and Verdery walked out of the mud and water upward on the boat ramp. At the top of the rise where woods began there grew a spot of grass and it held a pool of rainwater, and Verdery walked to the middle and sank ankle deep. "You think we can go on down and find a sandbar?"

"It's about six now."

"We got two hours of day left. It'll get us a little further down."

"Sure," said Dan Rhind, looking upward to nothing but gray and rain. "I expect we've seen the worst of all this mess."

"There's a place on your map called Kings Creek Landing, down a couple miles."

"That don't mean nothing, though. It might be just two ruts and a stump, or it might be less than that."

"It might, but we can try and see. Maybe there's a beach."

"Sure," said Dan Rhind nodding, then, "Hell son, it don't matter to me. Like I said we can go on downriver a little. We got some daylight left. You see I'm already half-wet."

"Alright," and Verdery made the same smile, his heart no more willing.

"You going to do any good alone in that big boat?"

"Sure. I just need to be in the back. I'll be alright."

They found Rhind sitting bent atop a smooth rock, vomiting into the Savannah River. Verdery went near and let him finish. "Come on, drunkard," he said, taking Rhind by an elbow and Rhind slapped his arm away, slurring something cruel and senseless, and he stood on his own stumbling along the shore, slipping and reaching when there was nothing there, and finding the Ouachita with his knees. "Drunkard, you're in front," and Verdery made Rhind sit with his ass to the keel at the bow this time, and Rhind sat heavy, a stinking lump as if asleep, his head back against the bowseat.

"Let's look for Kings Creek anyway," said Verdery, giving the rivermap away, and Dan Rhind nodded solemn while he looked over his son.

"You going to be alright alone in this thing?"

"I'm alright, I just need to be in the back. He's just ballast now. Counterweight."

"Damn if he ain't," said Dan Rhind, then, "hell, son," aspirating the words, and after a moment, after making a noise to himself, he went to the smaller boat and they started again over the water.

The rain eased spitting and an evening breeze blew from due south. Verdery rowed hard to warm himself and while he worked alone Rhind leaned to the gunnel and heaving vomited twice more, half into the river and half over himself.

Behind, the two bridges clouded in the steam mist became small in the distance. Verdery said a farewell to them, aloud, and no one heard him speak, and trailing Dan Rhind he worked the Ouachita amidst the bluegray for the next riverbend and wooded point, they alike all the countless others.

He followed for an hour, staying in the fast water, slipping wide around points, watching for strainers and dikes. The Corps numbered the dikes with green plates on the Georgia side and red on the Carolina side, counting down, downriver to Savannah.

The dikes were made long into the river, dual piers of blackened creosote posts leaning inward to one another, lashed together, serving as strainers against erosion and sediment. They reached out from shore well into the current, and white willow and sycamore and sumac grew from the post tops, and egret and white crane and great blue heron visited them, patient, regarding the water and too the boats with the men, sliding by, trimmed low, suspended upon the river's tensile surface.

Late this August day the water turned the color of umber, and the air solemn grayblue, dull as the steel of Alice May's shotgun barrel. They made Fennel Hill Landing and there was nothing save the name on the map, then within the next mile they made King's Creek Landing. It was as Dan Rhind supposed, just a clearing in the woods, enough to slip a boat in and be consumed by mosquitoes doing it. They did not even slow to look closer, and the rain came on. They made a stand of white willow at the head of a bend and they hoped to find sand just around, and when they cleared the trees there was a beach and an enormous sandbar, and they ferried into the slow water then slid halting in the yellow sand, their bows hushing in two succinct, separate breaths as they landed. Verdery wakened Rhind first, commanding him to wash the vomit from himself. He took an elbow but Rhind slapped his arm away and cursed a cruel warning, then lay into the water with his head going under once. Dan Rhind watched his son then the water above him and he did reappear and he stood from the water, his bath no more than a baptismal. And Rhind sat again ass to the keel, wetted heavy, ruined drunken, stinking asleep, as before.

The rain came on, spattering warning, presage, then when it had spoken whispering across the surface of all the river and the sand too, it came heavy, with intent. Dan Rhind took the tent saying, *I think the goddam thing does this*, and Verdery aped him righting it in the poor light and the squall. Dan Rhind quit for only a moment and he looked to his son, where the storm come an ocean washed down on him, his visage thieved of all expression—save a death mask—by the drunkenness. And he made a noise—not of adjudication or even pity, but of something else—to himself, and bent again to help Verdery.

They set the tent over a flat spot high from the shore, where the rain hardened the yellow sand, and scrambling they gripped the gear they would need for the night, and each trip into the tent carried wetness and sand. Verdery commanded Rhind shouting him from sleep, then he slapped his bare shoulder and wiped the vomit from his hand in the same motion. Rhind wakened, his eyes open to the pocking rain and he knew Verdery less than any spirit come for him, until he saw too the other man regarding him—yet again without judgment or pity, but more dour curiosity and inexorable sadness of knowing a thing unknown the day before.

"Will, listen to me," said Verdery, commanding against the rain and the thickness of stupor and indulgence. "Before you come inside you need to get this off you. Before you come into the tent with us, you need to wash."

Rhind swung a fist in the air and as a final warning pointed a forefinger at Verdery slurring, "don't goddamit, don't," then he crawled from the boat, his fists and bare feet digging heavy into the yellow sand and he fell through the tent door in a stumbling dive bringing gobs of sand and rain with him. He fell in place to one side on the bare floor and there he slept on his stomach, his arms down by his side, paralyzed, mouth breathing liquor and vomit.

Verdery tugged each boat high on the beach, each heavy again from the squallwater, then went to the tent, and while Dan Rhind held the doorflap for him he looked a last time at the boats and the river—the river the same gray as the air, as the rain, as the sky, as all the apparent earth—and he went second carrying gobs of sand on his feet into the puny shelter, and Dan Rhind went third.

They sat and it rained a terrible hardness. The remnant squall born so far away of the warm Atlantic fell a volume inestimable and in such a noise that they spoke nothing against it. It drummed heaving down, as if all of heaven might have tumbled, and in all the world seeable and knowable, in this day's failing charcoal gray dun, there visited only this terrific natural shudder.

It lay down over them and over the grains of the earth around them, and too into the ceaseless, tireless visage of the Savannah itself—storm and river born and grown of the same element, and enduring somatically now in the selfsame shared body. Into its living form, the river gathered all the flood, coursing fuller, darker, all washing in return to the mouth of the beginning ocean, likely in sentient transit, alive too, as it must be, whispering into the natural tremor, something alike, *come again, you come again, because I shall deliver you, without end, without finish, I shall deliver us.*

CHAPTER EIGHTEEN

Dan Rhind loosed the batteries then poured water from his flashlight. When he put it together again, it did not work. Cursing, searching in his gear he found buried a zippered pouch holding three stubbed candles, and in another smaller pouch a single box of matches. The candles were the fat kind, used, larger than votives. "She remembered the last time I came out, and she told me to do this, and damn if it didn't work. She said she just didn't trust tools sometimes. I think that's what she said. I think that's what she meant."

They set out the candles using their shoes for stands. In the small pouch he found a folded paper, and by the candlelight he read her handwriting, then put it away again.

"You hungry yet?"

"Yes, lord yes."

"I guess it's just two of us for supper."

"No, he won't be dining with us."

"My boy's got no quitting sense, does he Thomas?"

"Sometimes, no."

"You've seen him like this before?"

"I have."

"You been like that before?"

"I imagine I have."

"Hell, I imagine I have too, way back. That condition would kill my old ass nowadays."

They took the time to heat cans on the gas stove, warming themselves too, and they ate from the cans and drank beer without speaking, staring into the firetips, as the candles shadowed their torsos. *It's a good light*, thought Verdery, thinking too, *I'll remember to make it again*, thinking too a moment later, *I may never work again, and this light will never come again.*

The squall drummed a sudden rage, a missive, a warning told by the insane of the more insane, then eased, then came again. They ate sitting cross-legged in the wet and the sand, a small comfort the warmed supper, the full weariness of the day—that had begun fourteen hours before at Cliff's Folly, in the halfdark then too—settling over them. The squall eased.

"At its worst, this is a damn sight better than what they fed us overseas," said Dan Rhind, the candlefire luminous in a fine point within his eyes.

"This is warm. Thank you," said Verdery, knowing Dan Rhind was an Army man and overseas was Vietnam. Verdery learned the name of the place when he was a boy, too young to grip a football well, and it occurred so long ago that he tried to remember if it hurt, unsure now that it was the truth. He remembered it hurt his mother, and he believed his father too, but again he was uncertain. That day, when it must have been early spring, nineteen sixty-nine, his mother held him close, drawing his head to her cotton dress and her breasts, weeping openly, as if she were not ashamed her oldest son had died, third man walking in a foreign jungle, taken by strangers ten thousand miles from home. And because of that memory he always believed it true more than not.

"This rain is the same."

"As there."

"When it rains hard like this I think of there. Not always, but sometimes."

"I heard that, about the rain." Verdery meant that his brother hand scrawled it in hurried letters, that he wore his boots without relief on his feet for a month, that the rain had not quit for that same month, and that he wrote it to his mother not him.

"Sure, it rained. It rained like hell."

"Sure," said Verdery. "Were you going to shoot her?"

"That woman? No. No, I wasn't going to shoot her. It was a sorry sight, wasn't it. I'm sorry. No. She didn't . . ."

"That's alright Dan. I didn't mean to, we didn't mean to . . . I mean, we don't have to worry about her. That's alright. It's like you said about leaving it. It's just been a long day. It seems like more than one."

Verdery got them two more beers and they finished their supper searching the candlefire, as if gathered in the amber tips there burned clues to why women care beyond what a man understands, and how they know when to quit. They made their beds from the soaked bedrolls, and Verdery half-covered Rhind in his, and Rhind did not move. The drum of the sky falling consumed them, and they were alone huddled against the storm's might, this world full dark and not another witness, save three uneven candleflames. They sat cross-legged on their bedrolls, Dan Rhind weary bemused from the long day, remembering rain from a time and a place distant, but not yet vanished. Verdery listened, a sudden deafening weight he had never known, then it eased, as if done with them. Dan Rhind lay upon his back. "We went down to the swamp one weekend. Okeefenokee. I drove home from Fort Jackson, and got him. It was just me and the boy."

"That was when the fish jumped in the boat."

"The fish. He told you."

"Sure he did. More than once."

"He told you."

"He did. He told about the fish, and the car."

"That old red Mercury."

"And about the mosquitoes."

"Gators, bowfin'll take your fingers off. Spiders as big as your hand. We had a good time just me and Danny. Two makes for different times than three."

"Always seems like it."

"We camped just one night and fished from the bank, catching those damn bowfin. We let them flip themselves off the hook, because I learned fast about putting a finger in their mouths. A damn gator was watching us, and the next one we caught this gator rushed the shore and took that fish off the line. Just like that, then backed down into the swamp with the fish, just damn like that. Then waited there, you know, for the next one we caught. And we figured those gators out, and there was two of them, one on either side of the camping platform, you know. Just two and no more. And we fished and let those gators take the fish off the line just for the amusement of it. Danny too."

"He said that. A little hard to believe it happened that way without being there."

"Well hell," said Dan Rhind, then he made a noise, and folded his palms upon his chest. "You believe it?"

"Sure, I believe it." Verdery blew out the candleflames, and lay to his bed-roll, between Dan Rhind and his son. He listened at the uneven squall near and distant, it coursing and beating over the land and water. Dan Rhind's breath steadied, long and even pulls and releases, and Verdery listened to him sleep.

Sometime in the immeasurable night the beach had taken all the rain it would hold and the runoff wicked up through the tent floor. In the pitch dark he listened to them sleep deeply and he lay in pools listening to the squall and their breathing, and smelling Rhind. He worried if he had pulled the boats high enough, but he hesitated to check on them. Sometime later Rhind wakened all at once and went out, and when he did not return Verdery went out after him. Rhind passed him without seeing or slowing and fell again into the tent, bringing fresh cold rainwater and fresh gobs of sand, and after checking the boats Verdery followed him inside, cold wetted, listening to them grunt and snore baying on either side of him, and too smelling Rhind, and now he reeked of vomit and shit.

He lay in cold pools waiting for the light. He guessed the time and time passing. He fell asleep at first light, when the rain quit. He dreamed a dream the kind he knew. All a jumble. A fondness for a woman, a hill and a smooth lake. Flat lonesome land, and a cold, dim theatre. Everywhere the lighting units hung random, untended. He knew he had lost a day's work, then suddenly, seamlessly, another. He left himself alone fixed upon an empty stage, and the figure leaving and the figure remaining knew there was still much work undone, and the time for the work lost and the distance for traveling beyond reckoning.

He wakened alone, in the same position as when he lay down, and the dreams endured heavy. He ruminated and he sorted them, and he wondered if he should try to keep them as the day began and passed.

The sun peeked half through the low, fast clouds, and overnight the river had risen upon the beach and gained speed, its body darkened of umber. Rhind sat hunched in the boat on the sand and ate purposefully something out of a can, his hair and back wet from his bath. Dan Rhind stood away, shirtless, smoking, intermittently searching across the water, reading the rivermap.

"Good breakfast for you?" said Verdery.

"Good enough," said Rhind, husky voiced.

"You got in a solid twelve hours."

"Sure."

"So you must feel fine right about now."

"Sure. I feel the fuck great."

Dan Rhind finished his smoke and he joined them with the map open, speaking to Verdery, speaking out over the river channel. "We ought to be about one sixteen. We did a couple miles past the swingbridge, and it's Saturday morning. Hell, thirty-nine miles to Blue Springs, and it's Saturday morning."

"We did good yesterday."

"Seems like it."

"You want to go in the big boat today? I can take mine."

"No, hell, I'm alright. I think I slept some."

"You slept a little."

"Rain like that'll make you sleep."

"We got time for coffee?"

"I could drink a pot of it."

Verdery made coffee on the gas stove and they emptied the boats of their goods and they dumped the stormwater.

"Can you clean this now," said Verdery.

"Yes, I can fucking clean it," said Rhind, and he rinsed the vomit from the underside of the Ouachita's bowseat and gunnels. They emptied and rinsed both boats and struck the camp and repacked the gear, then they lay their wet clothes over all the gear for the sun to dry. Verdery and Dan Rhind drank hot coffee, and Rhind sat hunched in the long blue canoe and waited.

CHAPTER NINETEEN

They cut the channel steady performing to a gathering of yappy crows high atop a sycamore, all travelmates to an unhurried great blue heron measuring distance and time aloft. They made places called Green Log Point and Red Bluff Landing, and Poke Patch Bar, and they saw nothing of people and nothing manmade, save their own vessels and themselves. They made Seven Day Baptist Point then the Brier Creek oxbow, and they pulled up to the beach at Friday's Dream Point on the South Carolina side. Verdery lighted his stove and he warmed a stew for their lunch. They ate the stew with crackers, accustomed, agreeable to the sameness, and Verdery and Dan Rhind drank beer. The sun came full clear and with the stew warmed them and they sat upon the beach watching the steam rise from the umber channel, the steam grayed, wiry, alike the rebel hair of an old insurgent head, as thin as visiting spirits.

Verdery lay back with an arm across his eyes. From upriver there came the faint sawing of a distant outboard. It worked steady to make good time in the fast current and Verdery let the motor's calling put him into a shallow sleep.

"I believe this rain is done," said Rhind, still dry and rough voiced, to his father.

"I hope the hell so," said Dan Rhind, looking to upriver to where someone with a machine plied upon a swollen brown river.

"I imagine it is."

"Well good, because my ass is weary of being wet."

The machine and the effort of it neared, its pitch swapping as it made the bend and worked the flow, steady, searching, purposeful, as manmade noises profess themselves to be. The boy eased the throttle and turned for them, and Dan Rhind stood alongside his son and he put on a shirt. When the boy quit the throttle, Dan Rhind spoke first, and Verdery wakened and sat upright when he heard Jesup's voice answer.

"How about it," said Dan Rhind again, but there was already only worry speaking it, because he saw now all three who had come in the johnboat. The grandson sat in the rear with one hand to the outboard throttle and the other holding fast to a shotgun across his lap, and in the middle just in front of him, her hair wind-worked all about her like fruit of a smoke tree, sat Alice Mays. As soon as he could Jesup scrambled out of the johnboat, stumbling off the gunnel, boot heavy, slogging through the shallow water. "Now y'all wait just a minute," he said, for the second time.

"Alright, Mr. Jesup," said Dan Rhind, taking all of them in again, and finishing at the old man, then the boy and the gun. He recognized it as a variety of shotgun, but different from the one the woman had held on them the day before.

His mouthed worked soundless, despite all his rehearsal, despite the convincing and the intent he had hauled for the entire half-day, since sunup. The clouded gray eyes, they now completely hopeless, searched the men he had given the fish and bread. "We see how it is, now," he managed, his voice pitched, and sharper now than two nights ago, cutting with worry and tragic loss, "we see how it is."

"Alright, Mr. Jesup," and Dan Rhind nodded to the boy, watching his hands, now that they were both in his lap, and the boy only looked down at his own bare feet. "We already know that one there. We already settled with her, and with the law too."

"I ain't worried about that woman."

"Mr. Jesup, is that boy checked out on that gun he's sitting with?"

"I shoulda knowed that one was a mistake as soon as I seen her, but she said she knew something, so we brung her. We got her gun from her, you ain't got to worry about that. I ain't worried about her. We come to see about Kerrenle."

"That's the one you need to see about," said Alice Mays, pointing, an arm leveled at Rhind. "Right there," she said, then turned reaching for the shotgun.

"Jase," said Jesup, and the boy held the gun away from the woman.

"He's the one," she said, turning to them again. She wore a tasseled wedding fichu wrapping her shoulders, and when she raised an arm it hung as if she were winged. "It's what I was telling you all this way. That one is the trouble. Now if you ready to give me my rifle back, I can show you how he'll talk. He'll talk awful, but he'll say it like I said he would."

Verdery stood from the beach and he went to Rhind and his father and stood alongside them, purposefully close, already thinking, *this is a show.* Already thinking, *this is a piece of goddamed theatre. Look at these goddamed countrified people, and their goddamed show.* He said thinking *countrified* the way his mother used it to describe Southern people who only knew and believed of this life what they had eyeballed and been told as truth, what they had gathered within hearing and eyeshot as verifiable, for all the length of their living.

"Woman," said Jesup, his voice cutting higher than hers, "nobody was talking to you." He cracked a laugh of continuing disbelief, wagging his head with his hands to his hips, making other noises of disbelief. "I see the man standing right here in front of me. Now let me talk to him."

"I'm just telling you," and she moved to stand and the boy put a hand on her shoulder, to the fichu, as if he knew how by now without instruction from his grandfather, and she sat again.

It was the fourth time the boy had touched the woman. Taking a hand he helped her into the boat and helped her to sit and she was soft as he imagined when he saw her standing on the small, worn dock, with her hair loose as riversmoke, and the shotgun cradled, likely warm in her arms. Inhaling the cedar and plain soap of her clothes and skin for those morning rivermiles he laid his hand upon her next near White Woman's Landing, to calm her as she told vibrant stories of the future and the past. The third time was when they made the last bend and she saw the canoeists upon the beach.

"Mr. Rine, weren't it?"

"That's right, Mr. Jesup," said Dan Rhind, thinking he did not know if it was the old man's first or last name, thinking too it mattered least of all things.

"Well, alright then," said Jesup, groping the beach, then the white willows that began the treeline. "Well alright then. Did she run up into them woods when she heard us coming? She's smart that way."

"Did who do what? Did who run," said Dan Rhind, looking to where Jesup looked, then again at the boy.

"Oh lord, oh lord god," he aspirated, exhaling all at once hopeless again, with a gaunt hand to the back of his neck, wagging his head, searching now downward to his scuffed untied boots, and to the sand and the water that held them.

"He's talking about his grandaughter," said Rhind, speaking to his father, then the old man, then to the rest of them, "aren't you, Mr. Jesup. You're talking about the girl."

"Oh lord. She said she seen you with her when you come up to her place yesterday. That's how I knowed it was y'all. She said it all just like it was, three of you, both boats and all. That's how I knowed it was you all. She said your boy here had her in the boat with him."

"Had who," said Dan Rhind, then knowing his son was right about the girl. "Are you talking about your granddaughter. Is that who you come looking for?"

"Oh lord, I do love that child. I do love that child, I don't know why she wants to do no such a thing to me."

"Is your granddaughter gone?"

"She wouldn't leave," said Verdery.

"All this way she's been saying how if we found you, then we find my girl. I don't know that woman from Adam, but they weren't no one said they could help us until we found that one there. Like she was waiting for us. But y'all ain't got to worry none, we done took the shotgun from her so nobody couldn't get killed."

"Did you empty it."

"Empty what."

"The shells. Did you empty them," said Dan Rhind, and Jesup only looked to his grandson in the johnboat, and put his hands to his face rubbing at his eyes, wagging his old head. "Did she go missing," said Dan Rhind, fixed still upon the boy, counting the possible shells the chamber might have held, getting to a number, while the boy began to silently cry into his own palms, a sorry mimic of his grandfather.

"Oh lord, I know as good as the next one how a woman makes you do what you don't want to. What you ain't thought about doing. And I know them young ones is the worst at turning a man inside out. But all you got to do is tell me, when I go up in them woods, if I'm bound to find her up in there."

"Look at those boats," said Rhind, again speaking to all of them. "Do you see any room for four people?"

"Ask that one again," shouted Alice Mays, raising an arm and the fichu half to Rhind before he finished. "Let me ask that one again. He knows he can't tell nothing but the truth when he's talking to me. *I'd* a been in that boat if it was up to him. They got no good in them, just one standing next to the other, all ghosts on my property. I can count too. One, two, three, that's what you all come to show me, wasn't it. One, two, three, come for me. But I don't believe it. I don't believe it."

They let her speak—Verdery thinking as he heard it: *she said it like the other woman said it*, but he did not recall when and where he had heard it the first time, until revisiting it again that night—the boy in the johnboat's rear silently weeping, his hands to his eyes as if to obviate the shame of it in front of men, and not hearing all she said for the fragrances rising off her clothes and skin— Jesup, his head wagging slowly, neckbent, as if he were reading the very grit of the barsand, and Verdery saying again, his lips probably moving indiscernibly at the words, *this is a piece of goddamed sorry theatre. This is a goddamed stage production*, and he checking the sun, the angle of the light, as an instinct, his training and craft for making make-believe.

"Woman," Jesup said, weakly aloud, then he started, boot heavy in the beach sand for the white willows.

"Mr. Jesup," said Dan Rhind, then, "stay right here," watching Jesup go, looking a last time at the johnboat. "Watch that crying boy with the gun in his lap, and don't worry about what that woman is going to say. You hear me?"

"Yes, sure," said Rhind to his father.

"That's right, you don't worry about the words, you watch that crying boy. When I come back, I'm walking straight for that little boat, and I'm sitting down in the back, like we're leaving. I'm coming right back, with the old man."

"Sure," said Rhind, and Dan Rhind went where Jesup had, upward across the sand, to the white willows that began the crowded treeline.

Alice Mays turned and spoke, nodding to the boy while she spoke, then she stood and he did not try to reseat her, and she stood from the johnboat, holding to the shoulder wrap, and to her pleated cotton skirt—the same skirt or one much like the one from the day before—holding it out of the water to her thighs, and barefooted, wading, she went to Rhind and Verdery upon the beach.

When she came near Verdery saw for the first time that her eyes were green, the emerald of the river with the sun out. She spoke to them, more to Rhind, as if telling secrets, so that only they could hear it.

"Why do you want to be coming down this river, causing so much trouble to everybody and their brother? You all think you going to find something by coming down here. Channel Two, what do you think you going to find? Teacher, what you think you going to find, coming down here on this river, disturbing the way things are. You think you the first people to come this way? To come up and down this water? That's what it is, isn't it. You all think you the first ones to come down this river. Think you going to discover something or another nobody else's found. Think you going to explore and find us, and everything's going to be alright. Well, we already here. Here before you. We already been found."

"All that's alright, miss," said Rhind, thinking too, *the boy can fish, but can he aim?*

"I wasn't going to shoot you yesterday. You don't know that one, do you? But I got another rifle, and I'll get another one besides that one too. And the next time or the next, you don't know what I might do."

"Ma'am," said Verdery, not even pleading now, but saying it only as a fact, the same as telling her eyes were no color other than green and her hair wild as a sleeping child's. "We don't mean you harm. We never did."

"That's alright teacher. Nobody means to hurt nobody, do they? Which one of you was talking to that old man's granddaughter? See what I'm saying? I knew when I saw the two of you, that I was going to have to shoot you for a reason. You see, how it is up in my house, *He* talks to me. You see, *He* tells me these things. Then, I got to go out in the world and see about all these things I know the truth of. All these things I learned from *Him*. He tells me where I can get me a rifle too. No worry about that. And you know what, *He* ain't your Daddy, that third man, like you want me to believe. He never was."

"Which one is him," said Rhind nodding to the johnboat, nodding to the boy who watched them, her, upon the beach, who had scarcely batted his pink, brimming eyes since she had raised her skirt to her panties and stood into the water. "Is that him?"

"That who?"

Rhind nodded again.

"Him? Lord no. Are you a fool? That's that old man's grandboy, only not either. I remember when that youngun was brought back with his sister, his mama holding one on either hip. And that old man never had the sense to understand who that boy's real daddy is. He thinks just because it was his daughter, it made him his grandboy too. He never had the sense to look up in that Big House and see who the genuine father was. Like everything else around that land, around that entire county. Covington had something to do with all of it. When I come here I knew him, like everybody else knew him. That's how I remember him, like everybody else. Coming out the water, going in the water."

"Does Covington get you the guns?"

She looked at him as if he were the most absurd thing to see on Friday's Dream Point beach that day, her eyes widening and emerald wet as whirlpools.

"No, Channel Two. No. A dead man can't. Don't you know that was his house you stayed in the night before last? No, there's none of them Covingtons worth mentioning, least be the sorry boys he left behind. And this youngun here. And his sister. No, Covington ain't *Him*, Covington's dead."

"Who is *Him*?"

She looked up and down Rhind, as if he were a fresh mirage—surveying through his blood and bones and reading the arrangement, the order foreign—as if the question were never asked, and the asking bizarre too, and the curiosity as unimportant, as misplaced, as tedious as a housecat's ghost.

"That don't matter, Channel Two. What does matter was that one of you was talking to that girl, weren't you. I'm right about that one, am I not."

"Does it matter you lied to that old man about us having that girl?"

"Ooh, listen at you, Channel Two. If he don't know where she is, you think it matters where she's not? Besides, how do I know you all didn't put her off in the woods somewhere before you come on my place causing trouble. I know you stayed with the old man on that property. And everybody's afflicted after that."

"You know better than that. We don't have that girl. If your voices up in your little house and your head tell you the truth, you damn well know better than that."

"Don't you be cussing at me. Don't you do it. And I'll tell you another thing too, they're not voices. I didn't say they were voices. I'm no lunatic. I said it was *Him* that told the truth to me."

"But *He* is not a man."

"No sir. I said that, too."

"And you are not a lunatic."

"Don't try me, Channel Two."

In the johnboat the boy wiped his eyes with the back and heels of his hands, and he watched her with the grown men, and the grown men watched him the same. Alice Mays wafted of the cedar and the plain soap, and with her eyes as near as stolen jade and her hair disarranged about her head, Verdery thought again, *look at these people acting in this goddam stage production, and look at me standing here in the middle of this shit.*

"You see all this, Teacher? You see what all this has come to? You were tired, weren't you, Teacher. You were tired of all of it, from Augusta on up to the high north places you come from. But you see now what all this comes to. You're not the first man to come up and down this river—you never was. But you going to try and come down here and get some relief, because you tired of that north world, up there. But you see, we all tired, too. We're all worn down, down here. You're not the first man to explore this water, you surely are not. But you going to try to leave your mark. You, like all the rest of them that can't stay in one place, you going to leave your mark, then you going to move on away from here, and just leave behind what ruination you brought to us, before you go on to your next."

"Your voices tell you that too?"

"See, you trying me now, Channel Two."

"No, I'm not trying you. What you need to do is go on and sit your crazy ass down on the beach until they get back out here."

"I told you about that cussing. You talk to your pretty wife like that, don't you, Channel Two. Is that what you teaching your baby when you talk to your pretty wife like that?"

Rhind drew his hand up to cover his mouth, and he exhaled a long steady breath, and he put his hand again to his hip.

"Where's your drink today, Channel Two. I know you're not going it alone, are you. You need to get that drink going, just like home. Sure, that was the other thing I saw, and I've seen it in a bunch of you."

"I'm going to tell you one more time woman, go sit down."

"Will," said Verdery, "how does she know?"

"She don't know shit."

"No, listen. How does she know about what she just said?"

"She said you lived up north. You told her that yourself, yesterday."

"No, not just that. The rest of it too."

"That you're tired? That you're here? What. Hell, I'm tired, and I'm here too. Goddamit, Thom."

"It's the same thing I told Caron Lee."

"His granddaughter?"

"Yes, we talked."

"Yes, I know, I was there too. We all talked."

"No Will, listen. It was late. She came out late. We talked."

"When you didn't come in the house."

"Yes."

"You see what I was saying?" started Alice Mays, smiling hard and painful, her eyes brightening, painful too, consumed with disaster. "You see? I knew it was you. That's what I was told. I knew it."

"Goddamit Thom, you're not going to tell me something about you and that little girl, now, are you?"

"No, Will. Nothing like that."

"Like what, then. Please don't give this woman here something else."

"I stayed out, that's all. And she came out late, and we talked for a little while. That's all—we talked."

"Is that what you calling it," said Alice Mays, "talking?"

"She wouldn't know this," said Verdery nodding to her, "she wouldn't know what she knows, if she didn't talk to the girl herself."

"Teacher, why couldn't either of these people in this boat tell me the same thing?"

"Because they wouldn't know. Because Caron Lee would not have told them so."

"Oh, I see it. So you saying it was between you and her, and nobody else. Oh, she and you."

"And you," said Verdery.

"He's saying *she* told you," said Rhind, his voice rising. "He's saying you know where the girl is, and you know she's not with us. He's saying there is no *Him* that talks to you, and he's saying you need to go back where you came from, and show that old man where his granddaughter is."

"No, see now. See here, Channel Two, I'm not done with you yet. I got one more thing to tell you."

"This goddam foolishness is finished," said Rhind, his pitch rising again and breaking as he spoke, and now carrying full to the boy in the johnboat.

"You can treat that pretty wife of yours bad—as bad as you want, because you going to anyways. It hurts inside, don't it. But you need to be good to your daddy."

Rhind turned from her and started across the beach for the small boat, and she went with him.

"You hear me now Channel Two—you hear me now. He ain't going to make it off this river."

Rhind stopped heavy in the sand and he turned to her with his fists balled now, hanging down either side of him, and she did not stop until she was close to him.

"What," said Rhind, it coming out a burst, a short ragged breath.

"That's right. You be good to him while you can. Only a fool believes something or another will last forever. Only, it can't last forever. It's always got to end."

"Woman," said Rhind, raising and leveling a forefinger to her.

"You hear me, Channel Two. You hear me. People don't even get a chance to know, but I'm telling you. I'm telling you what people can't never know. Your daddy ain't going to make it to Blue Springs. He ain't going to make it off this river."

Where the white willows gave to pine, near where a single alligator rutted the sand, Dan Rhind found the old man, squatting, with the heels of his palms digging his eyes. He squatted too with his bare feet heavy into the thin layer of switches and cones and straw.

"Oh lord, oh lord, they done come and got her."

"Who came," said Dan Rhind, touching Jesup at the elbow, and knowing then that Jesup's only weapon rested in the boy's lap, in the johnboat where they left him.

"Oh lord, when y'all put her up in these woods, they come and took her away."

"Mr. Jesup, you know better than that. You know we don't have your granddaughter with us. You know that. You know we never did, despite what that woman says. You know that, don't you, Mr. Jesup?"

"Mr. Rine, what you saying to me."

"You know nobody came and took her away. Not any alligators either. You know all that didn't happen, because that girl of yours was never with us."

"Don't be telling me that."

"Mr. Jesup. It ain't loaded, is it?"

"Oh lord, she's pretty like her mama, she is. And her mama's pretty like Junie too. I see all them when I look at that child. Seems like it was made that way, so you can't never forget—it won't let you forget. Sometimes I don't know she ain't Junie. Sometimes they just don't seem to be no difference between them. And all I do is try to forget seeing it in no such a way. But it won't let me. It won't never let me. Oh lord, if I could see that pretty child just once more. Oh lord, I hope I ain't run that girl off with my ways. It's just sometimes a man can't forget, it won't let a man forget."

"Sometimes it's not like you think it is. Sometimes younguns do things just because they're younguns, and most often it's not nearly as bad as it seems."

"I knowed that woman was trouble when I seen her standing on that dock with that gun. I always knew she was trouble, and here I done come all this way just to worry somebody else with her. No, Mr. Rine, I done threw them shells in the river, way back when we found her. I told her that was the only way she was going to see y'all again. I knowed she was trouble."

"Well, we know her too. We had a time with her yesterday, and we want to be finished with all that, and go on our way. That's all we want, is to go on our way and to leave some of this worry behind us."

"Lord, I done come all this way, and I couldn't think about nothing else all the way down here. All I saw was my girl's face, like she done become a dream to me. I come all this way, and here I find it all comes to nothing."

"Mr. Jesup, that girl's alright. I know she is. Both of them children are smart, and they both have good sense. I could see that first thing when we met them. That girl's alright. What you need to do is go on back up to your place and talk to the county sheriff. That's Burke County, isn't it. They can help you if you need it. But you know something, I'm betting you won't need a thing. I'm betting you will find that granddaughter of yours as soon as you get back. It's like I said, sometimes what younguns do isn't nearly as bad as it seems."

"Lord, Mr. Rine, we done come all this way for nothing but causing worry. Foolishness. That woman's mouth was working all the way. She claims to know things. Said somebody told her we could find my child down here with y'all. After a little while that was the only thing I could see the possibility of— and that woman causing worry amongst us, talking on and on, like she knows something or another."

"I imagine she knows what she knows, like anybody else. But you see, your granddaughter isn't here. She never was."

"She was talking and talking."

"That's right, Mr. Jesup. Don't you see that's where you might need to go back to. If your girl was missing, and that woman knew so much about it all, then don't you see it?"

"It ain't the Lord she talks to."

"Mr. Jesup, let's go on back to the boats."

"I said, who is it you talking to all the time. I said, is it the Lord?"

"Mr. Jesup, let's stand up from here and go on back to the boats and see who it is holding that shotgun you brought with you."

"She said it weren't the Lord. I said who is it then you talking to all the time? She said nevermind about all that. She said, what we got to do is find the Lord, only then can we find what goes with the Lord. Did you ever hear anybody talking so crazy as all that?"

Dan Rhind knelt into the pinestraw and the thatch, to ease the pain in his legs. He put his hand again to the old man's elbow, to draw his eyes again to him. "What I'm going to do when we get to Blue Springs, is, I'm going to come back up and check on you, at your place. We'll be in Blue Springs tomorrow at noon. After that, I'll come back up by your place and check on you, and your granddaughter."

"I know you not coming all that way back up the river."

"No sir, I've got a ride coming to get me, and we're driving back, and on the way we'll come by and check on you, on our way home."

Jesup looked to Dan Rhind as if seeing him for the first time that day, and in his sudden regard he might have beheld an entity unlike a somatic man. He dug at his eyes with the heels of his palms and looked again, and the old clouded grayed eyes, hueless as a cold day's end, had reddened, and his mouth worked, soundlessly at first. "That woman, I said for her to shut that talking, that telling, but she kept on and on. I told her she didn't know everything about people. I told her she couldn't tell if somebody or another was going to live to see the morning. I said she just as well be talking about me, but she said she weren't talking about me, though."

"Mr. Jesup, that girl is going to be alright. What you got to do is get back to where you came from. That's where she will be."

"Everybody's got an idea of someplace for me to go, seems like."

"I'm just trying to tell you what I think is best."

"You know, she weren't talking about Kerrenle."

"She wasn't?"

"No sir." Jesup looked to him expecting him to know too. "She was talking about you, Mr. Rine."

"Me."

"I told her to shut that mouth, but she kept on and on."

"About me."

"Yes sir."

Dan Rhind stood against the pain in his legs. Steps away he leaned straight armed against the near sea pine, this tree garlanded by wisteria, the vine full conjoined to its host body and limbs, climbing to the highest point. He bowed his head to the straw-covered earth, palming the vine, closing his eyes, speaking to himself, softly, as an exhalation, the way a weary, unwashed, godless man prays not knowing the prayer. "Damn, these people. Goddam these people."

He straightened and he looked deep into the pinewoods and the sugar-berrys crowding too, and there was nothing but the understory and the distance where sight failed. He went again to Jesup where Jesup remained squatting, lost and purposeless, patient in hopelessness, and he spoke down to him. "Mr. Jesup, I need to go back to the boat to see about that shotgun you brought with you. I'd appreciate it if you were to come with me out there, but I need to go on and see about that."

Jesup looking up began to weep. He put his hands to his eyes, and he shook with weeping. "Lord, lord, help us. I don't want nobody to die. Lord, help us."

Dan Rhind knelt again into discomfort, bare knees into the straw cover, and he put a hand again to Jesup's elbow, and he spoke rough, gently suffusing his anger for the insane woman and the stupid squatting old man. "You need to come on here, with me. It don't matter what somebody says. It don't matter what some fortune teller says, for a thousand years, it don't matter. All that matters is what we do. You need to come on here, and let's go on back to the boat. All that matters is what we do. Right now."

He rough gently coaxed Jesup to stand, and Jesup allowed him then spoke soundless and Dan Rhind leaned closer, and Jesup spoke again.

"I want to look where it is you looked."

"Alright," said Dan Rhind, glancing the pinewoods, then toward the beach, then again to the woods. "Sure, then we're going back."

"Shore. Yes, sir."

He walked Jesup past the canopy of the wisteria into the sugarberry. The sun shone warm upon them in patches and they reached a clearing where the sand turned whiter. The trails of a single alligator remained carved in the damp sand and the straw, circular and vanishing into the undergrowth. Jesup groped the reaches where sight failed. In the clearing Dan Rhind heard the rising of his son's voice and he turned listening.

"Alright then," said Jesup.

"You see," said Dan Rhind, his head turned a quarter for his son's voice. "Alright then."

When he hit her, it was all in a flick of muscle, a clap of a rage, and his feet stayed the same in the sand. He snapped his right arm, fisted, all in one sudden bolt, stopping himself short in order not to kill her, and she folded, then crumpled, and lay with her eyes closed, her face fallen of expression and nearly peaceful, with the tangled hair all about her face and shoulders and the fichu covering her like a rustic pall. He let his arms go loose by his side and he went to his knees in the sand, and he watched her to see that she slept and was not dead. He looked to Verdery—to Verdery, seeming to come to him, speaking, but not hearing the sound of his words, and he did not even see the boy, even after the boy was over him. The boy ran the beach, his wide, flat barefeet digging the sand, and he used the shotgun like a tree limb, as if he had never fired one. He leapt upon Rhind from behind with the barrel at Rhind's throat, and the boy wept over the grown man he intended to strangle. Rhind staggered standing and the boy hauled himself up hanging all his weight with the shotgun choking Rhind, and he meant to choke him to death. He mouthed pitiably crying a mash of words drawling and he spit on himself and on the visitor he meant to kill. Rhind lost his good air with the cold of the gunmetal crushing his windpipe, and he tasted the tears and the boy's spit, and he stumbled kneeling again when Verdery seemed to come for the second time.

Verdery came from the Ouachita, actually speaking aloud, sternly, as if instructing, foretelling, *this is enough of this, goddam these countrified people, this is all there is going to be of this shit*. He swung the oar level like a baseball bat, how he learned as a kid ballplayer. He swung careful with the blade flat against the air, careful not to cut into the boy and so landing it made the ribs. He swung one stroke, and the boy heard it thump first then felt it go into his lungs, and he released wailing suffering for air, for the sudden fire in his back and chest and heart. Verdery took away the shotgun then slung the oar back toward the Ouachita, and he stood above the three of them, the boy curling alongside the still woman, and Rhind in the sand too, palms and knees, coughing and spitting vomit, wrenching for air. Verdery had never held a shotgun in his life but he held to this one by the barrel and stock over the three of them.

"Goddamit, this is the finish of this. Do you hear me, this is the finish of this shit. Goddam you countrified people, goddam you all." He spoke raging now to an unconscious woman and a boy deaf burning with pain, and the rage birthed a fury, and he spoke it then to Rhind. "Get up, Will. Get up and help me put these goddam countrys into that goddam boat. Get up Will, goddamit, get up."

Out of the woods Dan Rhind saw first that Verdery possessed the shotgun, and he thought, *he doesn't hold it right*, and when he asked aloud, *hell, what has happened here*, it was only half a question, he already knowing half of it. "What has happened here. Jesus, what has happened here."

"Goddamit," breathed Verdery. "We're going to put these countrys in that goddam boat, and they're going back to where they came from. Goddam these countrified people."

"Easy son," said Dan Rhind, watching the boy roll and cough, and curl up to his palms and knees in the sand, watching Jesup totter to him and kneel the same. "Easy, Thomas," and he put one hand on Verdery's shoulder and he gripped the other hand over shotgun barrel, coaxing Verdery to lower it straight down to the sand. Dan Rhind surveyed the mess of his choking son and the boy and the half-sleeping woman waking, groaning and he kept the barrel gripped.

"Don't do that," said Verdery. "I want these people in that goddam boat, now."

"Sure son, we'll do it. Easy though, we'll do it."

The boy crawled through the sand toward the johnboat, and his grandfather released him calling after him, his entreaty a look of dumbstruck defeat and aimlessness. In the johnboat the boy sat to the hull at the bow, half-lying on the gunnel, holding himself, his false ribs.

"Danny," said Dan Rhind.

"Goddam me. I'm alright."

"You sure."

"What did I say. Yes."

Dan Rhind knelt and brushed the matted hair from the woman's face. He helped her to kneel then stand when she was ready, all the while brushing away loose bar sand, careful of her ruined eye and all that side of her face swelling in misshape. He spoke softly, just between them, and straightening her fichu, stained of sediment and backwater, he walked her to the johnboat.

She walked with her skirt in the water and he sat her in the same seat where she arrived, wetter and filthy, fowardbent—knotty, gobbed hair covering her face again. Dan Rhind attended the old man next, coaxing him, and when they waded Jesup wept newly. He waited patiently kneedeep and when Jesup was ready he sat him at the stern, and he freed the johnboat of the beach pushing hard turning it upstream, bringing Jesup at the motor close to him. He spoke to him nodding once, then again, and Jesup nodded too, digging his eyes with the back of his hands. Dan Rhind spoke once more and he let go the gunnel, pushing off.

Rhind stood now behind his father, speaking hoarse and ragged, a simple declaration, and nothing more, "Woman, if I see you again, I will kill your crazy ass."

The johnboat drifted, the river already taking them backward.

Said Alice Mays, with her head down and turned slightly to where she spoke, with her hair and her face the same thing, the sound of her speaking affected by the pain and numbness. "That's alright. Come on, me and you. We all got to die sometime."

Jesup pulled the motor's cord, it fired, and he set the bow to upriver.

The johnboat made the bend at Brier Creek and when it was gone from sight the motor sawed on, its pitch swapping in the struggle working hard against flow, and they listened for it until its weary calling was gone too.

"Let me see that thing," and Dan Rhind took the shotgun from Verdery purposely not checking for shells, and by the barrel slung it end for end, same as the Screven County deputy had the last one. "Pretty soon here this river'll be full as hell of scrap metal."

"Goddam these countrified people," said Verdery, "goddam them."

CHAPTER TWENTY

The afternoon warmed and they made Thompson's Long Round and Mosquito Camp Point, then Poor Robin Upper Cut Point and Poor Robin Landing. Just before rivermile eighty-six they pulled up at the landing to ease their backs and legs, and they stood apart and urinated.

A pickup truck towing a small v-hull drove in and an ageless dark black man came from the truck. He looked out over the river checking its color and he looked at the sky.

"Hey Cap'n," he said to the oldest of the three white men, "how you making it today."

"We alright. We trying to keep out of trouble."

"I know what you mean. I know what you mean. Where you headed today?"

"Blue Springs. We looking to get to Blue Springs, by tomorrow."

"Well, alright then. You just about there."

"Yessir. Good then."

"Where you coming from?"

"Augusta."

"Shore enough. Then you done come a goodlong ways."

"Yessir."

"Done any good fishing?"

"No sir. We ain't got the chance. My boys fish. I don't mess around with that too much. Maybe when we pull up tonight, we might throw a line in the water."

"Yes sir, I know what you mean. I know what you mean. We fitting to try some, me and the gal." The black man nodded to the pickup where his common-law wife waited patiently smiling, but they could not see her for the glass.

"Well, let us get on out of your way here. You need another hand?"

"Oh, no sir. They ain't nothing to it. Nothing atall. I got the gal. We going to stand here a minute and think about it."

"Well, alright. Y'all be careful. It got fast out there. It'll take you away from home if you let it."

"Yes sir, I know what you mean. We'll do it. I believe all this mess and rain is done for awhile. Blue Spring is down just a little bit. It ain't too much from here, atall."

"Yes, sir. Alright then."

They let the fisherman and his constant smiling wife have the ramp, and they went again upon the fast brown river.

They made Poor Robin Lower Cut Point and Bull Pen Point, then Cornhouse Reach where the river straightened for a long stretch, then Little Cornhouse Reach where it cut through the Blanket Point oxbow. At rivermile eighty just before Martin's Landing, where the channel turned back to due east, on the Georgia side they found a short beach with a high ground clearing and they made camp.

They tied off the boats by pulling their painters to the nearest trees where the woods began, and Verdery propped a tree branch under each line to make a clothesline and they hung everything wet for drying. The day remained warm and clear with a mild breeze blowing from the south and there were neither squalls nor warnings of storms. The warming sun declined aligned with the river's channel and all together they made camp and no one spoke of the old man or boy, or the insane woman who claimed to know the future.

Dan Rhind smoked sitting cross-legged on the beach with his worn hat in his lap. With the weight of the day remaining with him he watched his son and his second son fish, they standing knee deep in the river, and he thought more of the gentleness of his wife whom he had seen one night in three months, and he thought less of the hatefulness passed between them. The golding sun warmed him, and all he surveyed of the brown Savannah River was fast but smooth, and the tobacco tasted good, as good as he had ever known it in his mouth and lungs, despite his regret.

Verdery waded along the sandbar following his lure as the flow took it and he fished into an eddy that made a small slough, and he looked back to the west, the setting sun, as he worked his line. It was still heavy with him, the boy and what he did to injure the boy. *They should be in school, and I should be their teacher, not a man who hurts them. Where have I gone . . .*

This sun becomes crimson copper, then dims fading to lavender, as it slips behind the treeline into the horizon dust. This sun sets across western Illinois, declining beyond the black earth of the endless coming cornfields, and there is high ground to find to watch the last of the day's dying light. This sun in late May falls past the Cumberland Range and he drives a great distance to hold his father's hand while he dies. This same sun of the Berkshires descends into a flawless desiccate air, where already in early August the nights cool crisp and the maples turn vermilion, green of summer going, loneliness coming. And despite his regret, against this kneeling plum sun, Verdery fished and took two fish and he thought, *we have come a long way in a short time. We have come far. Very far. Where have I . . . I should be their teacher, not . . .*

Rhind swapped his lure and soon he took a fish. He stood knee deep still ragged from the night before and his windpipe sore and poor sleep coming that night. On his drinking nights he stayed in the basement, and in the mornings his girl wakened him by lying with him with her head close to his, smelling his breath the same as dirt and raw wood and unwashed clothes. Pretending to sleep she asks, *why are you down here*, and he says, pretending to sleep the same, *I just had some work to do.*

What work daddy?

Sleep some, baby Annie. Sleep a little bit.

A month before with the heavy summer enduring into the doldrums, at the end of their porch, Emylia Gray said to him, *Thom is up north, and you still do it. It is still the same.*

I know it. I never said otherwise.

Once you said it different. You said it was he that caused it.
You know better than that.
How do you want it to be?
I don't know.
Forget about me Danny, do you love it more than your child?
I don't know how much I love it.
Then you love it.

Dan Rhind cleaned and pancooked in butter the bass, and they ate the bass with beans and crackers, and they drank beer as cold as the last of their ice—and there was nothing that was not good about it, save the persistence of memory.

They put out their bedrolls one at a time, and went again to sit upon the beach and watch the smooth impenetrable river—de Soto's watercourse, and Chufitachiqui's before him—the same enduring water, come as ever, dividing the same ancient land. The air turned to the lavender and a great blue heron flew to upriver, unhurried, silent, as measuring time and distance with each leveraging of its wings. Dan Rhind studied the rivermap for the next day, nodding, solemn, less than grinning at how far they had come and the price of it. It would be only two miles more, and he looked a last time, then he put it away into the small boat with his gear.

From beneath the stern seat he took the pistol, and he felt the good cool common shape of it in his hands. He went to the beach and holding it by the short barrel he slung it, overhand, into the deep of the river. He watched a moment as if there were more to see than the dense umber water that had taken it, saying, as saying it to someone who might have listened, *damn, there's one more for you.* He sat again in the soft sand and they drank a last beer in the lilac cast, and finally Rhind spoke, his voice rugged from wear, and the fresh beer, and Alice Mays's shotgun barrel.

"I wouldn't kill her."

"No," said his father.

"No. I wouldn't kill her."

"I know you wouldn't. Sometimes though, people speak their truth, despite themselves."

"That woman."

"You say what you know to say. What you believe, to say."

"She was right?"

"No. She wasn't right."

"She was wrong, then."

"That girl's going to be alright," said Verdery.

"I imagine," said Dan Rhind. "I'll go see about her and the old man tomorrow."

"Will you do that?" said Verdery.

"I will," said Dan Rhind.

"She'll be alright."

"I wouldn't kill her," said Rhind.

They sat upon the beach until the moon came bastard amber above the treeline, and until the mosquitoes came too, and they went into their shelter and lay upon their bedrolls. Soon Dan Rhind's breathing slowed and evened, and Verdery and Rhind lay with their eyes open to the dark and the mooncast listening to Dan Rhind sleep.

"Thom, I love Emmy and Annie."

"I know you do."

A faint wind blew from the South, and it moved the pines to whisper. Across the distance, a single heron called, once, then again, a last time into the settling darkness.

"Hey Will."

"Hey."

"There's one thing I can't figure."

"One."

"Who named the girl."

"Which girl."

"Jesup's girl. Granddaughter."

"The missing one."

"Yeah. Who named her."

"Hell, I guess her mother or father. Or maybe the old man."

"Sure. One of them—had to be. Hey, do you remember when you came to see me in Baltimore?"

"Baltimore."

"The poor theatre."

"You said they're all poor."

"The one above the jazz club, where we heard Gillespie."

"We drank V.O. And we danced. And Gillespie said it wasn't dance music. And you said it is if you dance to it. And he laughed at us and played some more. And when we came out of that club, it was morning."

"Do you remember the woman who was with us?"

"Which one?"

"The pretty, darkheaded woman. She was with the company, at the theatre, come from Boston. And she had been raised in Surrey, England."

"The club was called Ethel's Place."

"She danced to jazz and drank V.O. with us."

"The club was on the bottom floor. I don't know if I remember her."

"No?"

"Seems like I would."

"I think of her."

"Sure."

"I think of her. You believe that?"

With a clear blanched and shrunken moon above they slept deeply in the night. Verdery slept as he had not for four days, and he did not dream. He wakened once and listened to Dan Rhind's breathing, and he slept again, in the same position he had wakened.

The spattering of Heaven's endless confusion yawed about the polestar, and the moon burned borrowed cool light, all of their element suspended in the unreckonable void. The morning star rose in the east and the sky washed saturate, deepest blue just before dawn, and Dan Rhind wakened to the first light. He listened for the sound of the daybreak, but there was nothing aloud, save the distant blue heron and the breathing of his sons. He lay upon his back watching the light come, listening to Verdery waken, then go out of the tent to make coffee. His son wakened and spoke to him.

"Morning dad."

"Morning."

"How you feel."

"I'm alright, son."

"Come on out and get some coffee."

"You go on. I'll lay here awhile."

"Sure. We'll keep the pot warm."

"Good then. Sounds good, Danny."

Outside Rhind found Verdery tugging the Ouachita onto the high ground, where overnight the river had risen, setting both boats afloat. Verdery found them side by side nudging the beach with their painters taut and all their clothes and gear tossed from the clothesline. Full around them the depression had filled making a flood eddy, making their bar an island. The river ran faster than the evening before, its color yet again darker to umber.

"Jesus," said Rhind, thinking to say *morning*, helping Verdery with the Ouachita, then walking the circle of their small island.

"It rained upriver too," said Verdery.

"Yes it did."

Dan Rhind heard his son and Verdery speak, but he could not collect the words. Of the baritone voices he found the pitch of his son's familiar and a comfort. He put his palms to his chest and he listened, and soon he slept again in the position he had wakened.

He dreamed of his wife, she at sixteen when he first saw her in a small German burg outside the place called *Zum Deutschen Eck*, where he drank bock on weekends. In the dream Dan Rhind remembered the first time they spoke, when he told his last name, and she said, *ah, bu bist auch ein Deutscher*, and he said, *no ma'am, Tennessee*. He explained and she laughed as he was already in love with her. He dreamed of her smooth face full of courage and the first time he kissed her, standing near the stone ruins of a small lost schoolhouse near her home, and in the dream there came an inscrutable sadness at the distance of time and the irretrievability of time gone, and his wife's face turned to the rains of Vietnam. He flew amidst the grayed rains, scouting, and he came to a full green hillside, and in the Huey he parted the forest with his rudder wash. Upon the trail stood his son holding the hand of his sister, and they were children again, and with them looking up to the machine's wind stood his wife, thin, with a lean young beautiful face, her loose summer dress blowing, and from each visage came the inscrutable sadness of irretrievable timepast. He let the forest close above them, and alongside him sat a woman born of Vietnam he once claimed to love, because she was nearer than an ocean away. They flew fast and rising, and the earth below was all green with the beach and the baywater coming fast.

You can never love another more than yourself, Danny.

You are wrong.

Then how can you know how to love.

I don't know. But you are wrong.

She smiled and bowed her head to him and then she was gone, with him alone above the bluegreen bay, with all the air white full around him, and he no longer needed his machine to fly—and the dream took only a moment of his living.

Asleep in the warming morning, Dan Rhind turned on his side and upon the Georgia earth, offering a last gentle exhalation, he let go his life. He died—as the quiet, ceaseless river moved alongside him, as in the hidden eddy from where it called alone the great blue heron took a fish, the act seen only by the heron and the fish—as his wife turned in her halfsleep and remembered something that had not occurred to her for many years, then slept again and dreamed a dream she would not remember. He died as his son poured warm coffee.

For half an hour Rhind and Verdery sat upon the last of the high ground watching the morning come, then Rhind went to the tent for his father. He called for Verdery, and Verdery went into the tent and found Rhind kneeling.

"Thom, what's wrong," said Rhind, speaking to where his father lay with the bedclothes pulled full around him. He spoke it with his voice thin and soft and hoarse.

"I don't know, Will," said Verdery, looking to Rhind, then the bedclothes. "I don't know what's wrong."

"Thom, can you help us?"

"Sure, sure bud," and he knelt alongside Rhind. "What is it, Will."

"Oh, Thom. He won't listen to me. I mean, no. No, that's not what I mean to say. What I mean is. Oh, Thom. Oh please, can you help us."

Rhind put a hand on his father, to the bedclothes, and his father was still, and he did not turn and say any such thing as, *can't y'all let a damn man sleep?*

"Oh bud. Oh bud, oh Will."

The morning sun warmed the tent, and the clouded water rose near to them and their shelter, and because there was nothing else, Verdery spoke. "Will, this is what we have to do now."

He waited only for a moment longer, because he knew even as he spoke aloud he would do it alone. And he went out of the tent and tugged the boats high onto the last of the dry land, and he borrowed the bow painter from each boat, and with the tieline he wrapped Dan Rhind in his bedclothes, struggling tying clovehitches and pulling the rope through until the rope ran out, when he tied doubleknots.

"Will, I need you to help me do this, now," and he wiped under his eyes, and he knelt close to Rhind and wiped his, and looked close at him. "Will."

"We need to let him rest."

"I know Will, but you have to help me do this."

"He just needs his rest. Not everybody was as good to him as they could be. And I know it just tired him out. I know it just did."

"Will, you have to help me."

"Thom, we can go home now. We're tired now. We can go home."

"Yes bud. We're going home, in just a couple miles. But you have to help me."

"Everybody made him tired. She didn't have to talk to him that way. There's no need for all that. It just wore him down."

Verdery put his hands on Rhind's shoulders and looked close at him, and he knew again he would do it alone. "Bud, you want to go out?"

"No. No, Thom. I don't know . . ."

"Sure bud," said Verdery and he let him alone, and he took hold of the rope at Dan Rhind's feet and dragged him out of the tent into the sand.

Rhind went too then, watching his father in the wrapping, walking the trail carved into the yellow sand by the bundle of bedclothes. "Thom, easy, Thom, easy—don't hurt him."

At the small boat Verdery knelt then cradled the bundle an end at a time and lifted Dan Rhind into the vessel. He lay his head forward, to the keel, all of him beneath the center thwart, and he went again to the tent breaking camp. When he came again he found Rhind on a knee with a hand to the gunnel, wagging his head slowly, speaking softly aloud. He heard some of it and some of it he did not, and of the parts he heard he thought, *that is what you say, because it is the last thing.* As he worked, he told himself too, *I must not slow.*

He loaded the Ouachita alone, then he arranged the gear into the small boat, all around the bedclothes, finding the tipped cigars and the rivermap together beneath the stern seat at Dan Rhind's feet. He tucked them together into the forsaken outback hat—thinking too that he should have found the pistol, then remembering that it was gone into the river, with Alice Mays's shotguns—and he lay the hat upon the bedroll, upon the wrap where within Dan Rhind rested. He looked to the tent, then Rhind, then again to the tent, and he thought both ways for only a moment, and he went and struck the tent and loaded it into the Ouachita. He squatted alongside Rhind and looked close at him, and he held tight his arm to make him quit speaking. "Bud. Bud, it's time for us to go. We have to go now, we have to go two miles."

Rhind bowed his head and then he knew his father had died that morning, and that likely he would not warm and waken from it. "Goddam her, Thom. Goddam that woman."

"No, Will, it's not her."

"Goddam her," and he sat heavy into the sand and water and he wept full and heavy, and Verdery sat with him remembering in his own heart and he waited holding to the pain of his friend, because it was nearest, and the only thing. And he would take it from him if he could.

The river lifted the Ouachita off the beach and Verdery went to it and tugged it to the last of the dry land. He searched full round once and finished at the fast channel, thinking, *he and the smaller boat will have to go in front, and I will be alone again with the longboat,* and he went again to Rhind and he squatted again close to him.

"Bud, it's time for us to go."

"I know it, I know it. I saw what you did . . . thank you bud, thank you. I just don't know what to do about the rest of it. Thom, I just don't know what to do."

"Let's not worry about that right now. Let's just go on, and we'll know what to do when we get there."

"Where we going? Where can we go?"

"We're going to find Blue Springs. Remember how we talked about finding Blue Springs? It's just a mile or two away, and the water's fast, and we'll be there in just a minute, bud."

Verdery waited near his friend and soon, when Rhind was ready to try, they stood together. Verdery turned the Ouachita bow out into the eddy, and he put the small boat full into the water, and he tied its stern painter to the Ouachita's bow. He sat Rhind into the Ouachita's bow seat, and Rhind sat to the hull, then he lay down on his side over the bottom hull, the keel. Verdery freed them from the narrow beach and he sat into the stern seat and he did not ask Rhind to work with him. He ferried alone, rowing backward, keeping the painter taut against the flow, until he made the fast water, then he let the swollen brown river take them.

He let the small boat lead and he stayed in the channel following the fast water wide around bends, struggling against the speed to miss deadfalls and strainers, and he saw the sign for rivermile eighty. He made the bend at rivermile seventy-nine where the water went fast into Willow Oak Point and became an oxbow. He took the oxbow and as soon as he made the creek he knew he had gone the wrong way. The creek took them fast to Jacob Jump Point, halfway around the diversion, and there the water slowed. Now, Verdery could only row backward, towing the small boat to where the oxbow put back into the river, downriver at Wildcat Cut. He worked the blade deep into the cloudy backwater and they spun counterclockwise and he worked the opposite gunnel and again they spun. He took a single stroke at each gunnel and with each stroke the painter tightened, and the small boat's weight tugged and turned him directionless, defeating all his work.

He turned in his seat to stern and worked the blade fast and low, full gouging at the water's body, penetrating deep with each stroke, passing the fluid volume beneath them, crawling, sliding the conjoined vessels along. He took them close to the Carolina shore where he hoped to find an eddy to put them back into the channel, and there he saw the watergrass leaning with the flow, leaning back into the oxbow, combed against him. The storm rain had caused it, this he knew, but he struggled against the evidence, against the clear beating sun, against the death he had in tow. He fought until his back and arms and fists were weak and burning for lacking oxygen, then he cursed them, and he cursed the sun and the river's spill, and then he quit too and he let the flood take them, the smaller boat leading back into the oxbow.

They drifted, the vessels bound, turning slowly, gunnel to gunnel, then apart, rotation torpid aimless. Verdery lay the oar across his lap and he leaned with his elbows to his thighs, and he gathered the strength and the air to curse himself, and to not weep, and to quit thinking because now he knew beyond redemption, *he is not going to waken when we get to Blue Springs. He is gone now, the same as my father, the same as my mother, the same as James.*

He let them drift past the old shoreline overcome by freshet and on into the wood where now the flood spread. A patch of pine and sweetgum had become an island, and there Verdery stood from the Ouachita and tugged both vessels, gunnel to gunnel, close to the remaining dry land. The sun had passed into afternoon and he had been on the river for less than an hour.

What he reckoned a moccasin scuttled through the undergrowth and into the backwash, and he cursed its suddenness. It swam for a moment, surfaced, then curled beneath the brown water diving like a whip, and he did not see it again. He searched carefully all the dry land and the backwash then he pulled the vessels close, and he untied the painter that joined them. He rearranged the small boat's bow to the Ouachita's stern, and he retied the painter to the eyes there. For only a moment he made himself look to the shroud of bedclothes to see that they were still tied well, and he tucked the edges that had worked loose, and he tucked the hat. Wading around the small boat he stumbled tangling himself in drowned shrubs, and holding to the gunnel he tipped backward into the backwash. He let go to save the small boat and he went under the brown water, it clapping closed above him. He fought to stand, all at once breathless, less than cursing now, and he searched keenly all around for snakes and no snakes.

He tucked the bedclothes again dripping over them, and he found he had gouged his palm on a stump. It bled fast and he bled onto the shroud of the bedclothes, and when he saw he stained them, he quit.

On the dry land he stood, slumped, soaked, hands to his hips, and the one palm bleeding into his shorts. He searched the oxbow as far as he could see in either direction, and now he actually doubted he remembered the way he had come in. He looked too across to the short bluff and the treeline at Jacob Jump Point, but he did not know it was called such a thing, and he did not know how he would ever see the river side of it again.

A small gathering wind blew into the oxbow in the same direction as the flood's flow. It teased the water's surface restless and with the sun's glare the water shimmered countless patches foolsgold. The woods over the island were grown thick with hedges and the woods behind the new shoreline grew denser, heavy with sumac and willow. In the shallows peeked craggy tree stumps, vertical as a hundred sentinels scattered sown at half-attention and disregard for the careless drama come of the living and the dead.

Slumped and bleeding, with the backwater now lapping at his canvas shoes, Verdery closed his eyes to a sudden weariness, but he knew he was yet alone. He squatted and it came to him as sudden as a palpitation, a sickly cough, misplaced and uninvited as a trinket given as proof of emotional love. Then, he found her on her bed, the same bed in the same house where she had raised him. It possessed the collected dust of a place unvisited, untended as always when he came home at the end of each summer. The room was cold, though August, and she lay over the undisturbed sheets and the knitted spread. She might have been a carving, artifact too, with her arms at her side as if posed, her face misshapen with age, with yet residue of worry at the eyes and mouth. He went to her across the groaning floorboards, but standing above he did not reach out.

She called for him, taking him out of morning class, *Tommy, I want you to come see mama. Tommy, when you going to come see mama?*

Mother, I will come soon. But I have to finish my work here, now.

Tommy, they don't come anymore. I can't help it if none of them want to see me. Mama loves you Tommy. Mama loves you the same as mama loves James. James would come, but he can't come Tommy.

Mother, James is . . . all of us care about you. We are all your family, mother.

I don't know why they want to be so hateful to mama. I can't make them come if they don't love their sister.

Mother, you have to be good too. You have to be good to them.

But you coming to see mama. When you coming to see mama.

I will as soon as I finish my work here. But I have to finish my work. That has never changed.

Come soon, son. James can't come. Come soon.

I will mother, and he hung up the phone, and he went again through the proscenium opening and he taught his young class that day how to light a dark stage. *Everything is angle . . .*

Then, a summer ago, she was small upon the bed. Reduced and wasted by what comes. *She is the size of a child,* he thought, then, *she has been my mother for thirty-four years, and now she is child-sized. There is dust in this room and we have no vigilance against it.* Somehow, he was not surprised and he was not saddened, now that it had come. He imagined the moment, but not anticipated it. But he was not saddened. He went out of her room and he called Dan Rhind on the telephone and asked what he should do now.

Don't you worry, son, he said, leaving his work for that day, and most of his work for the balance of that week. *Don't you worry, boy, you hear me? We coming right over there, and we going to do everything that needs to be done. But don't worry, son.*

Verdery buried his mother on the morning of August seventeenth, and it was already so hot, the way it gets, that the men could not wear their coats, and they could not have their shirt sleeves buttoned, and the few who came at all were compelled to speak of the heat above her grave. He buried his mother in the clay alongside his father, ten years after. Siblings wept with regret, but with less heart now that they were old and worn of lives long lived, and he looked at them, and he thought without speaking, *do you not know the house is full of dust, did you not know this,* and he was not saddened, only wearied.

CHAPTER TWENTY-ONE

"Was it a cottonmouth," said Rhind, from the bottom of the longboat.

"What," said Verdery, to Jacob Jump Point.

"Was it a cottonmouth."

"Moccasin. I don't know. It was something, yes."

"You wet?"

"Yes. I'm wet."

"It's flooded."

"Will, I need your help."

"I know you do."

"I tried."

"I know it. I want to take him home."

"I know it, bud."

They worked the Ouachita with the smaller boat in tow out of the bottom of the oxbow and it was a good quarter-mile back into the river channel at Black Creek. In a length of time, neither knowing how much gone, they made a creek on the Georgia side, and Verdery said the name aloud and Rhind nodded agreeable that it was Blue Springs. At the bend they ferried hard to the Georgia side, and the small boat passed them and slung them about. They worked their bow upriver and they made the eddy below the landing, and they worked back upriver along the shoreline a short distance in the slower water. They landed in a clearing on the upriver side of the ramp and they tugged the Ouachita high onto the clay and sand, then Verdery released the painter from the Ouachita's stern and he tugged the small boat ashore to the upstream side of the long blue boat.

They climbed the grade to the landing and they sat upon the boat ramp and they looked out to the bend where the river narrowed and the rain made it run fast, and Verdery cried. He cried with barely a tear coming and with barely a noise, and he rested his forehead to his palms, and Rhind let him alone to finish.

He cried for the four days and nights gone and for the sun and the wind and the rain that had come into him—for the river's emerald body gone to mud, and for Jesup and his grandchildren—for the early soundless mornings and the soft evening of yesterday when Dan Rhind cooked the fish in the butter, and for the mid of the night when all things slept. For Nepaug and the coming desiccate autumn air and the immeasureable distance, and for his mother and the dust and aloneness. He cried for Catharine, gone from him, and for Ginny Eaves who let him go too often, and for his friend alongside him, who had no quitting sense—and he cried for Dan Rhind and for Dan Rhind's wife, who did not yet know, and then he quit as he had began, nearly tearless with barely a noise, and Rhind yet waited. "I don't know this place."

"Dad came here."

"Is this where the telephone is?"

"Up the road, maybe."

"You can call home."

"How do I do that?"

"I can call for you."

A smallish, clean truck came along the dirt road and circled at the ramp, towing a silver v-hull johnboat—the kind that had last been made many years ago. A neat antique, but good running. It swung a full circle and it began backing onto the boat ramp. It stopped and the driver put on the parking brake when he saw that Verdery and Rhind had not moved. The driver let the engine run, and he and his passenger stood from the cab and they walked the ramp. They were a pair of older men, one leaner with more height, wearing his best fishing hat, the other bareheaded, his hair silver and windblown from the drive. Sun tanned, each wore a style of plaid madras shirt, though each a different pattern and colors, and khakis too, also of different hues, and expensive walking boots. The taller one came to them, unhurried, smiling, with his hands backward to his hips.

"Whoo, look at her running today. It flooded all the way up to Anderson. Killed some folks up there. Whoo, she's fast now."

Verdery nodded and Rhind did the same after Verdery.

"I don't know if I ought to take his old ass out in the boat today," said the taller one, nodding to his companion, where he had stopped at the top of the ramp. "I can hardly keep him still on the good days. How you men doing?"

The other one called to them, "Where you men coming from in these boats?"

Rhind let Verdery talk and Verdery told that it was four of them, and they had all come from Augusta, and just now two of them had gone up the road.

"We didn't see anybody coming, did we Lee?"

"You men come from Augusta?" said the one near to them. "Whoo, that's a good long ways. You hear that, Mr. Creech, where these men come from? Well, we just come from church, and I was determined to get out here today, so we left the wives there, shaking hands and making plans. Now, they can do what they want, and we can do what pleases us. That so, Mr. Creech?"

"Yes sir," said Creech, nodding, still looking over the boats and their gear. "What all you men got in there."

"What," said Verdery, getting slow to his feet, and going to the one named Creech.

"You men come all that way, like you said, I'm just wondering what all you got in those boats."

"It's just gear."

"Damn, and an ass of it. Looks like you hardly got anywhere to sit."

"What," said Verdery, and Rhind stood, but the hatted fisherman spoke next.

"Creech, why don't you stop worrying these men. Half-blind as it is, and worrying over something and you can't even tell what. Now, why don't you bring your old ass over here, and help me to put this boat in this fastwater."

Creech put out his hand to Verdery. It was weathered and tanned, and his palm thickly callused from decades of finish carpentry, and he gripped Verdery's hand with the strength and sureness of a patient woodworker.

"Names Creech. Bud Creech. That one over there is Mr. Lee. That one used to be the sheriff back in Guyton, and you'd think he'd be more curious about things than he is. He tell you his wife let his old ass come out here today?"

"Deputy Creech, you going to help me put this boat in today?"

The old fishermen nodded to one another, and Lee walked the ramp to the pickup and backed the v-hull to the water. Rhind and Verdery launched the johnboat, and Verdery held to the gunnel standing shin-deep in the water, while Lee drove the trailer up and away. He came again with a small lunch bucket and he gave it to Creech. "Thank you, men," he said, then, "you men alright?" as he looked closely at each of them. Verdery nodded and Lee nodded, and said, "Alright then. Whoo, Augusta, that'd wear me out too."

Lee sat to the back with his hand to the motor's throttle. "Now sit your old ass down," he said as Creech sat too, crouching, half-turning twice before he became comfortable upon the foreseat, with the lunch bucket in his lap. "Thank you, men," said Lee again, and, "thank you, men," said Creech, raising a thick sure palm to Rhind and Verdery, taking his dinner from the cooler and setting the cooler down at his feet, and the dinner upon his lap. A sandwich of cheese and ham his wife made for him that morning before church, and he already missed her. Rhind pushed them off, and Lee steered upriver for a backcreek at Blue Springs they knew would fish well despite the flood. They heard one of the fishermen speak loudly, and then the other, but they could not determine the words, only that something had been said between lifelong friends.

Verdery went to the small boat and let it back into the water, and he led it upstream in the creek eddy to where a stand of dogwood and myrtle overgrew, and there he tied off to one of the thin arms of the dogwood. He thought to look to check the bedclothes, but he did not, and he finished tying quickly and improvised a half-hitch to the sapling, and there he left the small boat and Dan Rhind resting in the eddy, hedge covered. At the ramp he found Rhind sitting again slumped and cross-legged.

"Is it alright?"

"I think it's good. I think I found a good spot."

"Good then. Good Thom," said Rhind, then, "Thom, I'm sorry, I just want to take him home," and he fought and it washed through him, rattling, and he said again, "Thom, I'm sorry."

"No, bud. No, it's alright. It'll be alright."

"How?"

"I don't know. But it will. It will. We'll get him home."

"She was telling the truth."

"No. No, that's not right."

"I could've been better, and look what I did."

"She could've been better too."

"I should have seen it. And I should have seen what to do. I should have been good to her, and understood. And look what I did."

"Sometimes we can't do better than what we do. Sometimes they won't let us do better than what we do. You didn't come here to hurt them. We didn't mean any harm."

"But I did it anyways, didn't I?"

"No. I don't know. I don't know."

"He's not going to wake up."

"I'm sorry, bud."

"I don't know what to do. I don't know what to do. How can I see what to do?"

"We'll see. We'll see what to do."

"She's not home. I don't think she's home."

"Emmy?"

"I don't think so."

"But she knew today was the day. She knew to be home."

"Thom, she wasn't there when I left. She had already gone with Annie. I don't know how he thought she was coming for us. I don't know how, because she was gone when I left. She was gone."

"We'll call somebody else, then. We'll call somebody here. They'll help us."

"No, we have to call home. Thom we have to call home. I want to be home. I want him to be home."

"Alright then, that's what we'll do."

"I don't know what to do. I need to see. I need to see."

A full-size, noisy truck came along the dirt road towing its motorboat, and it made the circle as if it would back along the ramp. The driver got out, then the passenger, and they walked to the top of the incline. Each bearded and heavy, each wore a baseball cap with an industrial logo on the peak. They looked out over the river and the driver cursed at the mud and the speed and they each wagged their heads, and without speaking to Rhind or Verdery they went again to their truck and drove the way they had come, deciding this Sunday to get drunk on the land instead of the water.

"I want to go to call," said Rhind. "I will call. I have to, I know it."

"Sure. We just leave the gear here. I can call if you want. But you can come too. I don't know this place."

"I want to come. I want to call. I know I have to. I want him to be home."

They walked the dirt road cut through sweetgum and dogwood. In the heat and the thick of the woods the air grew wetter, full of the odd bitter fragrance of sweet and sourgum and leaves fallen to cover, and the air rich with distance and the character of an unknown place, and all of it heavy for breathing.

Silent, rattling and empty, voided but for a single purpose, they paced for a quarter mile. They stood aside into the undergrowth as a beaten, old-model truck came towing its johnboat. The driver raised his hand from the steering wheel at them. They stood aside again minutes later as the old truck came the opposite way. The beaten truck was a model Verdery's father had driven when Verdery was a boy. He thought to call to the driver, to explain it all, but the truck groaned on, shifting to high gear when it was just out of sight.

They walked another quarter mile and they stopped, listening, looking backward, forward. Neither spoke and they started again through the heavy air, stopping next when they made a clearing. A few-acre cottonfield yet unharvested. Loblolly grew tall on three sides of the field, but there was nothing otherwise, save the blanch fiber and the green and browning shrub, and row and row of them, and they walked on nothing spoken.

How, thought Rhind, *how can it be . . . how can I tell her. Where is she now. She is standing over her garden. No—that is not right, because she is gone. She is gone from him . . .* Rhind stopped and he bent, with his palms to his knees. Verdery rested a hand to his back and they stood together, quaking and empty amidst a lost wood, and Verdery waited for Rhind to finish weeping a long, last time.

"Goddamit, we missed it." Rhind lay down in the middle of the dirt road, his back into the sand.

"Maybe we walk on," said Verdery.

"The old man said Guyton, not Newington. Blue Springs is off Newington, not Guyton."

"How do you know Newington?"

"You know how I know."

"Maybe it's on downriver some."

"You know where we are?"

"I thought . . . no. No, I guess not. No."

"You know where the map is?"

"Yes. In the boat."

"That's how I know Newington."

"Sure. Alright, sure."

They listened and waited for the fishermen from the river but the only noise was themselves and the mild breeze working the sweetgums and the pines, and the light crunch of the brown thrashers pecking in the undergrowth.

"If he told her Sunday, she won't know where we are."

"He didn't tell her."

"How do we tell her?"

"I don't know how."

"How long do old men fish?"

"I don't know. I imagine all day."

"Then we need to go back."

"Probably."

"We don't have a map anymore."

"Alright."

At the landing Rhind lay down and he covered his eyes with an arm listening for the outboard's sawing, listening for the change of the pitch that would tell its coming. The eddy water had risen half beneath the Ouachita and Verdery tugged it again onto the land as much as he could alone.

He had thought about it walking the road half-knowing the loose, hurried hitch was faulty. With a suddenness, now sure of his mistake, the way you know the truth of a thing, he let the Ouachita alone and went straight along the bank, knowing then that his knot was poor where he had not paid attention—simple, invariable care he would have given, with a factor of twenty, any rigging for a stage. Simple care and attention he had given half a thousand times before, because it is always the right thing. And looking out he already saw it and he knew he should have bowlined the painter, and he should have chosen a better tree.

The small boat had meandered just to the eddy line of where the creek entered, just behind the strainer the deadfalls made slowing the river. It spun lethargic and aimless, dumb sentient, regarding its choices. Then at once the eddy line nudged it about, sending it bow to stern, slow spinning into the fast water.

From a crouch Verdery sprang headlong into the brown water. When he broke the surface he saw the profile of the Katahdin turning away from him— the color of bone, its form upturned at the bow and stern as if shaped into an unsure smile or maybe too only pained—spinning end for end. He swam a crawl for where he hoped the tie-rope to be dragging, trailing the bow where the flow began to boil. Something nudged against his calf and he did not know what it was, and he cursed and thrashed and swam all in a spasm. With overhand strokes he bore into the river altogether inhaling fury and heavy air and cold dirty water into his lungs. He stroked raging for the painter, to swim even as the sluice took him, even as he cursed, and he quit only when he saw the white boat again, it spinning free of all device and restraint, assuming the sublime inertia—the gathering of five hundred miles' worth of watershed and gradient—now surely taken by the fast water. He groaned a supplication, but there was no answer and no pity, and now he saw too the land had gained motion. Behind him receded the eddy and deadfalls, and the greened dogwoods where he had botched one simple thing, inattentive to the care he had learned, taught, in his craft, his profession, hitches he had flawlessly wrapped half a thousand times, never once lacking, never causing harm, never letting go. He spun, now just keeping his head above, his arms and legs tight with the cold, and he looked once more to the smaller boat, where now it slid fast, its weight concordant with the surface speed, and he chose then to try for the Carolina side.

A clog of debris overcame him and took him under. When he broke the surface next his eyes cleared only half and he saw dimly the Ouachita and the ramp in recession, but he did not remember that he should have seen Rhind too. He burned, starving of oxygen, and his arms and legs suffocating and bound with cold quit the fight, and he could only stay above child paddling, and soon that quit him too. He saw a last time what he imagined to be the small boat's hull, in low profile a glint of bone, and he forgot now why the distance mattered. The wild flush took him and he fought a last time to rise and see the treeline pass, trees turning under. The river clouded to shadow all above him, and he tasted the water and the odor of the water. Under now, a meaningless noise, and he felt something against his shoulder. He crawled with the speed of the water rolling him, then knelt into the surviving bar shallow, only a spit of yellow Carolina sand enduring the flood. He knelt, bended in half, choking with the river to his waist and the taste of the river all mud and flotsam in his lungs. He lay over choking of bile, then it was all gone.

CHAPTER TWENTY-TWO

I'm sorry Thom, but we had to go. I'm sorry Thom, but he's lost, and we had to go. We had to go, and I don't see him anywhere . . . His coughing, less than choking now, wakened him with his face cold against the Ouachita's hull. He raised his head from the keel and the vomit of river water, and he listened to gather which had been the dream.

He needs us now . . . *He needs us to find him* . . . *I said we would come* . . . *You don't know, but that is what I promised him* . . . *But I don't know where he is, Thom* . . . *I just don't know* . . . *We had to go on, and I knew you were alright* . . . *I couldn't leave him alone* . . . *I couldn't do it* . . .

Verdery lay again to the cool hull, and in his senseless half-dreaming Rhind chanted, and soon the chant faded and he slept coughing himself to sleep.

He wakened with the sun warm upon him, wet and newly wetted sweating. He knelt to the hull and he cupped his palm into the river and washed his head and neck of the sweat and the bile, and even then Rhind did not quit rowing. Verdery took his oar and he began with Rhind working the longboat upon the bloated river, and he did not ask anything of Rhind, and Rhind told nothing too.

They slowed only to check eddies and backwater creeks, and when they saw nothing of the smaller boat's profile, they went again into the fast water. When they had nearly made the two miles of Hudson's Ferry Reach, Verdery, with his arms and shoulders and back worn sore and nearly afire, said it to himself, *we have missed him. We have missed my boat, and we have missed him. He could not have come this far, this fast. We have never been this fast over the water, and he could not have outrun us this distance. We have searched carefully, and he was not there. He has been nowhere. I do not know how long I slept or drowned, but we have never been this fast over the water, and we have missed him . . .*

At Fowl Craw Point, Rhind lay the oar across his lap, and he kneaded one hand by the other to ease the stiffness. He leaned to help the knots and the fire in his back, and with his head down, he said it too, but he said: *Jesus, we can't have missed him . . .*

At Rabbit Bar point they made the first of a pair of switchbacks, but they did not know the name of the place or know that it was named, and they did not slow. They made the bend and they could not see it for the afternoon sun, and for the glare burning off the river's top, until they were almost past. They ferried hard to the Carolina side, to the creosote pilings assigned with the red marker as dike eighteen. The small boat had broached, and now the current pinned it fast to the pilings, the topwater sluicing in then out again, the gunnels shuddering against the flood's weight and speed and the insensate volume. It was whole but it had been emptied, and now quaking it captured and held only the brown water and foam and the excess remnant rain gathered and expelled by storms and progeny of storms.

As they came wild with speed Verdery knew he could not lash off, and as they swept past he took hold of its nose just inside the bow plate, and he gripped with the last of his strength. The Ouachita broached now, just clearing the trestle where pilings had been eroded and were gone. It pitched and rolled and swung all at once, end for end, and they took water over their gunnels. Verdery groaned as the weight pulled him apart, and he rent the air with an aloud cry when the Ouachita had gone half-round, when he absorbed the full speed and inertia into himself. Mad, cold water sluiced over their bow and the speed and the insane rage of it overcame him until he was blinded and starved of strength, and he let go the small boat.

He lay again as when he had drowned, but now he lay half under the riverwater they had taken. They drifted again into the channel, and the smaller boat followed—its gunnels and bow and stern points the only line of it visible.

Rhind watched it come near to them and groped searching all the water around them . . . *no, this is not right.* Each vessel yawed torpid, laden, and soon met, tapping gunnels . . . *this is not right. There is so much water . . .*

"Tie it off, bud," and Verdery knelt and coughed. "Tie it off."

Rhind watched and Verdery took hold of the small boat's gunnel, and when he had choked his lungs clear again, with his hands failing clumsy with cold and soreness, he lashed the vessels.

Neither worked an oar now and they passed where on the Georgia side it became Effingham County, and there was nothing on land to tell them so. Releasing out of the second switchback, at rivermile seventy, they made Goldwire's Reach, where the river straightened for three miles. Verdery bailed until his fists quit him, then he slept, with his head just above the covering riverwater. He slept for only minutes, and he wakened with a start, and first he remembered the morning, then he remembered his hunger and thirst. He looked to Rhind and Rhind with his head down did not see him, and he began to bail again, and Rhind did not rejoin his effort to do the same. In the distance, dissolving into the haze of warm thick air, the river narrowed to a single point. It reached beyond good imagination, and it was another hour.

Verdery did not see Cedar Bluff Landing until they were upon it. He stroked the oar blade once and half again into the river but he saw that it was useless and he quit, searching again across the umber stretch, guessing it another half hour to where the channel disappeared in the distance, to due east.

At a bend they missed a beach and Verdery cursed and struck at the water they had taken, and at their uselessness, and he bailed again. He spoke aloud, and to himself, "We're going to do some good here, bud. Let me get a little bit of this going. We're going to put out and get us something to eat. We'll be light here again soon . . ."

He dipped water until his feet were showing, then he pulled the small boat abeam and he began bailing it. He sat into the small boat amidst all the dull water and he dipped a pint at a time, swapping hands as they tightened, until it drew light again. He spoke aloud the same and he grew encouraged, and when he was satisfied he got again into the Ouachita. Passing Duck Cut Verdery found an eddy, and, with the small boat coming about and taking them around, he found the slow water, then a beach. Speaking aloud to Rhind he held him by an arm coaxing him to stand and he sat him upon the sand, and he emptied the Ouachita alone.

He made the camp high on the beach, close to the willows where a single, small alligator had sunned itself that day. He emptied the Ouachita of all its laden gear and he tugged both boats high on the land and tied them to the willows, checking his knots, cursing at himself. He warmed a stew and beans and he found one good sleeve of crackers. He cursed again when he caught himself eating and he put them away until the supper was ready. He served the supper, "here you go, bud," and he got the last of the beer for them, and they ate sitting the beach.

They ate quietly and purposefully, Verdery more so, despite how brown and cluttered and fast the water ran, despite that they were only two. Verdery served the remaining stew and Rhind refused the last of it. In the daylight they slept despite their worry and loss with nothing between themselves and the sand, and Rhind dreamed a short dream of his wife and child that was already vague when he wakened. He wakened when the day cooled, his eyes opening to the small boat, and he sat up not brushing the sand from himself, looking out across the river full of speed and debris, the dream of his wife and child clouding then fading from him . . . *it's not right . . . it is so full . . . it's so fast and so full, and we are not three . . .*

The sun had made the treeline at their backs and soon obscured it cast a roseamber to the far shore. An egret flew silent in the distance, to upriver—a single point of white pinned in the finishing day's hued warm cast.

"In the morning, bud, we'll find a landing and a phone. I can handle the boats again now."

"We're not going out again today."

"No, bud, I don't think so."

"We should have asked the old men if that was Blue Springs or not."

"We didn't know to ask. We know now, but we didn't know then. We thought we knew."

"You missed it."

"I went around, and I went the wrong way. The other way could have been wrong too."

"But it wasn't, was it."

"I don't know."

"How did you miss it."

"I don't know how. I didn't know which way. I didn't know."

"Georgia is on the right. Has been all the way."

"I know where Georgia is. We're sitting in it."

"I don't know how to get anywhere, somewhere."

"We have one way to go. It will take us. We'll get somewhere. I remember on the map a place called Lake Parachuchio. I think that was it—I remember how to spell it—I think that's how you say it. It comes in from Carolina, and it showed there's a boat ramp there too. We'll look for it, and we'll find a phone. I can handle the boats now."

"I can handle them too."

"Sure, alright. Good, that's good . . . *the boats are light now, and you know why that is . . . do not be dull, do not be careless and unkind . . .*

They watched the far shore awash in the cast light. It tinted richer just before turning to lavender. A whitetail deer came from the woods to drink. It waited before lowering its head, then chose not to, and bolted to the woods from where it had come.

"I can't do anything about calling now. If we find a phone or not. I can't talk to her—it's too late."

"We have to say at least where we are. It's Sunday. I think it's Sunday. Yes."

"I don't know where we are—where this is. Do you know where we are."

"Yes. We are on the river, about near Blue Springs. Tomorrow we will be at Lake Parachuchio. We will tell her that. You will call Emmy, or I will call Emmy, and we will tell her what to do."

"Goddamit, Thomas," said Rhind exhaling, leaning with his elbows to his knees and his palms to his forehead. "Goddamit, how did you not tie it?"

"Will."

"Did you tie it right?"

"Will."

"No, I mean, what happened. How did it happen? How can I say what happened?"

"I don't know, Will. I don't know what I was . . . I was trying to make it right. I was trying."

"Goddamit, what do I say? Don't you see? I don't know—it's too late. After all her talking . . . twice she found us . . . you didn't tie it right?"

"Listen, you don't say it was that woman, and you don't say it was the river—you just say it happened. You tell them they have to understand, and we did what we knew to do—and it just happened."

"Goddamit, Thom . . . why didn't you tie it right, or leave it alone."

"I don't know, Will. I don't know—I was trying . . ."

In slow pain all the world turned bruising dim, a soreness descending, a last offering. The far shoreline grew further distant in the dun, and they watched the river, full of speed and debris—and Rhind, searching until his eyes failed in the dusk, waited for the shape of his father to pass.

CHAPTER TWENTY-THREE

Verdery did not try the lantern. Just before dark he took what had half-dried and what was only half-soaked and within the tent he made places to lie. And when he could see nothing more of the channel and the mosquitoes came, Rhind went into the shelter too—into the dank and the wetness and the fust of the floodwater, and the odor of themselves. He sat cross-legged, full wearied of sadness because the river had gone black, because the night would meander, the way it does when you need light, and when he became drowsy he lay down alongside Verdery.

"They weren't together," he said, speaking upward to nothing, the dark.

"Who."

"Him and Mom."

"No."

"She's gone. They said it was enough. He gave her the house, but she left anyway."

"We have to call."

"I don't know how to call—where."

"She needs to know."

"He guessed she was in Tennessee."

"Tennessee."

"His family. He guessed. But he didn't know. And he didn't try."

"He called Emmy to come. No, he said work. He said there was someone at work."

"He didn't call Emmy. And he didn't call work."

"He said it wrong."

"I don't know. But he didn't do it."

"Then we will call Emmy."

"That's all I've been saying—I don't know how we get somewhere. And it doesn't matter. It really does not. It's all the same, no matter what."

The cicada had begun their steady rising, falling, wobbling chant. They listened for each other's breathing and to the cicada's shrill, and to the soundless, boiling river.

"Thom. We have to find him."

"Alright."

"We have to."

"I know it. We will—in the morning. Then we will take care of the rest of it."

"We have to. Or else she's right."

"She's not right. She never was."

"I don't want to leave him."

"We won't. But we need to think straight."

"Straight."

"We have to find the law."

"Why."

"To tell them."

"To tell them what."

"What happened."

"What did happen, Thom. What will you tell them."

"We will tell the truth. We will tell the truth, and they can help us."

"Will you tell them about that woman and her guns and her buddy the deputy. Or about that old man and his kids, and the one you were up all night with—who nobody can find—or the one you knocked the shit out of. Or maybe you can tell them about how you didn't tie that fucking Cherokee's boat up right."

"Goddamit, I will tell them everything. Like it was. Like it is."

"Then you go call them. We have two boats. You take one and go call them—I'll take the other, and go find him."

"You have to go back sometime, whether you find him or not. It doesn't matter about me, but you have work, and Emmy, and Annie—and everybody needs to know. They can't not know—they knew him too."

"Who needs to know, Thom. She left *him*. Who needs to know."

"You only get one chance when it happens. We can't change it—none of it. But you only get one chance, and there are other people—and you have to let them know, so they can know."

"He was alone, all the way around. He moved out of the house, and at work they said it wasn't right—didn't look right. Almost sixty years old, and he couldn't live in his own house, and they had something to say about it downtown. They said he *had* to go home at night—leave the property, the offices.

154

He had nowhere *to* go. What difference does it make whether he stays at work, or he goes home five blocks, to one small room. What difference. They said it just didn't look right, and they couldn't pay overtime anyways, and they said he didn't care about that either. They said it didn't look right, and they weren't talking about the work—but he couldn't live in his *own house.*"

"He said this."

"Goddamit, I knew before *he* did. They call me to his office when he was out—asking for me at my work. I thought it was work, shooting a stupid-ass story. They tell me, they say, because they know me, because I carry a goddam camera—because I know them. Hell, what in the hell was I supposed to do?"

"But you didn't let him be alone."

"He never told me. He never said it."

"You didn't say it to him."

"No. No. There are some things . . . I don't care what anybody says . . . he was sixty, and he couldn't live in his own house, and the people he helped get their jobs told *me* first. No, goddamit, there are some things . . . no."

"And she's probably not in Tennessee."

"Hell, I don't know. I don't know. All he did was work, and sit in that small room. It was a goddam transient house. He was sixty, and they know him in a dozen counties, and that was what he had. And they took his work from him."

The cicada cried all aloud, numbers intoned as single voice, choral and feral—a thin crescendo, decline—rude and sage insistence, their natural world.

"The goddam gun . . ."

"The pistol."

"He took it everywhere. He kept it in his desk—this is what they told me. He said it wasn't for anybody else—just himself. I wanted him to come here, with us. And you know what I even thought too?"

"What."

"It would be better here. That's what I thought. I thought better here, than in that little room. That little beggar room. Thom, that's what I goddam thought. His own son thought this. What was I . . ."

They quieted, and there were only the cicada amassed in the nightfall and their breathing as proof of the living.

"We'll make one call, at the lake, at the boat ramp."

"If there's a lake, if there's a ramp, if there's anything."

"There will be."

"Thom, how do we find him?"

"I don't know, bud. I don't know—we try."

They slept, and in sleep devoid of measurement the moon had come low above, it hued a rich nascent amber. It shone upon the wild river, its cast shaping the roils and debris in all its ceaseless agitation. The channel had taken the moon's color, and in its cast the moon and the river were the same, as if borne of a similar element, unkindly sharing a visage alike. Verdery wakened and the cicada were silent and they left the void of their calling in the quiet. He listened for Rhind and Rhind told of nothing hopeful in his breathing, and in the stillness Verdery slept again.

Upon an obscure beach of the Savannah River, at mile sixty-four and a half, they slept. They slept deeply, and no clutter or soreness or sadness kept them from it. The moon rose and reduced and whitened. It drew high away from the trees and the land and the water, and it shone blanched upon all things below. And in its reign it adjudicated all things, but more of anything it abjured the water and those who had come by it.

At rivermile sixty-four, at the outlet of a water once named Lake Parachuchio, Dan Rhind found an eddy, and slowed. Suspended in a gentle boil, he waited. Weightless, above the earth and beneath the sky, he loosed the shroud made of the bedclothes, and when the very early morning passed—the time when all things sleep, even the tempted faithful and believing—and no sons came for him, he went again into the fast of the river.

CHAPTER TWENTY-FOUR

Verdery knew.

When the light wakened him, and just before that too, he already knew he was alone.

Groping the distance to the nearest bend, he saw nothing of him. He had taken nothing save a single oar and his last bottle to drink, and Verdery thought, *it must have been at firstlight, because he could have done no good with only the moon. Goddamit why did you sleep.*

The water smoked and gauzed the distance, and he saw nothing of the smaller boat's profile, and nothing of a single oarsman in the haze and the low roseamber. In the eddy water he bent and washed the sleep from his face, and he looked again, searching the shroud of the steammist. With the river to his knees he half-chose what next to do, and took the time to strike and to save their gear into the Ouachita, and then he started for where he imagined the lake oddly, unlikely, named Parachuchio to be.

Passing into Jasper County, South Carolina, Verdery made the slow water, then the outlet at the lake's mouth. At the boat ramp he read the handpainted sign as it had been miswritten, but he did not know it had been spelled wrong. Half a year before, the lake had been renamed by and for an unimportant politician, but the original sign had survived unchanged.

Two riverbends before the gray clouds had come, and now it rained—the remainder of the next storm traveled from the otherworld horizon, this one once named for a woman. Verdery squatted beneath a bald cypress and the sky squalled and all of the lake and the sky turned to Payne's Grey, as if washed hurriedly, loosely, by a single brush, shaded strokes of a single reckless manipulator. He did not remember that the storm had been named for a woman, but she rained hard upon the misnamed lake and the watertree and upon him, and he only crouched in an abiding silence, and he waited and endured, because he knew to do nothing else.

An old-model and paint-faded truck came with its lights and wipers working. It parked with its engine running quiet, and its wipers and lights working until the squall eased. A black man, likely Verdery's age, stood from the small truck and he walked the boat ramp to the lake's waterline. Although he had come to fish he wore his laborer's boots and his blue uniform slacks. Mismatched, he also wore a type of colorful madras shirt his wife had chosen for him in a yard sale two years before, bought from an elderly white woman neither of them knew. His face and forearms were a soft color of brown, and he smiled unashamed and unworried when Verdery came near to him.

"Whoo, man, you alright?"

"I'm wet. I'm alright."

"That was a good storm. You know it's going to start up right when I get here. You sure you alright? You get out in something like that, and you got nowhere to go."

"I'm alright."

With their palms to their hips they regarded the lake, as if gauging its possibilities, as if searching for simple, difficult, apparent truths. The rain had caused the steam to rise again, and it wafted, hundreds dissolute spirits, a legion's worth dissolving into the August morning air.

"I need me one of them," said the black man, nodding where the Ouachita rested in tall border grass. Left alone it seemed abandoned, and it had taken squall water again. In the persistent drizzle it seemed a purposeless vessel, a single thing assigned a designless chance, luckless, as improbable as the rising ghosts of the lake. "I could do some good in one of them. Only thing is, my wife sees it different. I tell her, I make my own money, why can't I spend it how I want. But hell, that's alright. She's a good one, every other way."

Verdery smiled and nodded and waited, taking care to seem unhurried, standing straight-backed to seem less worn.

"I need to get to a phone."

"You need a phone?"

"I do."

"You alright?"

"I'm alright, I just need to call the house."

The black man looked to Verdery—a simple quick glance, a gentle estimation—and he looked again to the lake and its watersmoke.

"You been out here awhile."

"Sure. A day or two."

"Where you come down from?"

"Augusta."

The black man made a noise aloud—an opinion of half-amazement—a judgment of foolishness, and envy, and respect, all in a given single blow. "Whoo, you a long ways from home."

"I am. I just need to call, and let some people know—let everyone know everything's alright."

"Sure, I reckon so."

"I can pay you to drive me to a phone."

"That ain't no problem."

"I'd appreciate it."

The black man smiled, unashamed and unsimpering at Verdery, but Verdery could not do the same in return.

"Thomas Verdery."

"Jimmy," said the black man. "I got some coffee in the truck, and we can run up to the store."

Verdery nodded once, and he did not try to shake Jimmy's hand, and all the drive to the store on the rough sloppy clay road he did not try to speak.

The store was a small painted blockhouse, set where the Stakes Bluff Landing road met a narrow two-lane backroad. It was the kind of structure you see out on county blacktops, in that odd color of blue paint, the blue that somebody sold a lot of to somebody else. It showed beer and bait signs in its only window, and inside dusty wooden shelves held sweetrolls and cans of beans and motor oil, and beer. Jimmy spoke to the white man and woman behind the register, by name, and he bought a single pack of cigarettes, and went out-side again, to check the sky. When Verdery asked for the phone, the owners' eyes betrayed their surprise and unease, and Verdery looked away from them imagining how he appeared to them, and they had to explain again where the pay phone was.

He called twice to Augusta, and he went again into the store, and he bought canned beans and stew and crackers, and sweetrolls, the kind that harden still in the package. When he had paid, he went again to the back aisle, and brought beer and ice, and paid again, never looking up to the owner as he worked the register keys.

"Do you have maps?" said Verdery, laying out bills to the countertop.

"Maps? What kind of map. A road map?"

"No. No, I mean, do you have a rivermap?"

"A rivermap."

"Yes, of the river."

"Why, no. No, we don't have such a thing."

"Alright," said Verdery, and he let them alone with money he had earned at a place they had never been or imagined, and he went out of the store.

They watched him pass through the doorframe, their faces full of con-cern and conclusion, and they made noises of surmise to each other when the screen door clapped shut. Later in the mid-afternoon of that same day, the store owner stopped and made another noise, this time only to himself, and spoke aloud, *a rivermap*—and considering a last time the ragged unwashed man, who had come for the beans and crackers, and beer, his attention went again to his dusty wooden shelves, and poor inventory; and he thought too, that keeping maps of the river situated a half mile down the dirt road was half a good idea.

Jimmy smoked a cigarette and drank coffee, sitting near the Coke machine with his back to the blockhouse. He thumped the cigarette away when Verdery came, and he stood and waited for Verdery to put his goods into the back of the truck. He offered Verdery coffee and Verdery looked at the coffee and said, "no, thank you," and they drove again, silent upon the sloppy clay road.

"I need to go on," said Verdery this time taking Jimmy's hand, then giving him a twenty-dollar bill. "But I thank you."

"Oh now, that's too much," said Jimmy, now grinning easy at his palm.

"It's not too much for me."

"Where you headed, Thomas?"

"Savannah, I guess," said Verdery, already searching downriver, then thinking too to tell Jimmy some or all of it, and hoping too that he would understand it, and say that they were right to do it, and that all of it could not be helped—that they were not wrong—and that he was not wrong to slow and call, and go again, after his friend. And to resist sobbing. "Savannah. I don't know, Savannah."

"Well, this is too much, Thomas."

"It's not too much for me. Thank you, Jimmy," and Verdery went to the Ouachita and put his goods with the gear, and without bailing rainwater, he went again into the pouch of the lake, then the river.

With his palms resting to his hips, Jimmy watched the fast water take Verdery, and he watched until the longboat was out of sight. "Alright, then," he said aloud, and he turned to the lake and checked the sky, and he went to his poorly painted truck and gathered his fishing gear to walk along the high bank and imagine the good he could do with the fish in a longboat such as Thomas's, from Augusta.

And that early evening when he walked into his rented frame house, he lay the string of panfish into the sink, and he stepped behind his wife as she worked over the stove, and he held her waist and kissed her upon her smooth brown neck.

"You drowned?"

"Gal, I saw me a pretty boat this morning."

"You did."

"Yes ma'am, it was the kind I like."

"I see," she said, smiling at her cooking, at the bread she had going to serve alongside the fish she knew he would bring.

When his two children came into the room, he knelt before them, and he took the twenty-dollar bill from his shirt pocket.

"Y'all see this?"

"Yes, daddy."

"We going to share this four ways. But to earn your part y'all have to do something good for somebody, including your mama, tomorrow."

"Yes, daddy."

"You hear me?"

"Yes, daddy."

"Alright, then."

His wife smiled down at him and at their wondrous likenesses, then she turned again to her stove.

"James Herbert, you going to clean them fish?"

"Yes, baby. I will."

CHAPTER TWENTY-FIVE

With the Ouachita heavy of rainwater, drawing low in the channel, Verdery could not help but make good time. He searched by sight the eddies and backwaters and creeks, and the rain came furious and intermittent, causing the watercourse to steam. He made one stretch, then another appeared through the gauze, and he made that one too. Empty from the sadness and aloneness he took squall water and he drew lower, and the spirit steam rose about his vessel while he searched by sight for the slender blanch profile, as he trusted it would appear, lonely too a single passenger and pilot upon the river's tensile surface. He made places named for the lay of the land, named for their own shapes, places named for persons and events, but he did not know any of it, and he only guessed at the rivermiles. He made a fixed bridge, appearing suddenly out of the steam and the bluegray squall. He did not know it to be the Clyo overpass for Highway 119, and only as he slid past the footings did he understand how fast the channel actually ran. In a half mile he made a second bridge, this one trestled for a railroad, and soon after that he made the rivermile sixty marker, running wide at the bend, missing seeing it altogether. He made Sister's Cut, and the river switched back passing Goethe's Camp, then Sister's Ferry Landing, then Dr. Brauner's Camp, but he did not know the names or that they were named. There came Little Boykin Bar, Bowlmaker Point, Chairmaker Point, Zacharias Point then Frying Pan Point. And unseeing past the watermist, it growing thick as clouds, he worked his blade less steady, and for all he could know and tell it was only he ever upon the water, only he amidst the rain and smoke, and it had no end. Sore with sadness, he lay his oar across his knees and he let the laden vessel turn, then turn again, and he did not try to alter it. He sat down to the hull, into the squallwater, and he lay aside his oar and he closed his eyes, shutting them to the rising clouds and he thought without knowing, *he could be anywhere. He is no where. There is no one.* Inhaling the spiritmist he tasted the vapor upon his tongue and into his lungs, and he tasted the rain—all the world's rain come and spilled for them, gathered falling across half the enduring earth.

In his hearing the squall became a hiss, and a whisper, and it spoke as it had come, *I am before you and after you, and I am endless . . .* and it washed upon him.

I should not have come, he said inward where he held the truth of the rain *. . . I should not have come, because I am not ancient, and I do not understand. There is no place I understand. No place have I understood, and there is no place I can go.*

I have lost them, and I am alone, and I will not find them again. I should not have come, because I am not ancient, only tired, and that is not the same. And I have lost my father . . .

The squall quit as sudden as its coming. The silence and the leavening of the bluegray wakened Verdery.

He saw first the marker, and he watched it hard until he passed, until he was sure he saw the same numbers on the downriver side. "Fifty." He counted backward, and he subtracted from two hundred . . . *it is forty, no fifty, of course, and it has been how many days,* and he said some of it aloud . . . *it is Sunday . . . no, it is Monday today. The month is August, but I do not remember the number. It was Tuesday when we came . . . No, it was Wednesday, which made it Thursday morning . . . It was a good long day, and it is Monday now. People are working again, but I am not at work . . . I do not work . . . Jimmy did not work today. Is it a holiday in August . . . No, there is no such thing, but I am glad Jimmy was not at work—I am lucky too. Savannah is twenty-four, this I know without guessing . . . No, that is not right . . . Tybee is zero, and Savannah is fourteen miles up. Savannah is fourteen, and I am fifty, and that makes thirty . . . That makes thirty-six . . .*

A warmth came and burned off the steam and clouds, and the sun dried and cut the vapor and both shores appeared. A great long stretch lay ahead, and now he could see the waterway for a mile and a half, reaching, narrowing to a point where it dissolved into the blue smoke.

He bailed with Rhind's drinking cup, then slowly, after two heartless starts, he set himself to rowing. He worked steady, guessing at the time passed, searching the distance, twisting in the stern seat, checking back for what he might have missed.

The houseboat was just a dot, too distant along the endless stretch to even show color. Nearer, he guessed what it was, it slowly wagging in the flood-water, committed to an anchorline. It was only a box, made of studwalls and ply, sitting upon a ply deck, all of it buoyed atop steel drums. Painted a common barn red, weathered and peeling, and it had turned a tinted hue, something pinkish and salmon, something alike the dust of the earth at sunset. But not that too, all of it more something manmade, lacking a natural heart. At the boxboat's rear there hung a single window, and at the front another smaller window at a short uncovered porch. At the corner of the porch led a ladder to the house roof, and upon the roof there rested a single weathered lawnchair. Verdery steered close alongside, and as he passed he took hold of the porch's stud railing, and tied off. He groaned as he boarded, as his legs took his weight. Inside the porch window hung a sun-faded quilt, and to the right of the window an entrance, a ply door with a hasp but no lock. Verdery spoke at the window and he waited and listened and he heard nothing and felt no motion, save the fast water against the boxboat's drums. He spoke again, and he climbed the ladder to the upper deck. The lawnchair, wooden and caned, sagged from age and weather, and held as memory the shape of the last person to sit. Regarding all the water, he turned a full circle with the ply deck creaking beneath him, estimating the stretch he had come from and the stretch he would make downriver, searching all the while for evidence of one other person.

He went again down to the porch and he spoke a third time, then turned and urinated past the stud railing, into the river. He bent to untie his painter, and an odor he had known before came to him, and he straightened and went to the ply door and opened it by the hasp.

She squinted when the daylight washed upon her. He took a short breath to speak and he looked away from her, apologizing as if he knew her, but he had already seen her raise a small, knobby fist to cover her eyes, and he let the ply door close halfway.

"You're the third one," she said.

"I'm sorry?" and he coughed twice, inhaling the odors as they rushed for the opening.

"You are number three."

"What?" and now he looked at her again.

A single candle burned upon a simple homemade table, and blue smoke from a cigarette curled, rising, rearing, into the candle's cast. The daylight shone the room full of dust, it suspended, commingled into the body of the blue smoke, all of it stirred, disturbed by the ply door's motion, all of it fragrant from age, cloistral, mephitic too from sickness, and from the dark. She put the cigarette to her mouth, drawing on it, coughing into a flannel bedspread she wore over her shoulders—over her head and shoulders, as a petticoat—and she sat bent to the simple pine table, sitting upon a cabinet likewise homely in build, she had made into her bed.

"There was the one, and I said, was there anymore? Then sure enough come the second one; this one in a boat. And I said, was there anymore after that one, and sure enough here come the third one, after the first two."

Beneath the bedspread, her hair was drawn tight into a bun, the way Ginny Eaves wore hers when she danced or taught dancing. Impossible to judge how long her hair might fall when loosed.

She was an old woman, thin arms and walnut fists, a smallness. *She is child-sized,* thought Verdery, *she is the size of Annie. She is the size of my mother on the bed alone in the cold room . . . How can it be that she is so small . . .* then, "you saw him, and the boat. You saw my friend."

Unlikely precise, she lay the cigarette half upon the table, and she motioned with her head, but Verdery did not know her meaning, or if she nodded, or if she told anything at all. "I know it smells. I can't fix it anymore. It gets to where you don't know it so much."

Verdery waited with his head bowed, with a bare foot propping open the ply door and opening it no wider. "Did you see him?"

"I saw somebody. It was just him, and he came close to me, but he just kept going. He kept on while the first one stayed with me, and I never had the chance to tell him the first one's already here waiting on you."

"When. I mean, how long ago. Can you tell me that. Was it white— "

"I can't tell about the time. It seemed like a minute. But it was early when the first one came."

"I didn't mean to trouble you on your boat. I didn't know there was someone here."

"You're looking for the second one."

"I'm looking for my friend. Yes ma'am, he's in a small white boat."

"And the second one was looking after the first one."

"No. No, he was looking for something else."

"Well, I don't know. That first one woke me up this morning, early, against the drums. He hung on for a good long while, and I figured there'd be another one after him. That's just the way things go when it gets fast like this. I've seen them before."

"Thank you, ma'am. I didn't mean to worry you."

In the daylight and the candlelight, her eyes peered as small and as dark as berries of a cherry laurel. Now, in her face, he did not see the age her hands showed, and the odors came again to him, conjoined yet nearly distinct, and he knew three but he could not discern the fourth. He knew the smoke, it had drawn him inside, and he remembered the sadness of the dust, and the age and wetness of late August; but he did not carry the strength to name them. Later, in the river again, he would know too the fourth, and he would name it to himself, and he would know that she told it probably true about the first one come early that morning.

He bowed again, as if to go from her.

"When I saw the second one come, I said, that rain needs to stop. For the both of you, because I knew then you were coming too. But I haven't finished it."

"I appreciate it," said Verdery kindly, careful not to mock her. "It's rained since we started."

She let the flannel spread fall to her narrow shoulders, they actually not enough to catch it. She wore covering her head a wrapping resembling a tuque, it knotted in the back where Verdery mistook her bun to be, and now with the tuque drawn tight and smooth she seemed balding. He let the door close full behind him and squatted with the pine table and the candletip between them, and he searched the black cherry eyes, and they held only the points of the candlefire.

"You're alone."

"Yes, I am."

"Can I help you?"

"There's no need."

"What is your name?"

"It's kind of you to ask."

"Are you sick?"

"Yes, I am sick."

"I can bring someone to you."

"There's no need."

"I have to find my friend, but I can help you."

"Don't you worry about me. I chose it this way."

"But you're sick and alone."

"That's alright. It's the best I can imagine. It's my pick, that's what matters. There's somebody else you can do some good for."

"Somebody else."

"Others."

"Sure. I imagine so."

"Then you ought to do it."

"I will find him, won't I."

"Yes. I believe you will."

The candlefire wavered at their breath and in the black cherry eyes the flame quivered. "You're almost to Ebenezer."

"Ebenezer. Yes, I remember that."

"Ebenezer Creek. A little while away. There is a landing too, and there is a host there. Tell him you want to stay the night. He will say he needs to ask if it is alright. Tell him it has already been asked."

"There's daylight left."

"Yes, but that is where you will stay. Think of the tide, and then you will find your friend."

"The tide."

"You'll make the right tide."

"Alright."

She coughed once, shutting her eyes tight, covering with the bedspread, but it was not enough that Verdery could not smell the dying in her lungs.

"How do you make the rain stop."

"You ask. Then you show it."

"What do you show."

"That you mind."

He stood to open the ply door, and she spoke a name. "At Ebenezer you will need to tell him that name. He will know it."

"Alright."

As he sat into the Ouachita she coughed twice, with the same hardness, and as he slid away he smelled the sulfur of a freshly burned match. When he had made half the stretch he turned in his seat to upriver and there was only the boxboat, its odd hue complementary in the blue haze, its size reduced half by the distance. When he neared the point at the bend of Old Log Landing he looked back a second time, and he saw now the gray smoke rising amidst the blue. He ruddered the Ouachita about and he cursed aloud a single exhalation as it went afire in an instant and burned, now the size of a thumbnail, yellow and crimson. He stroked three times right-handed against the river and he cursed again, and useless, he quit, and lay the oar across his lap, and cursing and watching the boxboat burn he let the fast water take him wide around the bend to Ebenezer.

The river turned at a right angle just below the creek. There on the Georgia side he found the landing. He made the slough, it swollen brown with floodwater and flotsam, and he went easy to the shore beneath a bald cypress. He landed in the grass where the water came high and only the top of the boat ramp was visible where it turned to gravel and clay. Nailed high into the tree facing the land above a rotted picnic table, a handpainted sign of delayering ply instructed: *cars $1.00 boaits $2.00 payBill.* In the clearing rested a house trailer upon cinderblock piers, its wheels missing tires but the hubs still on the axles.

Verdery tapped at the door, half-thinking he had already been there, not fully thinking of Jesup, not fully thinking, *it's not as old and worn, and cluttered.* Slump-shouldered, searching his canvas shoes, he listened for a noise. His skin held the heat of the sun and it occurred to him because the flames were so pure crimson and gold that he had forgotten to drink anything, including the beer he bought with Jimmy. He put his fist again to the thin door, and it opened. The attendant she spoke of was an old man too, and Verdery thought, regarding him as he would anything known as inevitable in this life, *they are all so old*, and soon when he got again into the Ouachita, and the next morning too, he would think, *they are all so old, and they are alone . . .*

He was small, and smaller declining by age, and he could not stand well on his own. With a thin gray arm he propped himself to the doorframe and he grimaced, as if the light of day were painful. He wore a clear tube delivering oxygen beneath his nose, and in his right hand, between his first two fingers, he held to a burning cigarette. He spoke first, struggling breathless to make the words aloud, and he grimaced bowing his head to take oxygen.

"It burned," said Verdery. "She burned, when I left her."

"What was it?" said the attendant with his head bobbing, nodding slowly, drawing off the tube to gain good air.

"You know her. Don't you know her, she sent me here."

"Know who," said the attendant, rough whispering, nodding up to Verdery, his eyes wetted thickly with endless pain and rimmed crimson. He asked a second time, now with only his eyes.

"She was in the square boat, the houseboat. And I saw it, but I couldn't get back. It's too fast. It's rained too much, but she stopped it."

"Who did?"

"Did you send someone for her. Somebody must have. You must have heard that someone went to her. You have a telephone, I see the lines."

"Boy, who are you?" He looked past Verdery, to the clearing. "Where you parked?"

"I came from the river. I came past a houseboat. It was red, and she sent me to you."

The attendant motioned with his smoking hand and he surceased from the doorframe. Verdery leaned with his arm straightened to the trailer's skin, and he nodded down to his shoes, and he slowed himself . . . *this is what I must do. Now, this is what I must do . . .* He told himself with forbearance, the same as teaching a hopeful child . . . *you have to see it to make it. At the beginning, and before the finish of it, you have to see it . . .* He went up and in and followed the old man to the kitchenette, careful of the tube that came from beneath a bench seat. There was enough of it that the old man could wander inside, and when Verdery sat, he sat carefully.

On the tabletop was a single ashtray full of a mound of blackened tips, and the host lay the burning one atop the mound. *This is what I must do now*, thought Verdery, but he could not yet make the list in his head . . . *if I can find the first, then I can see what to do, but I must find the first thing . . .*

"Bill," the attendant rough whispered, motioning to himself, grimacing . . .

I know already, Bill. You are all the same. You are the same as the first one at the lock, and you are both the same as Jesup. You are all old, but you are not the same as she. She was not the same as you. I saw in her face and eyes that she was not the same, and you do not know her, Bill. You do not know her. She knew this place, that is why she sent me here, but you do not know her. She, is the first thing . . .

"Been inside for a month," he said, and Verdery watched his mouth to understand. He spoke fast, all a jag, in shallow exhalations, struggling for good air for his next words. "Doctor said be two more months," and he drew on the cigarette, and inhaled it burning. "My back, see . . . back gives me hell . . . doc said can't use it for three months . . . got two to go . . . been one, be two more."

"Do you have a phone I can use, and a book—a phone book. I can pay you."

"Say they was a fire? Say you know somebody?"

"An accident. I should call the law. What county is it?"

"This Effingham."

"Effingham."

"Stillwell right up the road . . . Rincon other way. Sheriff's number right on the wall . . . use that. Say somebody knows me?"

"This is Ebenezer?"

"Ebnezer, right. Creek over yonder . . . church up on the hill. They all know where's Ebnezer. Crazy happens all the time at Ebnezer . . . when river so wild and high, crazy happens all the time . . . they know it too."

Bill twisted and buried his tip into the mound of ash and refuse, and he spoke again something about how his back was ruined, and some of it Verdery understood, and some of it he did not see his mouth to know.

The trailer was cooled, and the cool and the acrid smoke the same as gathering places for drinking—same as the tavern on Bolton Hill, where there was no back door, just a hole in the bricks, and a sign reading *do not go through here;* alike the one on the side of the road in the Purchase, in Kentucky, where he sat with his friend who wrote stories and books, where on Saturday afternoons the farmers and old miners played reverently at chess and tabletop shuffleboard; the one made of cedarwood where he and Catharine huddled away from the snow in the dead of the winter, watching closely one another drink and speak, guessing at what comes next.

When will you leave me.

I will never leave you.

You told me . . .

I'm telling you. And they drank warm drinks, eager to finish and make the drive back to the hilltop, her room warm too.

So many of them I have let go . . .

because, then, my eyes were sharp and purposeful. Sharp, and there was tomorrow, and my eyes set for the next day. Some, I took their hands, and some, I held and kissed, and some, I loved. But always, we said good-bye, and do not be sad if you have the strength, because the next day comes and we follow the light, and our purpose . . .

I let them go from me too easily. What did I expect without them, to let them go so easily. I was careless, because they will not come again. I will not go to them, and they will not come again for me. It is the carelessness that is the sin. The forgetting is the weakness, and the carelessness is the sin . . .

we were young and hard and looking for the next day, and we let that go too. Too soon. It is all so far away, and they were never with me. They are not here now, and it has been so long ago, and I am tired, and they were never with me. I have let so much go, and the distance is too great. I imagine I remember the faces, but I do not remember how they laughed, because I have caused the distance and it is too great and truly it was only me . . .

A woman with a thick, kind accent answered, and Verdery remembered the second thing, and that was the finish of his list. He explained to the Effingham County sheriff's office all he knew, and in the telling he doubted he spoke the truth. He doubted he stood now speaking aloud telling what might have occurred only an hour before, and so irretrievably long ago. At the end of it she asked, "are you alright, are you crying," and he said, "no, I am tired," and she asked for his name, and he said, "no," again, "I have to go on."

He lay ten dollars upon the kitchenette table, and Bill wagged his head at the money, and Verdery let the money alone and went out of the trailer with Bill following, and the supply tube trailing him.

"Thank you," he said, and Bill nodded raising a hand to him, grimacing a smile, bowing to gain oxygen. "I hope your back gets better."

Have you seen him, Verdery might then have asked, but he regarded the old man she called the *host* for only a moment more, then he let him alone to his good and bad air and burning cigarettes, and went again to the Ouachita.

CHAPTER TWENTY-SIX

On the high bluff obscured by the grown woods lay the ruins of a church. Middle Europeans, Salzburgers from the Austrian mountains, crossed the ocean to settle and worship. Even as Savannah itself was being righted out of timber and stones, Oglethorpe delivered them upriver to the creek. Calling it New Ebenezer, they stood alone in this wildland, no trouble to Savannah and its Englishmen and unbothered too. Eventually and for a short while they were the only ones to raise silk properly. Working scrabbling fieldstone to make a foundation, they spoke a new voice, worship, laughter, prayer rising from them, into stands of burr oak and hickory. And too, nearby, a single hidden Creek or even Yamasee squatted at the edge of a glade, darkened bare feet into the blanched sand, regarding the rising hymns, thinking inward in the tongue that he or she spoke outward, *they have come, and the more will come.*

On a high bluff the Salzburgers lived and died alone, and they left behind a rubble unseen as Verdery passed. He searched the west for the sun and he saw that it had fallen behind the treeline, and too soon the daylight would quit him.

A mile below he made the first of four cutoffs, where the Corps of Engineers had straightened the river by plowing open the land at switchbacks. At each cutoff he took the long way around, the way the river meant to run. On the Georgia side at Little Keifer Point he came upon an elderly black couple sitting on overturned pails, bank fishing the eddy with canepoles. They wore hats of straw and hers a gardening style with a flowered band she added. Verdery spoke and they smiled together and each waved and spoke in turn. *Yessir,* they had caught a few small ones, though they couldn't tell *how in all that mud,* and *no,* they hadn't seen another man on the water. *No,* they didn't know of too many good places to stay on down the river, *but, you know, Ebnezer is a good place, but you missed that a little ways back.* He said her hat was a nice hat, and she said, *I shore thank you son, tell him,* and he wished them luck with their canepoles, and checking the sky for dimness he went again into the fast water.

Equidistant from shorelines with the sky shading to dusk he searched but he did not believe.

I can go on into the darkness, but no, that is wrong—the dark does me no good. At the bends where the willows are, there are also the sandbars . . . the water is high, but some of the beaches survive . . . soon at a bend I will make camp. But no. That is wrong too . . . you must remember right from wrong. I have forgotten to eat—but do not eat—remember right from wrong. If you forget now, you will never be able to regain it—so you must remember now. There is eyestrain . . . the distance is hidden by the dimness. You must be careful, because if you miss him, you cannot go back. You learned the first rule of perspective is what: the further away, the smaller . . . but how can that be . . . how can we change by proximity. I do not understand this, yet I know it to be true . . . just look, and you will see it to be true. But that does not matter, it is the dimness. This is why you must be careful when you work . . . it is the eyestrain . . . you lose them in the dimness. You cannot allow the mud in the lights, you learned that long ago. You cannot allow the mud and lose them in the dimness . . . do you understand this? You must remember to understand this. It is too dim for seeing well, and you would not allow this because I know better—on my stage, I know better. Remembering is knowing—you must remember, and do not sin. Do not allow the weakness, and do not sin . . .

Past white willows on the Carolina side in a slow eddy Verdery found what survived of a beach. He let the tent alone and he let dinner alone, and each time it occurred to him what to do to make camp properly he reproached himself, *no, you must not, this is all* . . . He took two beers and he sat into the hard sand of the beach where the waterline had risen that afternoon, and something in that watermark important—but he let it go. The sky washed to lavender and imbued the air of all the world the same. Evening dark spilled upward, first bluing, then dimming, and a southern wind less than a breeze came warm and fragrant of distance, of the unseeable, inestimable, and he drank a beer not thinking deeply of the next morning, outside of reckoning it might yet come.

He had forgotten the last marker, and he tried to count back to where they had imagined Blue Springs to be, but he could not. He did not know if he and Jimmy had ridden together this last morning, or the morning before, and he could not remember if they had ridden on a Sunday, and he quit that too, and he did not try to count the days.

He stood against his bone soreness and waded into the river, and underhanded he tossed the second beer to where the fast water began. He took and drank another beer with the river to his knees, and he watched until the blue was gone and it was night. He sat, then he lay upon the beach on his side with his palms together beneath his head, and he slept. He slept even in the night air and with the dew settling upon him, and with the mosquitoes. He wakened once and stood into the river and when he had finished pissing, he drank another beer, listening to the hum of an unsilent earth, watching the night glow. Alone in this world found he thought to say aloud, *forgive me*, then he lay again into the sand near the same spot where he had first slept.

In the late mid of the night, when even the mosquitoes slept offering peace, he dreamed. He dreamed of Bill at Ebenezer, Jesup, the lockkeeper, and it was of a wistful, longtime past, and they were three in the same, and not any one of them needed a tube to breathe. There was the small red boxboat, and Dan Rhind had come aboard, as she knew he would. They spoke gently to one another, he simpering as he did, not ashamed, but kindly acquiescent, and he told her she would not die, and she believed him because she was as small as a child.

Alice Mays stood alone upon a beach, and he did not slow for her, then she stood again upon a wooden dock, and with each stroke he gained strength and speed, and when she saw again that he would not slow, she sat, and wept soundlessly, with her palms covering her face and the now colorless eyes.

His father sat with his mother as she died. He brushed the dust from her, and he sang to her in his rich baritone, the way he sang for his children when he lived, and he sang until he was sure she could no longer hear him. Outside, the clapboard siding had whitened again, dry of the mildew and the overgrowth of privet hedges cleared, and dreaming he knew he and his lost brother would not fear and dislike coming home again.

He dreamed he and Catharine swam in Lake Nepaug, and he promised for both of them he would resist the restlessness, and emptiness, and never leave her behind. The water held the color of the sky and the air the taste of inestimable distance, and next, he flew just above the hemlocks, and he saw all the lake as large as a proud eye searching upward the world, and he watched her upon the grassy peninsula, lying in the sun, and she rolled on her back, that she might feel the weight of the man she lay with upon her breasts and stomach and thighs.

He dreamed he piloted the resurrected sea cruiser, and the vessel cut the water fast, with the water pellucid, and Verdery saw everything beneath its surface, but he discerned nothing he knew. He crossed a large pond where the river ran backward and beneath a high bridge he found Rhind sitting upon a small hard beach, and he sat with a woman. When he came near to them he saw that it was not a woman he knew but Caron Lee. He sat with them, and they did not speak as they watched the cruiser depart from them, upriver, to where it abided as before, low sunken and disused.

He wakened in the same position as he lay, dew wetted in the morning's first lilac, and a soft wind blew, less than a breeze, already warm, already thick.

In the night the beach had gained a second watermark, lower still, resting the Ouachita higher, and through the morning's steam and firstlight he saw the river's color had begun to turn again away from the mud and the umber.

He sat cross-legged abiding in the soundless hum of isolation, abject solitude. A great blue heron flew to upriver along the shore. Full of purpose it did not settle or slow, making for the bend vanishing into the gauze the same as it had come.

He would have first made warm coffee, but with the dreams yet clinging he did not. When the steam cleared and the far treeline appeared he slid the Ouachita into the eddy, and he left behind the place mapnamed Hickory

Bend, and in half an hour, past a nameless creek that fed spoil areas, he found the rivermile forty marker.

It is only sixteen miles now. How can that be. Twenty-four from forty is sixteen . . . that is not right, it is fourteen at Savannah . . . that is right, that is what Dan said, and he spoke the truth as best he knew to . . . then it is twenty-six . . . but no matter, I will be there soon . . . it is early and I am fast, and I will be there soon. If I do not find him, then I will be in Savannah . . .

He had settled to his rowing, working easy and unhurried, and cautious, to survey each diversion he came upon, when he found what remained.

At the pierposts signed as dike three, he knew first the oil drums, they gathered and captured, strained against the creosote pilings. The ply, blackened buckled and all a ragged pile, hung with the river awash sluicing through it. The fast water took him close, and he remembered the name she had given for telling at Ebenezer. Amidst the strainer, the offal, there survived a shape, and he looked away. He did not then tell himself that it was again child-sized, and too, he did not confess the second shape, a tangle like something slayed and knotted amidst the charred, ragged heap, and he only understood—allowed himself to see, as slow as learning that love is not a promise—in the next half day, that Rhind would not again find his father.

The fast water took him, and he did not look back. He did not consider the law now, and he did not consider whom they had left behind on this earth, because, now though he only suspected, in the next rivermiles he would come to know that he could not repair any of it.

At a landing named with a signpost Purysburg he stood at the top of the ramp, searching all directions. There was no one and no structure save a weathered outdoor table, and he went again to his boat.

At Moody's Cut he took the long way around and he made a stretch, an alligator pool where the water seemed to slow, where they dwelled in great numbers, and where they behaved differently from the upriver breed. They crawled for the water, and they appeared, watching curiously and unashamed and lacking fear, the long, thin, silent vessel, with only the knobs of their eyes and foreheads breaking the surface. He overtook a great wildgrown male, and they traveled alongside one another until the creature knew he was not alone and he quit swimming, backing gently, sliding beneath the surface.

Opposite the mouth of Big Collis Creek he made the rivermile thirty marker, then an enormous yellow sandbar on the Carolina side. It spread larger than any he had encountered and he landed the Ouachita half along it. In its center he stood searching in a full circle testing all directions, even where the reeds and canebrake began. He walked its length checking the far eddy and the creek that bordered it, and he returned checking the sand for evidence that someone might have come before him, and there was nothing, save the windworked carvings and shapings, and the empty imprints of his own feet and weight.

He took a beer counting by sight what remained and in the pure sun it cooled his palm and his stomach and made him feel a small drunkenness. He stripped and he took his bar soap, and in a shallow sunwarmed pool he bathed, careful of the dropoff where the water drew cooler, careful not to go deep. He bathed himself, then swam to rinse, then washed himself again.

This is thirty, and Savannah is . . . no, fourteen . . . you must remember, Savannah is fourteen. Something else is fourteen, and you have already forgotten. If you forget, you are lost. Fourteen from thirty is sixteen . . . yes, that is right, and sixteen is only three hours. You have done ten miles in how many hours . . . you do not know. Two hours . . . and sixteen is half again what ten is, and that is three. If you do not find him in three hours, then you will not find him. It has been so many hours since the beginning . . . and you are at the end, nearly . . .

At age thirty-five he still held the form of an athlete—thick shoulders and back, and good legs. He had broadened in ten years, but his shape was still good, if no longer thin, boyish. He searched the length of himself, and in his chest and stomach and thighs he could not see the same lines that Ginny Eaves or Catharine or the rest of them, with their slender hands, their willing eyes, had known. He swam again now into the deep and the cool, not remembering to stay shallow, and when he had finished he dressed and sat again into the Ouachita, and went again upon the water, where Rhind had gone, fatherless too, before him.

CHAPTER TWENTY-SEVEN

He made the last sharp bend of its kind, the last switchback for the remainder of the river's run, then he made Abercorn Creek, the creek that defined the island, and the river widened into a pool, and when he cleared the point he saw the high bridge, with the insect traffic crawling its back. He slowed without knowing it and he ferried across the pond to the Carolina shore, that too without knowing it, and there the hue of the river's body changed to the color of rust, or tea, and he saw that a single sycamore leaf suspended beneath the surface—perfect in its shape, its points stretched as a reaching hand—flowed against him.

He quit his blade to see if it was true, and soon the Ouachita quit too, and soon again it backed to upriver, as the leaf. He rowed and quit again, testing to see if it was an eddy pool or boiler, but soon again the tidewater backed the Ouachita to where it had been, and in the first moment of knowing, it became true to him as if true from the beginning and before the beginning.

He let his boat pivot in the tide pond until he faced where he had come from. He saw now where it widened, where the ebb and flow met in opposite strengths. He lay a palm into the pond and he tasted of it, and he was unsure if the brine was him or the Savannah, or if it was there at all.

Seven years before as he walked Riverside Park between twofer Saturday shows, a woman with a man, she speaking in a variety of European accent, had asked him of the Hudson River, *is it saltwater there?*

I don't know, ma'am, you would believe so, thinking too, *I suppose we could taste it. That's how you know, taste it.*

And she frowned and made a pouty expression as he seemed so unsure and went on asking the same of the next couple they met, and Verdery did not hear their answer.

He searched backward the point he last made where the river's body folded into the tea color, the near memory of the channel's lost speed. *They had said tidewater . . . one of the old ones . . . was it Bill, or her. Was it Dan. He had said it . . . no it was her, and she is gone with him. It was a word she used, but I chose to misunderstand. It was how I heard, or chose not to hear. The rain . . . he spoke of the rain . . . but that is not it . . . I am sure. You knew it would come . . . you have always known of the tide . . . why were you not prepared to know the times of the day? You grew up in these places, Isle of Palms and Port Royal Sound. Carabelle, remember Carabelle? Where the shark took half of the grouper before you could get it into the boat. In Astoria, at Hell's Gate, you saw the river run both directions . . . you knew this . . . but you did not know. This has never been done . . . by you it has never been done. You did not know, and now you must row against it . . .*

He turned the Ouachita about, facing across the pond the high bridge and the traffic crawling steadily its back, rowing toward what would soon come to be the full, exigent bearing and volume of the floodtide.

It turns twice a day. That is twelve hours—no, that is not right. It turns four times a day . . . that is right. There are two high and two low—yes, that is right . . . you knew that, you knew that all along. There is so much that you forget, but you have not forgotten that. Two tides twice, but when . . . you should have known the schedules. Bill at Ebenezer said it . . . no, he did not, and he did not say the times . . . you should have known to look at them, but you did not even ask about Will. He would have told you everything, if you had only asked. You let that go too, the same as the rest of it . . .

you should have known to ask, and he would have told you everything . . . but you did not ask . . .

He knelt to the Ouachita's hull and he worked his blade deep into the body of the tea-colored water. He pulled in long, full strokes, his bow cutting fluid burls off the tide pond's top, gaining on the high bridge for what he guessed to be Interstate 95.

Thomas Carpenter you should wear the watch Catharine gave you. If you did so you could tell the time, and you could count six hours . . . yes, six times four is twenty-four, and that is the day. But it is less than six hours, now . . . yes, because you did not know when it began, and it has begun. And there is one more thing you do not know . . . you do not know which tide he made, when he came into this very same pond . . . there is so much you do not know . . .

He made the high bridge along the Carolina shore. Just before the piers he made a steep, hard beach of dark color. There, cut into the sand survived a single keelmark, and he knew it, guessing, as the carving of his own boat.

He had bought the Katahdin boat in Nepaug from a scene painter who claimed to be displaced Cherokee—relocated, because he had been fired by an opera company's fussy and mostly drunken and almost gay general director, and had been forced to take a job in the North, far from his home—and claimed his Cherokee name to be Adahy Dancingfire. They put in Lake Nepaug together and the Cherokee demonstrated the vessel to have a soul and made Verdery promise care for it. *See*, he said, *see how it cuts the water, it is the way it smiles at the keel. It smiles even when it is let alone to sleep, and you must promise care for it.* And when he was satisfied Verdery understood and his intent mostly wholesome, then, he said, there was only one other thing, and Verdery said, *yes, of course, cash.*

With the keelmark there were the foottracks. A set that might have been Rhind's and a set that were small in comparison, child-size, or from a woman with feet alike Ginny Eaves's. Walking the beach of Sullivan's Island and Ginny ahead of him marching alone because he had said the wrong thing, and he trailing and thinking of how endless the ocean and when he would drive away from her. He became unsure, then doubted all that he saw, because truly he had seen it upriver too, and there it had resembled the markings of travelers, and there it had been the alligators.

It was someone with company. See, Thomas, they are the lucky ones . . . probably they did not give one another away. And they are so very wise to have one another . . .

Upon the hard beach he saw too that now truly the river, waking the bridge piers, chose to run backward. The traffic clopped above at the high bridge's expansion joints, and he urinated a last time before he would stand again in three hours, at a place named Port Wentworth. He lingered in the foottracks and he scuffed at them with his bare feet—the dirt and sand and silt the same color as the floodtide—erasing them back into the beach.

In a half mile he made a bascule railroad bridge. A workman stood upon the rails on the Georgia side and quit his work to watch the canoeist, and they regarded one another across the distance—the workman as still as a stone post benchmark, assessing the man alone in the longboat bearing headlong into the floodtide: a curiosity, an envy. Verdery quit for only a moment and nodded once, and the man upon the rails seemed to return it, and Verdery rowed on for a wide, long-around bend, passing into Chatham County, Georgia.

He made McCoy's Cut, a passage that led into the Middle River, and the Little Back River. And the tide came full against him now requiring that each stroke, each pull, be deep and long and nearly flawless, that he should not lose speed, that he should not lose anything measured in feet and inches he had gained. He kneeled to the hull to make his best stroke and he bore right staying in the Savannah River proper where the channel had grown wide, where on his left the marshes began. He worked close along the right side hoping for eddies, and he measured himself against the mossed bald cypress and sea pine, and he saw that he only crawled. The tide stretched the beards of the watergrass to upriver and bent the sawgrass and the cane, and caused the stalks to shiver in the flow, and he pulled against all of it.

At each stroke his bow cut the brine, laying burls to either side of the hull—each pull labored, an opposition to an ocean and all that he could see, as far as he could see. The wind came up and blew at his back, and for this he spoke aloud, *thank you, goddam thank you.* The pure sun made his palms wet and the blade loose in his hands, but he took care not to falter. The alligators slipped from the canebrake into the river, their knotted eyes and snouts surfacing to observe the guide and his vessel, and he came alongside a wild grown one as long as his boat, the tail graceful, powerful and sublime steady coursing its ancient form just beneath the surface. When it saw the smile of the bow, it hesitated—as if considering the Ouachita, and its master, in their displacement, their toil—then slipped backward, beneath the cover of the tea colored river, its eyes vanishing last.

He made Ursla Island on his left, where the only thing seeable was the level spartina of the marsh. The wind caused it to hiss leaning this way and that, and it hissed while the wind rolled the water's top. Since the hard beach and the keelmark it had been an hour, and it was an hour more when he made the wide bend at Drakies Cut, and he saw the swingbridge for Port Wentworth.

He quit where on his left Steamboat River made Onslow Island and he tied off to a cypress bough, and the tide sent the Ouachita about, tauting the painter. He sat into the stern seat and drank water he had saved in Augusta. He turned around in his seat facing opposite, straddling the gunnels, his feet in the coming tidewater.

Halfway to the bridge a motorboat with a canopy top lolled in the mid of the channel—a type of bay boat, made for fishing; or not, if you cared not to—carrying dual powerful outboards for working the tide. The pilot had shut its engines down, and he seemed to busy himself all about it, one side then the next, bow to stern and back again. Grimacing to the sun, with his flesh and muscles hot and worn weary, Verdery watched the bay boat, bobbing and soundless, guessing at the captain's work—searching beyond that too the length of the wide wind-rolled channel, studying too the distant, low bridge, half-believing too that its pourings and bracings and all evidence that it actually stood before him might wizen to dust in any next moment, mirage undone, taking with it the first man and craft he had found since Rhind left him alone, since Jimmy—and in his doubt he drank more water.

Past the low bridge, in the summer haze, he could see now too the port-dock cranes of Garden City. There were three viewable from Drakies Cut, they cerulean blue, mimicking the sky's hue, they only trinket-sized, rested, rising, thin-armed atop the marsh plain, mantis or spider-like, yet awesome, because over such a stretch they rose above all else. In the past he had only seen them from the highway, but now they emerged, sublime, overawing, granting a low, soundless, humming fear, at men—machines and time's industry—beyond common knowledge or comprehension, beyond what the eye could salve into the heart, beyond what the heart might hold.

If the openboat comes, I will tell him everything. I will ask that he help me. If he comes to me, I will tell him truly that it is too much, and that he may help me . . . and he will tell me that he has seen him, that we will find him again. If I wait here, then it may be only an hour, or it may be two, but it may be six . . . but, no, that is not right . . . it cannot be six, because you have come to here, this far, and it has been some time. It has been an hour, or it has been more, but you do not know, because you cannot tell the time, because you did not prepare. Catharine thought of you, but not you of her. It is less than six, but you cannot wait five, or four, or one or any. If he does not come, if he does not even see you, then what . . . and you cannot wait, and there is too much in the distance . . .

take the water, then another . . . take the blade, as you have done since the beginning. When the river turns again, you may never find him, because it will be this strong the other way . . . so you must take the water, then the blade, and you must bring the bridge near to you. Do not worry that you cannot hear the noise, it will come when you bring it near, and then it will sound the same as home, as Beech Island, and the others, and you will know the sound . . .

but it is so far, and you only crawl against the ocean. Thomas Carpenter that is why you must start . . . go to your knees and begin. The water was good, and the rest was good for your back and for your arms, and now you must go to your knees, and again to this river . . . this river . . . this river you told about . . . you told them all, you told them too much and too often, but you cannot tell them this . . . this they will never know. You told too much, and you did not tell it true, and now you must go to this river again, and it is so far . . .

He watched the bay boat drive for upriver cutting the rivertop and disappear behind the marsh. He watched until he was sure it was gone and he loosed the painter and he went to his knees. Pulling long, deep strokes, he came about, setting properly the Ouachita against the floodtide. The tide slapped at his bow and broke apart in a white wash despite the tea color of its body, and he pulled steady against his weariness and against the exigent, tireless, insensate ocean that had come for him, and he measured himself against the cypress and the sea pine, chiding himself to watch the land not the water for what he truly gained.

He could not know when the man in the bay boat had seen him, he only heard it seeming to come nearer, and he saw when it passed him thumping hard at the tide, the engines laboring, cutting a fluid path of white, then slowing and coming about all at once, as if the driver were pacing it, making it work its best. He idled until the tide brought him near to Verdery and they reached for each other's craft, with Verdery holding tight to the bay boat's gunwale.

It was fitted with bench seats along the bow—comfort for taking a drink, for observing the unfortunate landbound—and a cabinet housing the pilot wheel at standing height. He shut the outboards down and only then did Verdery know what he spoke. The boatman was tanned with a full head of windworked silver hair. He wore a madras shirt, like Jimmy's at Lake Parachuchio, alike the old men at the place that was not Blue Springs, but of yet another style. Chewing something he smiled easily and broadly, with a portion of Dan Rhind's grin, already knowing secrets of Verdery and the blue longboat.

"You a man after my own heart."

Verdery tried a smile, but he was never a natural, and too the last of it was beaten out of him, and he quit and only managed grimacing at the boastful sun's gold upon the rivertop.

"You see, that's what I'm trying to get back to. I'm trying to do it today."

Verdery nodded and he looked over the boatman's vessel checking for lashing cleats at the stern, and he checked too the distance to the low bridge. It had been only a moment since they joined, but already he had lost some of what he had gained, and already they were assuming the tide's speed upriver.

"Soon as I get rid of this tub, that's what I'm going to get me. I had one years ago, and I messed up and sold it, and all this thing does is drink money. Everytime I look at it it's fifty dollars."

"Yes sir."

"Yes sir, you a man after my own heart. I need to get back to how it used to be. I used to go all over the place in that thing. Just like you, sitting right there."

"Yes sir," said Verdery nodding . . . *remember, remember, do not forget to ask, because it is so far yet.*

"Yes sir, I envy a man of freedom."

"Yes sir, sure, sure. Can you tell me where I am?"

The boatman looked upriver, searching likely the marshes—because of all things to be seen in their sameness they draw, demand, the eye—then he looked over the Ouachita and its gear, and he looked again upriver.

"Well, son," said the boatman, then hesitated, then looked to Verdery. "You know this is Port Wentworth."

"No sir, I don't."

"Well, I don't mean right here, but I mean back here at the bridge."

"Yes sir."

"That's Houlihan Bridge, and just on the other side is the Port Wentworth landing. It's a good landing. That's where I put in. I came to sell this thing today. I'm showing it here before too long. Yes sir, you a man after my own heart."

"Is that Savannah," said Verdery, nodding to the far portdock cranes.

"Oh no. You got a little ways before Savannah," said the boatman, chewing with attention, still considering Verdery's first question. "Like I said, you got Port Wentworth, then you got Garden City, then you got all the portdocks, then you got Savannah. All on the right side."

"Is it far."

"Savannah?"

"Yes sir."

"No. Not too far. I mean, it's a good ways, but not too far. You going there?"

"I don't know. Can I get there?"

"Oh sure. You stay on the left, all the way. See, on the right side you got all the industry, all the way down. On the left, starting in a little, you got the spoilage islands, you know, from where they dredge, you know, to keep the channel clear. Son, which direction you come from?"

The question ran through him—*this is where I have been*—and it ran as a fluid filament, winding and woven through, as serpentine and binding as the full stretch of the gradient watercourse he had made . . . "Well. I came, I started. I came from Augusta," he stammered, and he tried to count back, and he remembered he did not know what day it was.

The boatman quit chewing and looked at Verdery as if he had said something secretive and ludicrous, and his face grew sullen with awe, and he looked upriver to where Verdery by his testament must have come from. He looked to his wrist and with his mouth open adjusted the band of his watch over his tanned forearm, and he searched again the upriver channel where the vessel and its guide must have come from—and when he spoke next his voice had thinned, its pitch another pitch.

"Lord, son. Lord. You know where Augusta is? Well, I guess you do. How long you been at this? I mean, Lord, son."

Verdery wagged his head at the low swingbridge that yet receded from him, and he took care not to look at the boatman, because it was true and he was amazed the same and he did not know that he could endure the awe of another near person.

"A few days."

"Well, hell, I guess so. And you going to Savannah?"

"I don't know."

The boatman bowed his head and put a palm to the back of his neck, then he looked again upriver and he smiled at the interminable marshland, his eyes narrowing in the glare, full of admiration for such a place that he loved every day he was near and away from it.

"You just came through the reserve. That was Ursla Island, this next one here is Onslow. That cut takes you through to the Middle River. But you want to stay on the left of the main channel if you going to Savannah. Like I said, all your portdocks are on the right."

"Do you know when the low tide is."

"It's going to be about six or seven. You'll know it."

"Yes sir. Do you know what time it is now."

"It's about four."

"Yes sir. All I need right now is to make the landing."

The boatman looked at his watch a second time, and he twisted searching in the direction of the low bridge.

"I got to get back and sell this thing today. My people should be there by now. If I see you at the landing, I'll talk to you again. But let me go on and see about these folks. I might be late already."

"Is there a store? I need some water—I forgot more water."

"Well, you wait on me when you get there, and we'll see about that. There's a store a half mile up the road. You don't want to walk that. I can run you up there. I got these people waiting on me for sure, and this thing . . . well, I just want to be done with it today."

The boatman cranked the busty outboards and he made a tight turn, idling ahead and clear of the Ouachita, then with the power of his engines he lay the floodtide white to either side of his hull.

Now again to Verdery's left was the second cut he had made when the sun was not in his eyes. He watched the bay boat bouncing in the glare, cutting the tea water, laying it aside in a line of thin blanched foam, and he went to his knees and he pulled a long, deep stroke—one, then another, then another. In fifty strokes the boatman made the low Houlihan Bridge and passed beneath it, idling again, into the Port Wentworth landing.

This swingbridge still worked when needed and it was low overhead when closed. The openboat had passed him wide again in the channel, headed up-river for the marshland, and he had seen it carrying three instead of one. He did not ease, fearing losing the feet and inches he had gained—only allowing himself to read the pier postings for the horn soundings.

He eased into the ramp eddy and in the same moment of recognition—when his muscles knew that he could quit for awhile, when all his body remembered how it was to quit—he remembered too that he should have been looking for Rhind and the small boat. In that same sensate, undivided moment, he saw he was not there—not at either ramp, upon the fishing dock, not in the grass or the lot, and the realization washed him, soaking deep into his chest and stomach. And knowing and sore aching he quit rowing and let the Ouachita with a gentle whisper slide into the tall fescue grass of Port Wentworth Landing, in Chatham County, Georgia. From the interstate bridge at the tide pond he had struggled for half a day and in that time he had made six miles.

CHAPTER TWENTY-EIGHT

A man could not walk that fast . . . it is as fast as a man can run, and it will not quit . . .

of course he is not here. The man in the powerboat would have said so . . . he would have said something, if he were here . . . he went with the good tide, and I did not, and of course he is not here . . .

Verdery looked to the sky, over his right shoulder to find the sun, to guess at the time of day.

He had said four, and that was awhile ago. An hour and more, remember you went backward. He had said six or seven, but this will never quit . . . I will need water . . . everything else I have. But I will need water . . . when I find him, he will need water too . . .

A county sheriff's car came from the swingbridge road into the landing lot. The deputy let the engine run after he parked. His passenger was a uniformed woman and they spoke to each other with their heads down, for a half hour, nodding their only gestures. The deputy looked only once to the dock, and from his car he would not see the boat ramp's bottom, and when he did see Verdery his thinking was elsewhere—not even too on the woman who spoke to him, but on another altogether. When the deputy had given her the half hour he promised, and he could raise his head again, he drove them out of the lot the way they had come, he yet behaving as if listening, nodding, his mind no less on the other woman.

I will have to call. I will have to call again, soon . . . it is only fair . . .

He counted back by half days, and he tried once, and again, and the third time the pieces of memory did not fall apart.

It is only Tuesday night tonight. I have spent only one night alone. And that was the night of the day when I met Jimmy, and did not think of the water to drink . . . but that cannot be right . . . that was only yesterday—but it is right. It was so long ago, and far upriver, but it was only yesterday, and today is Tuesday night. Savannah is near. I will take the six-hour tide into Savannah, and I will walk up on Bay Street, and when I do not find him, I will call again. It is only fair, and then too, it will be the end. What will you say. You do not know, but it will be the end . . .

The bay boat came beneath the bridge, thumping and cutting the river, then idling down and easing to the out-ramp. Verdery helped the three of them ashore and he helped the boatman hitch his vessel to the pull trailer. He waited while the tanned boatman smiled and shook their hands and wished them a good evening, and hoped they would enjoy the thing as much as he had; but he, *just wanted something simple, now.*

They stood alongside one another, Verdery searching the tide, doubting that it might quit before dark, the boatman admiring the seventeen-and-a-half-foot Ouachita—its bow-to-stern lines seated in the water, and how it moved with only the strength of a man to encourage it.

"Yes sir, after my own heart. I sure hope they take that thing from me."

"They seem . . . they seem . . ."

"Sure. Just married and all that."

"Sure, sure."

"Son, I got to thinking about that out there, and I wanted to make a point of telling you so. I could've took a minute. You get where you don't think so much about it when you got horses behind you."

"That's alright. I made it alright."

"Ain't it something, though. Ain't it something," said the boatman, to the marsh across. "Every day, it's some-kind-of-thing to look at."

"I never knew."

"It is . . . What you need up at the store?"

"I need water. And maybe more ice. But water."

"Well, I'll run and get that for you. You might want to stay here with your boat, and your gear. I don't know, but you might want to stay here."

"Sure. Is there a place to stay tonight?"

"How do you mean. To camp?"

"Yes sir. Is there a place?"

"Well, you can try here in the grass, but they'll just come and worry you about moving on."

"No, is there a place toward Savannah."

"Well. Well, you got your spoilage islands all along the left here. That's where they dredge the channel, you know, like I was saying. That's all bluff. You can probably get you a place along one of those bluffs."

"On the left," said Verdery, groping the far tide, the low grass, to where he spoke of, seeing none of it.

"Sure, you want to stay to the left."

"Am I a fool to want to go that way?"

"How do you mean."

"I mean the traffic. Am I a fool in this thing?"

"I tell you this, you don't want to be in the backwater or a slue when one of the cargo ships come along. It's best to be out in the open. Sometimes there ain't much to them, but sometimes I've seen them take all the water out of a cove. They've done that to me—left my whole boat on the dry land."

"They're big ships."

"They are."

"Will there be much traffic tomorrow?"

"It's hard to say."

"And I'm not a fool."

"If you stay to the left, you'll be alright. You ought to be. You know small vessels have the right-of-way."

"Does that matter?"

"No sir, it don't. It don't."

"Is there a place to put out in Savannah?"

"Well, you got your public docks. But you have to cross over to the right."

"Where do you cross?"

"Look for the suspension bridge. Rope-stay, you know, to say it proper. Just below, that's downtown. River Street, and all that. Cross at the big bridge, and look for the public docks. Listen, let me run get you that water. I owe that much to you. Now, what else?"

Verdery wagged his head and he gave the boatman money and the boatman went for his truck, and he stopped with the door open and came again to Verdery.

"You know what. There is an island. It's called Way. That's what I know to call it—Way Island. It's right down on the left. It was a spoilage island, but it's all grown up now, you know. Tall trees and all that. Sea pines and scrub oak, up on a bluff."

"Where is it?"

"Let me run get this, and I'll show you when I get back. You need something besides the water?"

"No, I don't think so. Just that."

"You said ice."

"No, I don't think so. Just the water, a couple gallons. I forgot more water."

"Alright then, just the water.

From across the bridge highway came two young black boys running for the dock with their fishing gear wiggling as they ran, and giggling both of them, like boys playing. Each had a cane pole, one a tub of nightcrawlers. They were thin boys, lean like boys who play all their food out of them, and they argued concerning technique, both impatient with their lines and corks. The smaller one, after he tried the fish and did no good, let his canepole alone, and he went to the grass with Verdery and he sat with him.

"Junior, you better watch this thing," called his older brother.

"It ain't bothering you," said the smaller one, then to Verdery, "that your boat?"

"Yes. That's my boat."

"What kind is it?"

"It's a canoe. An Ouachita."

"A who?"

"An Ouachita, from Texarkana, Arkansas."

"Whoa. You from around here?"

"No. I came from . . . another place . . . up the river."

"Where you going in your watchitall?"

"I'm going down there, looking for my friend."

"Is your friend in a watchitall, like that one?"

"No, he's . . . yeah. He's in one like that one."

"You going to find him?"

"I hope so."

The older boy still concerned with the fish called, "Jordan, leave that man alone. That man ain't worried about you," and Jordan looked to Verdery and waited for him.

"Jordan's alright. He ain't worrying me none," said Verdery, loud enough that it was friendly, and the older brother shrugged his shoulders, "alright then," he said, and his attention went again to deceive the fish.

"You the watchitall man?" said Jordan, now sitting cross-legged the same as Verdery, facing the same direction and watching his brother fish in the slowing tide the same as Verdery.

"I don't know. Seems like somebody told me, a long time ago, I was the Ghostman."

"Ghostman?"

"Yeah, Ghostman."

"You don't look like no ghostman to me."

"You ever seen a ghost, Jordan?"

"No, I never seen a ghost. I'd be too scared to see a ghost. I wouldna know what to do, if I ever saw a ghost. But I don't bleeve you the ghostman. I bleeve you the watchitall man."

"Alright," said Verdery, and the taller brother slung nightcrawlers to the river, and the younger brother looked where Verdery looked, and Verdery searched the tide and he did not yet let himself believe it slowed.

"My brother ain't a good fishingman, like me," said Jordan, the way a grown man renders sometimes a political opinion, when asked or not.

"You're a good fisherman?"

"Shore I am," said Jordan, the way his father said *shore*, at home—his father who worked in heavy boots the Garden City portdocks, and who came home sometimes smelling of fuel oil, and sometimes creosote—and said *whew, lord* and *shore*, and called both his boys, *hoss.*

"You a good brother?"

"Shore, when he is."

"It's important to be a good brother."

"I know," said the boy, and all in one weightless motion he got to his feet and went to his cane pole and his brother Joseph, so named for his father's brother, Joe. And together they took a medium-small yellow perch from the line, and they strung it and lowered the stringer into the river and fished again.

Verdery now yet did not tell himself that it was true, and he waited to see that the boatman said it right, and that in its slowing the tea clouded river did not lie to him.

When he comes again, I should ask . . . I know the others, but I do not know his name . . . I should ask . . .

He lay back into the grass listening to the boys fish, hearing too the clap and sigh of traffic upon the Houlihan Bridge, and oppositely the drone of Port Wentworth's industry, and beyond that Garden City. And he imagined too cluttered amidst all of it a bustle song of Savannah itself. The chorale obscured, folding into tints and stirrings, blending into the half-void of sleep's thinnest cover.

I did not eat, but I must not. I must save the water for him, because it has been days and nights, and we are alone. I have remembered the day, and what night it will be, and I will remember again, but we should not be alone—he should not, but I do not know how to cure it. When she died alone, it should not have been so, but I could not cure the dust, and I could not cure the fire, and I could not cure the aloneness. Ginny should not be alone, that is too much, and I have saddened Catharine, and I should not have. Listen to it in the air . . . you know the sound of it, and you know the dryness will come, and then the air will become, sad . . . each sound is a distant one, and nothing is near to you, and in the dry air they will all be alone . . .

you must remember all of it, because forgetting is the weakness—each day, each time of day, each, one after the other. Remember the last words with Ginny, and where, and when . . . Catharine, and what her eyes seemed to see when you left her . . . and remember flawlessly, how small she was last upon the bed, alone, and the odor of the dust, how old it all is . . . how old . . .

you must save the water, and the water will carry you, and you must save his sup-
per, because forgetting is the weakness. And the air will become dry as the dust, and
they will be left alone, every one of them . . . and the sadness will choke you, because
you cannot repair any of it, because the distance is too great . . .

do not behave foolish in the sadness . . . do not be ridiculous . . . you are too old,
and grown beyond the fascination, and there are many, many greater sadnesses. So
do not behave foolish, because you chose all of it . . . you chose the leaving and you left
them behind, because you chose, and there are many greater sadnesses, so do not behave
ridiculous . . .

do you know why you left? Do you remember why you allowed it—do you remem-
ber why you caused so many years distance? The driving and the distance and the
aloneness? Each time the aloneness was not only with you . . . you see this now, you see
how it is the same. You left them alone, but do not be foolish, because there are so many
greater sadnesses . . . remember his, and the water and the dinner, because the sadness
he carries is greater. He is alone and his father is alone, and it is endless, because you
touched it, and you did not tie it . . . son . . . son . . .

"Son," and Verdery sat up all at once.

"We did good on your water," said the boatman, raising both arms holding
to a gallon jug with each fist. "I about run over those younguns, but we saved
the water."

At the dock the boys were gone, and then he saw it, and only then chose
to believe that he actually witnessed the watergrass and loose stacks of sea
rye, stilled. But too, more than that, it had not only quit but it had started
back—nearly indiscernibly, one inch and another, it moved the seafoam and
oat debris oppositely, toward Savannah, and the ocean.

"I went on and got some ice. Hell, if you don't need it I can take it to the
house. But hell, if you do, then you got it. But anyhow, we did good on the
water."

"It's going out."

"What is it?"

"It's going out—the other way."

"Oh, sure. It's six-thirty. That's your ebbtide."

"Ebbtide."

"Sure. That's what you been looking for. It's like that song."

"Song."

"Sure, the Mercer song. I always liked that song. Makes me think of it
everytime I see the river running back out."

Holding to the water the boatman sang the notes of the first verse, and he
quit, and for a moment he seemed to adjudicate his abilities, then he shrugged

and he gave the two gallon jugs to Verdery. "Well that's how I remember it anyways. But I sure do think of that song. Was it Johnny Mercer, or another fellow?"

"It's a good song," and Verdery did not know if it was Mercer or not.

"Well anyways, I already set your ice in your boat."

"Let me give you some more for that."

"Oh hell no. It was just a little old dollar or two. It's not worrying me. What you need to do to camp . . ." and he explained how to find the spoilage island called Way. He told there would be a short bluff to make, and no one should trouble him, but he might stay out of the river channel's sightline to be sure. Last he told that Verdery should take care to be inside before dark—of this he must pay attention . . . *when it gets dark, and there's no wind, it's all the worse.* "Yes sir," he said when they stood together again near the Ouachita, "you after my own heart. You got the right idea . . ."

" . . . Why don't I take you in my old boat, and show you just where I'm talking about. I can make it up for leaving you out there fighting that river alone. Let me do that for you."

"No sir. You're all put away, and it's going my direction now, but thank you," and Verdery offered again money for the ice, and again the boatman refused, not even looking at the bills.

They nodded a last time to one another and Verdery watched the boatman go to his truck and drive, hauling the bay boat, and he waited until the boatman made the bridge road and disappeared past the cabbage palms. He waited a moment longer then waded the Ouachita bow out to the river and sat to the stern seat and started again. With measured, easy strokes he coursed into the ebbtide. He had made a quarter mile when it occurred to him that neither had asked the other's name, and he turned in the seat, looking back to the low swingbridge. There was only the low structure stretching across the smooth channel, going small in the distance, and he turned again to downriver.

CHAPTER TWENTY-NINE

At the Port Wentworth turning basin he worried at the rich color of the late day sky.

Do not behave ridiculous . . . they are blameless . . . behave like a grown man and you will remember this . . .

To his right the terminal came into sight. The portdock cranes were stilled this time of day, asleep and powderblue, but the stacks behind worked brooding ceaseless letting go their heavy smoke steam into the roseamber sky. Vessels were docked for the night and along the stretch of channel he saw nothing coming for him, and he looked again to the rich sky and in a sudden moment as quick as a cough the volume of another doubt rushed to fill his chest.

Thomas, you should have stayed . . . there was a grassy spot. They might have come for you, but then it would have been done. And too, you don't know if they are looking, and too, the girl is home by now, and Jesup has forgotten all of it. They are all so old, except for her, and none of it has been written yet for her, because she is not the same as them . . .

yes, you should have stayed . . . you do not want to work against the tide again, but there was flat ground, and he should have told you so . . .

you do not know what they know: Jesup, Caron Lee, the law. How will you call when you do not find him? You cannot now . . . it has been too long, and it has been too much, and you cannot make this last stretch. It can only be six miles, and that is an hour, but how can you make it?

there has been too much to turn back, and there are so many to see you, and they will say that you are ridiculous, and they will turn you back. You are a flyspeck against all of the inventions, and they are too great—and it has been so long ago when you saw him last, that you cannot hope to see him again . . . and you must call her to tell her so, and how will you do this . . .

He let the Ouachita pivot about and he felt the air cool for the first time since that morning. He stroked against the ebbtide twice, and he quit and lay the oar across his lap. He leaned with his elbows to his knees and wagged his head at himself.

There it is. It is already gone. You have just been there, and already it is lost to you. The light is lost and there is no good land . . .you should not have come . . . it was so very easy to see . . .

you do not know this place. This is their home, and you have never known them . . . they know how the river goes, and they know how their machines work, because they made them, and for you it is too much . . .

in Nepaug they knew their home, and they only suffered you. In all the diverse places, they only ever suffered you, and you should have known that he did not want to be found. They let you go, and you let them alone, and it will never be otherwise, and that is the proof that you have no home . . . that is the proof . . .

When he came about he saw where the marsh began, and a cut-through, and on the other side of the backwater he viewed the white sand of a bluff and stands of scrub that grew upon the plateau. He stroked again, gently disbelieving, making the still water of the cut, checking the sun and reckoning how many half hours of the day remained. The marsh grass grew higher than he could see standing and he searched the island's bluff through clearings, not yet ready to let go his doubt. The cut was full of turtle and they flopped to underwater again to clear his way as he slid soundless above them, and he could not help but admire their size and numbers. Half around the spoilage island the marsh closed and he turned and went the way he had come. He viewed a stand of seapine but saw no good path, and he went on again toward the mouth of the slough and there to the left he found a passage through the marsh—an entree to the white bluff—it luminous, the sand the color of bleached bones and the late roseamber cast. The narrow passage rounded gently then opened to a small pond, where he eased across the still water. The Ouachita's keel scraped short, stopping at a five-foot beach where the bluff began. He put away his oar. He had landed close enough to lay his palm upon the Katahdin's gunnel—knowing the caned seats he and the Cherokee had reworked—and as he bent forward with his elbows to his knees he only coughed then cursed at himself for disbelieving, for believing anything at all.

It was empty—the same as when they found it straining against the dike with the river running through it—save three things, the oar Rhind had taken, Dan Rhind's ruined hat resting upon the stern seat where his son had laid it, and a single pair of smallish canvas shoes beneath the bow seat.

The ebbtide had left its first watermark upon the beach and upon the small boat's hull, and Verdery tugged each craft to the beach so that the bows touched the bluff. He took both oars, only half-knowing why, and he went atop. The bluff rose standing height with a rain cut for climbing and from it he could see the river again, and on the far side he saw too the papermill sending its steam gauze into the late roseamber sky, and the ball of the sun three-quarters down the length of its stack. Nearer to the south, behind the island's treeline of hog apple and seapine another stack rose, this one higher, the exhaust of a powerplant so looming Verdery could not tell if it was on his side of the river or not.

The footprints were alike those at the interstate bridge, two pair, one much larger, as the pair of a father and child, and Verdery could not remember if he should know Rhind's foottrack . . .

His will be larger than mine . . . He guessed at the half hours of daylight remaining and he searched the channel and there were no boats, then he let it alone and walked for the scrub oak. He came to an imperfect circle of young liveoak and he entered and that is where he found him, sitting in the scuffed, blanched sand with his back to a scrub tree.

"You alright?"

When she heard him she sat up all at once as if wakened by a gunshot or the poor finish of a poorly invented dream.

"We're alright," said Rhind.

CHAPTER THIRTY

At Ebenezer he landed the small boat fast, and she did not step to one side or the other and she did not turn away. He drank the finish of the gin from the clear bottle, knowing he had a good last one in it, and he had all of it but the last one.

"There's people looking for you," he said, thinking too, *she's wearing the same clothes as the night he fixed us supper* . . .

"I know it. I mean, I guess so."

"You don't mind worrying them?"

"I'm not going back. I can't help it if he's worried."

Rhind stood from the small boat and he went near the worn picnic table, thinking again—the same as when he saw her from the channel, as when he first knew it was her—*it will steer better with her in the front* . . . and he urinated to the far side of the bald cypress. *I ain't got a dollar, Bill,* he said aloud as he finished, then holding by the handle the clear jug and backbending he slugged the last of his gin. At a well spigot nearby the trailer he knelt and filled the bottle and capped it and he went again to her and Verdery's boat.

"I'm going that way."

"I know it."

"You coming."

"Yes."

"This is all we got," and he gave the water jug to her. "Come on then."

They slowed in the gunmetal blue squall only once on the way, at a strainer to retrieve his father's battered hat and the woolen blanket Verdery wrapped him in. Rhind put on the soaked hat and he had Caron Lee lay the blanket across the thwart for drying. Near dark they made the tide pond at the interstate bridge, and Rhind put them fast to the hard beach. She turned to the rear facing him and they sat upon Verdery's and the Cherokee's caned seats watching the tidewater and the sky fall to night, and it was a minute longer before she told him she knew.

"What do you know, Caron?"

"I don't mean to say the wrong thing. It's what she told me."

"What did she tell you."

"About your father. About how . . . I'm sorry. I don't want to say it wrong."

"He's gone now. She was right. She told us right."

"I'm sorry for him . . . for you."

"I could've made her tell it different. But you know Caron, I didn't. I didn't do it, and now he's gone, like she said."

"Did your friend go home . . . he said he wasn't."

"What? No . . . no, I don't know. I don't know . . . he's . . ."

"I can go with you all the way. I mean I can . . . if . . ."

"All the way?"

"To where you're going. I know what to do. I'm not going back."

"He's worried about you, your Grandfather. By now he's called the law."

"No he didn't. He can't."

"He can't."

"He can't. When he gets close to me I can smell him, what he's been drinking, and I know he won't call the law, because he doesn't do right. He'll lose me if he calls the law. And I won't go back."

"Alright, Caron."

"Did he go home?"

"No. I don't think he went . . . I don't know."

"Are you going where he said?"

"Where did he say?"

"Savannah."

"I don't know. Savannah, sure. Let's go to Savannah."

"And then you're going home."

"Home?"

"Then can I have your boat?"

Rhind laughed a hard, fast laugh at her, and it seemed to him odd that he should laugh, and in the empty dusk air bouncing off the high bridge it sounded like an odd thing to have done. "It's his boat."

On the hard beach she sat close to him. She drew her knees up, and she saw that he did not try much against the mosquitoes.

"Did she bring you to the boat ramp?"

"It's called Ebnezer."

"Ebenezer."

"Ebnezer. No. A man brought me there."

"Did you know him?"

"He didn't want anything. When he let me out, I went one way, then came back the other way."

"When I left, I didn't see my girl. Her name is Annie."

"I told her she might not be right. I told her to quit telling me those things, because I knew you and your friend before she did."

"She liked to stay with me downstairs. It didn't matter to her. When she sleeps sometimes she tries to talk, and I don't know if her dreams are good ones. I wanted them to be good ones."

"I said she wasn't right about everything."

"What did she say, Caron."

"She said everything, and I told her to quit, because I knew you first, and I knew she wasn't right. I said we could tell our own stories . . . about how they end up, about what happens to them, to us."

"And she laughed, and said that's only something people believe, and believing don't change what's fixing to come."

"I don't know . . . she said everything, and I left when she went down to the water with her gun. It was morning by then . . . and she already took her medicine."

"Caron, if you say enough things, often enough, then you're bound to be right about some of it. And she was."

"I know it, but we can change what's going to happen . . . your friend said so, and I know he was right."

"She said I was going home?"

"I don't know. I left. . ."

"And she probably called the law."

"Not unless she walked to find them."

Rhind laughed hard again and the air was yet empty and darker. The tires above clapped purposefully, with intent traveling, and the beams from the headlamps searched far above opening the dark, dissolving in their reach into the failing twilight. Caron Lee leaned to Rhind, her shoulder touching at his upper arm.

"I don't have anything—I didn't bring anything," and he thought too, *if I had something left to drink, I would drink it now . . . and I would drink until I slept . . .*

"That's alright. I can go with you tomorrow too, I know what to do."

"If I had let him go, if I were different, he would be home now."

When she slept, he lifted her from the beach and he lay her into the small boat, beneath the center thwart, and he patted her head telling her the bowseat was right near. He shook the woolen blanket and he lay it across her, and he sat again to the hard beach, and he waited for the light to come again. He slept at the first gray of the morning, and when he wakened upon his side, she was again with him, spooned at his back, and the blanket over both of them.

In the morning gauze the river ran toward Savannah, but it was only remarkable to him that the odor of it had changed from brine, and the color too. When she wakened he knelt to her and he brushed the hair and the sand from her face, and he cleaned his thumbs and took the sleep from her eyes.

"I didn't bring anything. Let's go to Savannah today."

"I can go. I know what to do."

At the short bluff of the spoilage island they put out to rest, and he waited sitting cross-legged in the bone sand of the glade for her to come from the scrub oak, and gripping the neck of the empty water jug he slept before he knew he slept. When she wakened him—speaking while she slept too, lying close to him—he brushed at her hair once, at the black ants, and he went to the bluff and he saw that the river now ran backward. *We are very close now, and when it turns next, we will take it the rest of the way, and it will be the finish of it . . .*

He slipped his wedding band from his third finger and in his fist he raised it to the marsh, and in the next moment he balked, and went again to her.

"I can go back, to the landing we passed, and I can go to the store. Find a store."

"I don't want to go—"

"You can stay here, and I'll come back when—"

"You won't come back."

"I will."

"No . . . if I go, they'll . . ."

"Alright, Caron. That's alright."

"When can we go to Savannah?"

"When the tide changes, we can go. We slept, and now the tide has to change again."

In the circle of the liveoak upon the drying, blanched sand, they slept. They slept deeply, and the curiosity of the black ants did not keep them from it. He wakened with her close to him and it seemed to him that much of the day had passed. With a dream still heavy with her she turned to him and she kissed him, as she imagined a grown woman should do, and he did not turn away as a grown man should.

CHAPTER THIRTY-ONE

"You alright?"

"We're alright."

When Verdery knew what he had found, knowing it true, he stopped, still holding the oars, and they regarded each other, with as little surprise as if one or the other had just come in from the porch. Rhind's face and arms and legs had welted from the mosquitoes, and Verdery looked down himself and again at Rhind, thinking too, *remember, you are as ragged as he*—and Rhind's greatest movement was blinking his eyes.

She slept an arm's length away, on her side with her knees drawn up for balance and with her palms together, beneath her head as a pillow. She slept right upon the white sand and the nutgrass, and Verdery allowed a guess that it was her, though truly in this first moment of half-disbelieving he already knew. He knew the woolen blanket that covered her, and that Rhind reclaimed it nearby where he found his father's hat, thinking too, *you did not tie that well, either*.

She sat upright in the scuffed sand, brushing the grains and the black ants from her, and last of all the things he understood in a heartbeat gone, that since he sat with her in the mooncast and sedge on the slope behind Covington's cabin, she had aged beyond her fourteen and fifteen years. She had welted the same and upon her once flawless complexion it was more, not simply exposure, but something more.

"You alright?"

He moved for the first time slowly closing his eyes and seeming to nod, bowing his head away from the tree and back again. "I bet you needed those today," said Rhind of the oars.

"I did. I didn't know I'd find you."

"We're alright," said Rhind, his voice coarse and unsure, as if he were just then remembering how to speak to another grown man.

Verdery looked away from her, and she from him, and while he stood there she did not raise her eyes to him again.

"I didn't call home," said Verdery, just then remembering that he had tried with Jimmy at the store, but there was no one, and it was the truth he told.

"Alright."

Without going nearer Verdery squatted like a storyteller, gripping the oars one in each fist, balancing himself to the sand. There impressioned amidst the scuffing was the track of a small animal, and there too was the track of his foot, and her foot, half-sized, and he waited for Rhind, though not expecting it, and Rhind did not speak. Verdery smelled the odor of himself, that his bath that midday could have been a better one, but that too was only a spit of a moment given to fugitive thought, and that too spirited from him. When his legs ached, he stood again, half-bent with stiffness, and he turned from them, searching through the oaks' cover to what he could see of the day's surviving light.

"You want some supper?"

"Yes. Her too."

"Alright," and he went out of the clearing to begin unloading the boat and hauling the gear up the bluff, back and again.

Silent torpid and practiced, Rhind joined, then she came helping too. Verdery had them set the tent into the clearing where the scrubtrees obscured it from view, and at the stove he warmed stew, and they ate stew and crackers and they drank beer and water. And each alongside the other they silently watched the earth's dust tarnish to copper the ball of the sun. They watched it decline, last hued bruised on the underside, then full round as a plum or sore flesh, into the gauze of the mill's steam. When it had gone and there survived only the persistent failing lilac, Verdery understood the boatseller's warning.

He knew mosquitoes like anyone knew mosquitoes. The night before they had worried him, the way they do. But now it was not the same.

Slapping and cursing, they as thick as an animate dust, he hauled first the Katahdin then the Ouachita full high on the bluff. He tugged one then the other across the nutgrass and sand, and across a fallen hogapple tree behind the shelter. Twice he told Caron Lee, saying her name, that he could do it alone and to keep the tent closed. He left the stove and all the gear in place and he put only the beer and the water inside and he closed the tent door fast against the dust and whine and insensate blood thirst of the mosquitoes.

He made a noise and cursed to himself and he went out of the shelter again, then returned with a package cursing a last time, zippering the door, succinctly with finality, shutting out the hell and the bearing of the swarm. He handed a sweetroll to Caron Lee and tossed another one to Rhind, saying, *here*, and breathing hard he sat heavy and lay back.

"What you got here?"

"It's something I found at the store. A fellow took me to the store, and I got some things, and I got that."

"Where did you go to a store?"

"Back at that lake."

"What was the name of that place?"

"I don't know. I don't remember."

"I thought you said it, the name of it, way back."

"I don't know. I don't know what the name was."

"Was there a phone at this store?"

"No."

"That's unusual, isn't it."

"Unusual? Yeah, Will, I suppose that was unusual. Caron Lee, have that if you want."

"Alright," said Rhind, and he took the cake and he lay it to the corner of the tent, and soon he had forgotten it.

When the night had come full, Verdery went out a last time to gather the bedrolls, and this time he did not curse. He wakened Caron Lee for only a moment and he lay his bed under her, and let her sleep again, and she slept between them the same as when he had found her that late afternoon—upon her side, using her hands as a pillow, with what survived of the woolen blanket, of Dan Rhind's pall, covering her. He put the second bedroll aside, and they let it alone.

The engines of the powerplant worked through the night—choking stop, coughing start—assiduously trading off rumbles and moans. And in the gripe and groan of tireless industry, each time an engine fired to replace another, Caron Lee turned and whined and through her thin, poor, half-dreams, spoke aloud in her sleep.

Verdery imagined Rhind already slept too, but he spoke all the same into the shelter's warm air. "Where did you find her?"

"Where?"

"Yes, where."

"I don't know where. It was a boat ramp. Big clear place. There was a trailer. But she was the only one there."

It was Ebenezer, thought Verdery, but he did not say it aloud.

"Why did you take her?"

"What?"

"Why did you bring her with you."

"Because she wanted to."

"They're looking for her. You know that."

"Do you know that? They can find her if they want to. She's right here. She was right there, and nobody was looking for her there."

It was Ebenezer, thought Verdery again, *and Bill's back is his trouble . . .* "Where did you stay last night?"

198

"I don't know. Under the bridge. It must be Ninety-five."

"I thought so too. I thought it was Ninety-five, but I couldn't remember right. He talked about it a couple times . . ." and Verdery quit when he knew what he said, because he was dumb weary, and careless, and he feared allowing all of it again.

An engine shunted awake and Caron Lee turned and moaned into the unquiet, and when she had settled Verdery spoke upward, again into the warm captured air. "It must have been late."

"When."

"When you hit the tide."

"It was dark."

"How did you know."

"Know what?"

"About the tide."

"I didn't know. Until I saw it."

"I saw it too. Did you sleep in the boat?"

"Last night?"

"Yes. Where did you sleep?"

"We just pulled up there and that was where we stayed."

"Was she alright, Will . . . is she alright?"

"I don't know, Thom. I imagine she's alright. She seems alright."

"Is she the same as she was before."

"Before. How was she before?"

"I don't know . . . tomorrow, where do you want to call from?"

"Call."

"Yes. I said I haven't." For a dozen breaths Verdery let the warm air go silent, and the want for sleep came upon him, and he was no good for thinking in order. "The tide should be out in the morning. It should be out to Savannah in the morning. We have to get it then."

"Alright."

Late the night cooled the air and they slept heavy and unmoving, and their wearied bodies gave and eased against the spoilage island's borrowed earth, and they knew little of the powerplant's rumble and whirr, less of Caron Lee's thin, fitful calling.

Six miles upriver of the Savannah, Georgia, public docks, upon a refuge built of alluvium, bottom sand and sediment, they slumbered as irrelative as differing species, as displaced as the very dredgings to which their worn, ragged shapes clung.

The tide ebbed until past midnight, and slowly it ceased to a standoff—a moment's fluid balance—then, beckoned by the sphere of the moon, guided by an incessant will not its own, it turned again for six hours to flood.

CHAPTER THIRTY-TWO

In the firstlight Verdery made coffee.

In the night he wakened once to hear when Rhind went out to finish the beer. Verdery went out too and pissing he asked, "you going off alone again."

"We'll go in the morning like we said."

"You can go either way with the tide."

"No, we'll go the one way."

When he wakened next she was half off the bedroll spooned at Rhind's back, and now he doled the grounds into his percolator brushing away the black ants.

It was six-thirty. He said that. You forgot to ask his name but he said six-thirty. That means it did not turn again until after midnight, probably one . . . that means it did not turn again until just now, and it will go out to Savannah until one or two. You have six hours, because there are four a day. Have you seen the twenty-mile marker to know it is only six miles more? You missed it or there was not one, or you have not made it yet . . . then you are no closer than six miles. Six miles used to be an hour's worth, but that has changed. If you had asked him he might have known to tell you, but he is asleep with his wife, and he cannot help you . . .

Verdery counted back by tens. He groped to recollect where each marker had been and where each boat had been in relation to the other as they passed each marker—whether near or far from one another. He counted back to two hundred where he knelt at the benchmark at home with Rhind standing above him and the late summer sun warming both their backs. Now at the marsh eddy the narrow beach was striped with the first watermark—an increment incalculable to him, distances gone—and squatting, sipping coffee, sore-stinking ragged, already he had grown weary of the day to come.

Atop the bluff, at his back, she sat with her knees drawn up and she stood when he stood, and she looked down into the sand and ants when he turned to climb.

He gave her coffee from the pot and he took the last of it, and he made more. He found the percolator one summer, put away in the house where his mother survived alone, and he had taken it and washed it and cooked in it right away. When he was a child they used it for camping in the north Georgia hills, and each time he watched its glass bubble turn brown he remembered his mother's and father's laugh, and how they loved to sing and to cook a kettle of fish stew outdoors high to a mountainside, and there was nothing that was not good about the color of the percolator's coffee and remembering the onions of the stew in cool mountain air.

She sat cross-legged in the nutgrass and sand and she held the cup with one small hand and the other rolled into a fist in her lap, and between sips she looked only at the steam and the dark body. Her hair fell to her face and she did not try to put it back, and she searched the coffee, as if in its hue and fluidity and sharp rising fragrance she might find a story shown dissimilar to her own—something of promise, a refraction of things done and undone—and that it might be enough.

She is the same girl, thought Verdery, then in the next pulse, *no, she is not . . .* "They're looking for you . . ." *her hair is a different color now. It is the color of umber I have used painting shadows . . . I should be their teacher, not . . .* "we saw your grandfather and your brother, and they were looking for you. We sent them back and told them they would find you."

She was barefooted and she wore the same denim shorts and a loose blouse and that was all, and all she had to wear, save the canvas shoes in the small boat.

"Did you stay with that woman named Alice?"

She nodded with her shoulders drawn up, as if expecting him to scold her, and in the rebuke he would tell things done wrong and how to right them, or not.

"We know her too, but that don't matter now. I know your mama's worried about you. She has to be. And your school's started too, hasn't it?" He thought to count back to remember what day it had become, but he could not recollect the twenty-mile marker, and he quit. "We need to eat before we go. You think?"

She shrugged then nodded, then without brushing the hair from her face looked to him.

"More coffee too, yes?"

"Yes," she said, only whispering, and he nodded, and for the moment his weariness eased from him.

He poured, listening for Rhind in the tent, and he sat again with her, cross-legged, as she. "Caron Lee, I might have been wrong. What I said before, it might not have been right. The truth."

"The truth?"

"When we talked before, I might have told you wrong."

"Alright," and she combed a hand through her hair and it fell again the same, and Verdery saw that she wore a ring on her finger, and he thought too, *she wore it last night, and you saw it then* . . .

"Caron Lee, the other night, the night before last, were you alright? Was he good, nice, to you?"

"What?"

"Were you alright, did he do right. Are you alright this morning?"

"I'm okay. I'm alright. He did right."

"Good. Good. Caron Lee, you need to call your grandfather. He is worried about you. Then you need to go back and make everything better. You can do that."

"I don't like it there. I don't like the way it is there. There's nothing. I don't like the way he is. He's not like you and Mr. Rine."

"Caron."

"I don't like it. My mother didn't come. She's staying away. Where she is. She sent a card with a picture on it for me and Jase. She wrote big, like when she doesn't want to say much. Jesup made me read it to him, then he said you have to expect something or another like that. Then he said we was his now, and he had to figure out who was needing to sleep where from now on. I should've read it wrong. If I was thinking right, I would've read it wrong to him. Before I left I told Jase I was sorry I didn't read it wrong to him."

Verdery waited for her, to say it again, and the second time tell it different.

"I like him—the way he is."

"Him."

"Mr. Rine. He's not like the people I know."

"But you don't know him. We are from a different place."

"I know it . . . that's why."

"Caron, we had trouble. From the time we left you we had trouble. When we get to Savannah, we need to settle these things—Mr. Rhind does too. He's got people worried about him too, and he needs to call and settle with them. And there is something else that I don't know if we can ever fix. I just don't know. And you, you have to do that too. It's different whether we found you or you found us. Do you see that?"

"I found him, and you weren't there."

"I see that, but it makes a difference when we get to Savannah."

"He told me."

"What."

"He told me what happened to you, and why there's only two of you now, and why he has the hat."

"What did he tell you."

"He said his daddy was gone, and you lost him."

"He said that."

"And he told me about his wife and his baby."

"What did he tell you."

"But I don't care. And he knows I don't care, and he said it too. He said he could make it right by giving me this. He said everything from the start would be alright if I took it."

He had seen it the night before, the yellow band ridiculously oversized for her, and she had to hold her fist balled to keep it on.

In that cleaved, lengthless moment, as sudden and passing irretrievable as a single failing pulse, when there abided no good air for a breath, he did not yet tell himself—the way men do not, regarding some truths—that it was the same Emylia Gray had given to her husband ten years before. In the next moment, their hearts, separate of purpose, concomitant in the need, beat again.

You saw it yesterday, when she stood from the sand and dust, and you knew it then, and you probably knew it before that—but that is not true . . . you knew it then, and maybe you knew it last night when the light had gone, and you knew it this morning . . . that day ten years past was a flawless late September day, with the air dry and the sky so pure blue it carried beauty and pain of equal dimension. A first wistful day telling the season's change, the air thin bodied, fragrant of chance and uncertainty. After the ceremony in an aged hotel's ballroom, portly Frog Holler and Milltown women danced the shag together, and he stood alone, more alone than an hour before. That day he leaned drunk in a doorway with wine of different colors in each hand watching the dancing, William and Emylia, a life beginning and something gone too . . . *you saw that it was gone from his hand, but you did not say so . . . then, you should have known, and said so, but you do not see . . .* "Caron, it's someone else's."

"It's mine. He gave it to me."

"Caron, listen to me. You can make this alright again. But you have to do some things. You have to do some things now. You have to do something right now."

"I didn't do anything wrong. I didn't say anything wrong. *He* gave it to *me*."

"You have to give it back. We can fix this. We can fix this whole mess, but we have to do one thing, then another." Verdery knelt from sitting, and on his knees close to her he smelled in her breath the coffee and desolation, and he smelled himself and her, unwashed. "You see this, don't you? This has gone wrong. Nobody wanted it this way, it just happened. I might not have said the truth . . . one thing then another happened, and nobody caused all this wrong to happen—it just did. But, now, we can repair it."

She stood away from him without brushing the sand and black ants from her. She stood with a palm covering the ringed hand so that both small hands were the same, a single fist. She put her hands to her chin and closed her eyes when he reached for her, still kneeling.

"Young lady. Caron."

"What."

"You just have to see it . . . how I see it."

"I ain't done nothing wrong. He gave it to me. He said he wanted to."

"I know it. I know it. But it's just been one thing and another—and nobody caused it. I know this. But now, right now, we can start to settle things. All we have to do is one thing, then another—you have to know this."

She looked to the tent but Rhind was not there, and he was not there when Verdery looked.

"Caron, listen."

"You said you couldn't help no one but yourself. That's what you said."

"I said I might be wrong about all of it."

"But you said the other first."

"But it all has happened since then, don't you see? Don't you see it has all happened since then, and now you can start to settle it—now you can fix it. There's so much time."

"He did it all. I didn't do any of it. He asked, and now I have it because he gave it to me."

She wiped at her eyes with her fists balled the same, and she raised her head to look past Verdery, and without turning he already knew Rhind stood behind him—and he spoke loud enough for Rhind to hear.

"Goddamit, young lady, you can fix this."

He saw her search down to what might have been Rhind's feet, then up again to where their eyes must have met and held.

"You fix it, Ghostman."

Verdery turned on one knee and he saw the same as she, but not that too, knowing this remainder heap of a man. *My only friend . . .*

"You fix it."

She went to him and leaned beneath his free arm. He stood, as tall as he was, in as bent a pose of disregard—with she under an arm and gripping an oar with the opposite arm—as if he were urinating, or sleepwalking.

"Go on for a minute," and he raised his arm to let her go, and she went into the tent and left it open behind her.

Rhind stepped close to Verdery with the oar's blade cutting a thin row through the sand, standing above him in the same bent, slope-shouldered pose—worn and sour and unwashed, bitten welted, eyes swollen from sleep and sleeplessness and waking knowing desolation, or the lie that comes in place of it.

"Will."

"Yes, Ghostman."

"You don't have to say that."

"Alright, then. I won't."

"Will, this can all get better. But we have to see it right, to fix it."

"I see it. I've seen it—all of it. Now you fix it if you want it fixed."

Verdery stood from the sand not brushing himself, and it was as it had ever been between the two of them, Rhind a half-head taller. "We can go either way from here. We can go back to Port Wentworth, or we can go on to Savannah. Either way we'll get a phone and make a call."

"A phone. You're not going back anyways—who you going to call?"

"I didn't call anybody yet. I knew you should talk to Emmy. Not me. Not alone."

"But now none of us are going back, are we. So who needs to be looking for a phone."

"What I said before—that isn't right. I didn't say it right. That's what I told her. I told her I didn't say it right. And you have Emmy and Annie."

"She was gone, Thom. She was gone with my girl, and she didn't say where."

"She'll come back. You just have to quit. You quit and she'll come back."

Rhind turned his head to the marsh, an unheard calling, and he took in a long breath searching across the channel, seeing nothing he would remember. "We can't go back now. It don't work if you don't go with the water."

"Then we go on to Savannah. It's what we said. It's what I said from the start, when everything was right."

"No," said Rhind, exhaling, as if he were speaking to the open, into the rising wind that teased the river's back, "you know better than that."

"Will . . . I've found you now . . ."

"No," said Rhind, after a moment, as if the effort itself unimportant to him. He turned facing the west, to the marsh searching past to the watercourse, leaning less to the oar now.

"Did you see him, Thom."

"See him."

"Did you see him. Did you see . . . did you see him."

"Will."

"Thom, did you see him—I never saw him."

"You found his bedclothes."

"That's not him."

"No, Will. I didn't see him. Not again . . . not again."

"When he was gone, he was gone. And all you had to do was tie it right."

"I don't know how it got to be this way. But some people need to know."

"We know, don't we. When he was gone he was gone, and now none of us are going back."

Verdery stepped close to Rhind, but Rhind did not turn from the west and the wind and the open channel. "I've been alone. I am alone, so it doesn't matter about me. But you've got to call, and you've got to call about that girl —and you've got to take that goddamed ring off her goddamed finger."

"You know how it is with those young ones. You know about it, Teacherman."

"Goddamit, let her . . . leave that much alone. Will, the next thing we do . . . might be right."

"You know better than that too. All you had to do was tie it, like you say you teach them . . . and everybody's gone."

"Will . . ."

Rhind turned on him—as if he had been touched awake—but with his eyes full open, lacking worry and shame, and his voice steady, shameless too. He took up the oar and lay it across his shoulder. "But now we're going on down."

Verdery blinked, then bowed his head exhaling the coffee and the wear and the six days gone in the same breath. "Goddamit, Will. Sure. Let me get the tent down and we can go on."

"No. No, just us."

"There's three of us."

"No, just us."

"Goddamit, Will, no . . . goddamit, no."

"Just like when I found her."

"Goddamit, *she* found *you*."

In the mid of the channel and the morning steammist, riding the ebbtide, Rhind thought, *I don't imagine I broke his neck* . . . He had said so aloud, speaking to his father.

The first swing, he swung roundly with the blade on edge, and caught the oar high against Verdery's shoulder—the speed and the weight, and the dumb resistance to motion, staggering both of them. They stood upright again in the sand and grass, now further apart. Verdery knew only to curse—not at Rhind or himself or her, but likely at the blade, and at the volume and the weight of all the water it had plowed to bring them here, at the miles joined end for end, at the inertia and the insistence of habit and insensate unlearned will, and the failing to know better than all of it.

He cursed through the sudden fire of the pain, and he missed catching the blade the second time, and this blow seemed by the succinct, crisp noise to finish the arm. He fell sitting heavy, at once, and he could not lay over.

oh goddamit . . .

Against the third Verdery did not try. Rhind quit the same as he had begun the last stroke—without a cause, purposeless too—when the blade wrongly made his neck, letting it rest on edge for only a moment against the skin of him, before dropping it into the sand.

"Goddamit Thom," said Rhind, accusatory, choiceless, and he let go the oar at Verdery's feet, where it fell across him, *goddamit, Thom Carpenter . . .*

He tugged the Ouachita clear and he took only the second oar and in a single rush he put it over and down the bluff. He remembered and he went to the small boat and he took his father's hat and put it on. He said her name at the bluff and down he said her name a second time, and in his strained and aimless calling he set the Ouachita three-quarters into the marsh's off-colored backwater, with the bow out to the passage.

She knelt to Verdery, where he lay on his side, the side on his good unbroken arm with his legs drawn up. His breath moved the black ants in the sand when they came near to his mouth, and she brushed away from his face the ones near to his shut eyes. There was no blood and she did not think to look for it. She brushed his face with the back of her fingers, and her fingers were wet with her tears upon him. She washed a spot of his face clean of the dust they all wore. She spoke soft down to him, and all Rhind heard of it was, "I will," then Rhind took her by the arm under the shoulder and stood her to her feet.

"Come on—come on Caron. You can't stay here. He'll be alright after awhile. I don't imagine I broke his neck, too."

"He didn't cause it."

"Goddamit," said Rhind, saying it to himself, "how does it matter . . . goddamit."

"He told it right. He said it right."

"Goddamit, there're two boats here. I'm going in one of them."

"Alright. Alright."

He wakened to see the stern point of the Ouachita vanish, sliding away into the sawgrass marsh. It was an hour before he knew what it was he saw then, and it was the afternoon before he made a noise greater than an aspiration. A whitetail doe discovered him, she tracking where she had been with her nose low to the earth. When he groaned aloud she bolted and she did not slow until she had made the sea pines at the backside of the spoilage island.

Near the left bank the ebbtide took them fast into Kings Island Turning Basin. There, three bearded workmen, already soiled for the day, labored upon a salvage barge, their skin the same rust color as their scrap metal. They paused their work to watch the blue longboat and the girl at the bow. The laborer nearest straddling the ruddy cords of scrap raised an arm to them, but Rhind did not ease. "Damn," they said when the Ouachita had gone by. "Damn."

At mile eighteen the Garden City Terminal stood cluttered of squarish browned warehouses and factories, emanative of smoke and steam, the air cumulative of their odor and noise. The great portdock cranes, powder blue as Verdery had seen them from Drakies Cut, stood aligned, dream-slow in motion, inestimable at their work, lettered and numbered in diminishing order to downriver: *Port of Call, Savannah, Georgia, USA. No. 8, No. 7, No. 6* . . . They came upon the first of the great cargo ships rested to the dock, its immensity too beyond an accurate telling at first sight. At Garden City, then the Ocean Terminal, the freighters were named and lettered in painted block the size of house walls: *Yang Min, Hanjin-Frotamanns,* and *Patty,* a grain ship. *Hoegh Minerva, Lauritzen Bulkers,* and the *Lilac Wave.* Workmen, small and dark as mites, roamed atop the containers setting the bridles, the rigging for hoisting, and the containers floated into the air beneath the arms of the great cranes—newborn possessed to mother.

As they neared the rope stay bridge it grew in all dimensions, cables in the early sun thickly woven artful, suspension webbing purposeful of design and invincibility, the roadbed clearing above beyond reckoning, and too in proportion to the glint of the vessel that carried them beneath it, unfathomable.

Rhind set the bow into the wake of a hurried passing tug that did not slow, and they rode the rolls until it had eased, and the tug was the only traffic that threatened them that morning. With the sun showing ten o'clock, three hundred yards past the high bridge he ferried to cross the channel and he made the southwest bank where old downtown began at River Street. They eased past a single docked tugboat, next a restored gaff-rigged schooner, and last a paddlewheeler.

At the public docks he tied off to an oversized lashing cleat, making figure eights, and they walked the ramp to the riverwalk promenade, then across to River Street. They stood together opposite the store fronts, both barefooted, welted, rubbish-like and sour, and the shoppers, out-of-towners, saw fit to walk a clear path around them.

An aged, stooping, black man who slept out of doors approached them, said his name was *Tyrus,* and he *shore needed some medicine,* and he *might could sing for them a spiritual song for a dollar or two.*

"No sir, Tyrus," said Rhind, thinking too, *we're the same, but one of us has a song.* "I can't afford a song."

"Thas alright," and Tyrus's brown eyes smiled and pained together. "Thas alright, I'll sing you one anyways, godbless you," and he went and he sang *Amazing Grace* to no one but Jesus.

"Alright, girl." He put into her small hands the last of his coins, the last of his bills too. "You should go on and call back to Girard. This is River Street. Tell him you're at River Street. Tell them what you think you ought to tell them. They still have a phone line, right?"

"You'll be here?"

"I'll be here. You remember where we stayed last night."

"Yes. You going to call?"

"You go on, I'll be here."

"Alright, I will," and she left him, crossing the stone driveway to the store fronts, gripping the money in her small brown fists, the left hand wrapped by the right.

He had come to River Street with his wife—when their life together seemed of a moment and they could look each other in the eyes without fear of being seen inside—and they had shared drinks and watched the water at twilight. He remembered she said, *It's old here . . . everything is old here . . .*

Is it good that it's old?

It just is.

That night they made love with rum in their lungs, breathing drunken and careless upon one another. And they had made a child too, and late into the night he looked out over the river a last time, and there was nothing upon the water save the luminous threads of streetlamps, incidental, wavering, and when he lay down beside her next, he did not sleep.

A thin man and woman—each soiled, beaten by the things of this life they never knew to expect—came to him for money, and they said the amount they hoped for, and Rhind said, "I don't have a thing," and it felt good and simple to him that it was the truth.

The sun and the wind were warm over him, this he knew, and now the black ants were not troublesome. The sand held a fragrance, and it was something he had known, but he could not name it amidst the dust of his dreaming. The marsh grass sighed with a sudden gust gone through it, and the soft noise—motion, travel, one place becoming another—wakened him for only that moment. He bled inside only where his bone broke in his arm and where his neck at the base of his skull had steadily intumesced, and now in the mid of the afternoon his breath shallowed.

The grass wakened him a last time and that is when he saw himself leaving Way Island. He saw the white profile—the good boat only ever a smile upon the water—slide into the spartina passage and vanish. Then he was upon the channel again. His craft moved well with the tide, the warm wind at his back. The channel shone emerald in the clear sun, its best color, a new morning unexplored. Across the distance he saw the old city gathered upon the southwest bank, austere and a glimmer, its gold leaf aging, and each unhurried stroke eased the land and water past and the distance near.

She and Rhind and Dan Rhind waited at the docks as he ferried approaching the tidewall. They stood close to one another, and there were no marks on their bodies and no worry in their faces. He imagined he smiled and nodded at them and he saw that they understood as he went on with the good ebbtide, and let them, with the shimmering mirage of the aged old city at their backs, become small again. He watched until he could no longer descry that it was a lived place, then he turned searching across his bow. The river narrowed and the liveoak and seapine grew high to either side, and ahead they grew overtopping the thin, emerald passage, meeting above where the sky might have been. The good warm wind brought sleep heavy upon him, and he lay to the smiling boat's hull, and he used his unwashed hands as a pillow.

With his eyes shut a last time he felt the course take him and his vessel, and soon in his sleep he felt again the warm sun upon him, and too in his hearing came the open ocean's first call. There he slept.

Rhind waited at the dock only a minute and a minute more.

In the Ouachita he did not look back until he made the tip of Hutchinson Island, where the Back River rejoined. He went fast and all the air was still. He went with little effort and there abided clouds only low and distant in the flawless cerulean sky, and it was a sky already of August passing. At Oglethorpe Channel he looked back once and the church with two spires was the last he saw of Savannah.

He met an immense freighter coming to port where the river bended a last time at Elba Island. A single watchman, a boy, blonded by the sun, shirtless, sat cross-legged upon the deck at the freighter's bow. This boy a carving, a figurine, but only trinket-sized—his assigned duties vestigial, his greater purpose an amulet, a periapt, a Captain's comfort—he and Rhind samesized, the disparity of their vessels in comparison ridiculous, untellable, the Ouachita only debris, a speck, a spitting. In his wonder and half-surprise, the boy may have nodded; and Rhind did not ease riding the wake.

He took the South Channel not knowing there was such a thing, and it was nine miles when he made the low bridge at the old fort named for Pulaski, and he did not cease. Soon he passed where the waving girl stood alone on Cockspur Island, and within the same half hour of sun he made where the water truly opened at Lazaretto Creek and Tybee Knoll Spit. With the air stilled the bay shimmered calm and he rounded Tybee Island to his right, and there rising behind the gentle surf and beach stood the lighthouse, in its sweater of black and white, and rivermile zero. He eased only for a moment, and there was something in his thinking, but less than retelling why it mattered now, what it mattered a benchmark two hundred river miles ago—when he sought to let his life go, as it had let go of him.

Over the Northbeach at the jetties, some of the children quit playing to watch him pass.

He set his bow to the east, to the mouth of the bay and the maritime marker at the breakers, the three masts that told the entrée to the channel. In the near distance approached a cargo ship with its containers stacked high, then beyond it, another, half again the size. And beyond the second a third emerged from the seahaze as only a nick disturbing the fathomless horizon.

He stroked to open water—calm and only gentle rolling, until the wind and maybe a coming storm of dusk—for the line where the ocean met the sky, a washy plane of dissolving hues, without beginning, endless too.

In the late mid of the afternoon he turned in his seat and all the land had gone from him, and he turned again. He took off his father's hat to let the sun on his face. He dipped it in the Atlantic Ocean and he put it on again, and he plowed Verdery's oar into the same ocean. It occurred to him that he was thirsty, and it seemed odd that he should mind such a thing where there was nothing else, and a promise of nothing else, and he made for the gauze of the void wherein somewhere lay the curve of the world.